DEAD RECKONING

A Rosalind Schmidt Genealogical Mystery

ANNA DALHAIMER BARTKOWSKI

Dead Reckoning, A Rosalind Schmidt Mystery © 2023 by Anna Dalhaimer Bartkowski

All rights reserved. Published in Chandler, Arizona, United States by Infinite Adventure Publishing.

No part of this book may be reproduced or utilized in any form or by any means, electronic or mechanical, including photocopying, recording, or by any information storage or retrieval systems, without permission in writing from Anna Dalhaimer Bartkowski. For information contact: anna@bart4.com

Bartkowski, Anna Dalhaimer
     Dead Reckoning, A Rosalind Schmidt Genealogical Mystery.

Book Cover by Anna Dalhaimer Bartkowski
Cover Photo by Anna Dalhaimer Bartkowski
www.annabartkowski.com

Printed in the United States of America
ISBN – 978-0-9790720-7-9 Print
ISBN – 978-0-9790720-8-6 E-book
Library of Congress Control Number 2023910335

1, Dalhaimer Bartkowski, Anna 2023 – Mystery. 2. Historical Fiction 3. Genealogical Family Saga 4. Murder Mystery

Dedication

This book is dedicated to the brave souls who answered the invitation of Catherine the Great's Manifesto and their descendants around the world, especially, Rebecca Ann and Ashley Maria.

Table of Contents

Dedication iii

Prelude, 1765, Bavaria 3

Part One 5

Chapter One, October 2014, Arizona 7

Chapter Two 12

Chapter Three 14

Chapter Four 16

Chapter Five 20

Chapter Six 22

Chapter Seven 25

Chapter Eight 30

Chapter Nine 33

Chapter Ten 37

Chapter Eleven 42

Chapter Twelve 44

Chapter Thirteen 48

Chapter Fourteen 49

Chapter Fifteen 53

Chapter Sixteen 59

Chapter Seventeen 64

Chapter Eighteen 67

Chapter Nineteen 70

Chapter Twenty 80

Chapter Twenty-One 85

Chapter Twenty-Two 87

Chapter Twenty-Three 90

Chapter Twenty-Four 93

Part Two 98

Chapter Twenty-Five, December 1765, Büdingen, Hesse 99

Chapter Twenty-Six 102
Chapter Twenty-Seven 104
Chapter Twenty-Eight 106
Chapter Twenty-Nine 107
Chapter Thirty 110
Chapter Thirty-One 114
Chapter Thirty-Two 118
Chapter Thirty-Three, October 2014, Arizona 122
Chapter Thirty-Four, 1766, Baltic Sea 123
Chapter Thirty-Five 126
Chapter Thirty-Six 129
Chapter Thirty-Seven 134
Chapter Thirty-Eight 136
Chapter Thirty-Nine, October 2014, Arizona 143
Chapter Forty, 1766, Kronstadt 144
Chapter Forty-One 146
Chapter Forty-Two 149
Chapter Forty-Three, October 2014, Arizona 157
Chapter Forty-Four, Russia, 1766 158
Chapter Forty-Five, Mariental, June 16, 1766 162
Part Three 164
Chapter Forty-Six, October 2014, Arizona 165
Chapter Forty-Seven 170
Chapter Forty-Eight 182
Chapter Forty-Nine 186
Chapter Fifty 190
Chapter Fifty-One 195
Chapter Fifty-Two 198
Chapter Fifty-Three 201
Chapter Fifty-Four 206

Chapter Fifty-Five 209
Chapter Fifty-Six 210
Chapter Fifty-Seven, Mariental 216
Part Four 222
Chapter Fifty-Eight, Arizona, October 2014 223
Chapter Fifty-Nine 232
Schmidt Family Tree 236
Acknowledgements 238
Bibliography 240
About the Author 243

"This is the story of our people, the Germans from Russia – ever-wandering, ever struggling, coming and going from one country to another –
in search of a special place, a place to call 'home.'"

Dr. Timothy J. Kloberdanz

Prelude, 1765, Bavaria

The sun's rays cracked open the earth in Ansbach. Christoph Schmidt reached down to touch the dry, barren land of his farm. He raked his fingertips across the pale ground. Dust filtered through his hands, revealing the rock-solid field below. The terrain was so tight there was no space for a seed to sink into the soil, germinate into roots, and grow tall into daily bread. A tear rolled down his left cheek. The countryside needed to recover for at least a year or more. If the heavens poured open with water today, a harvest might be celebrated in two years. Or not. Before the war, he had given his all to his family. The two-year drought stole everything he cared for…his wife and two sons dead, buried only two days ago, and his farm was infertile, completely unplantable. He had nothing left to lose.

No rain left his neighbors without a harvest and a hungry, desperate look in their eyes. Christoph had seen that look during the war, and he did not stay there to find out what those people were capable of. He moved on.

Christoph was not certain toward which direction to navigate. He had been west of Ansbach during the war, and he had no desire to return to the French provinces, despite their beauty away from the battlefields of the Seven Years War. Every night he dreamt of where he had been and the horrors he had seen. He preferred not to see any of it in his future.

Now he needed a new path. He had learned to track his whereabouts via the star Polaris. Should he set sail? Walk north? Wander south? He yearned to thrive alone with his Germanic customs, traditions, and language.

He walked from the farm toward the rectory hoping to talk to Father Trier before Mass. He trusted the pastor and valued his opinion, even if Christoph needed to confess his sins before Trier would explain the latest news to him. He had to understand the details of the pamphlet he had folded in his pocket. If the rumors were true, this could be his last day in Ansbach.

Part One

"There are four things our ancestors need from us: acknowledgement, validation, understanding and forgiveness."

Dr. Steven D. Farmer

Anna Dalhaimer Bartkowski

Chapter One, October 2014, Arizona

Rosalind Schmidt walked into the office as usual at 7 a.m. She believed it would be a typical Tuesday, until Anthony Findley once again found a way to shatter the calm of her existence.

After dropping off her laptop and purse in her office, Rosalind headed toward the break room for her first cup of coffee. The whirr whoosh of the copier grinding out paper matched her footsteps as she walked down the hall, energy bar and empty mug in her hands. She was starved since she skipped breakfast after her morning run.

Yesterday she explored websites until after midnight searching for her grandfather's port of entry to the United States. Ellis Island? No. Boston? No. Galveston? No. The mystery of her ancestors and proving her family line tracked to original Mariental settler Christoph Schmidt wasn't going to get solved in one night. Determined to pace herself, after hours of not locating her grandfather's name, she nodded off at her kitchen table, arms crossed over her laptop.

As chief accountant for Kelco Marketing, the bills, payroll, and financial duties demanded her attention despite her lack of sleep. Rosalind had established Kelco's reporting standards, aligning it with accounting models based on a monthly routine, which was sorely lacking when she joined the team over ten years ago. Rosalind preferred to forget the years between graduating high school and joining Kelco. If only it were possible.

She loved working for Kelco despite some mild hiccups along the way. A corporation with four locations across the mountain states, Kelco's motto was, "We're small enough to care yet big enough to make your marketing succeed." She shivered as cold air blew out of the vents and she pulled the front of her blue jacket around her for warmth.

The metronome sound of the copier running annoyed her. It was strange that the machine was already cranking as most people arrived closer to 8 a.m.

"Good morning." Rosalind glanced into the copier area, tossing her honey-colored bangs behind her ears. She expected to see someone standing there ready to collect printouts, yet no one was there. They must have stepped away. Whoever it was must have disarmed the building's security system. The machine pumped out pages flowing into a neat stack. The number of copies requested was 666. Rosalind pressed the "interrupt" button on the copier.

"What a waste of paper and ink." Rosalind assumed the 666 was an error. Yet, upon closer look, the copies displayed a replica of someone's bottom with the shape of lips clearly visible on one cheek.

"What the...? Who the...?" As Rosalind asked the question aloud, she realized the simple answer. Whenever mischief or shenanigans were afoot, there was only one culprit. Anthony Findley. He tried anything to cause uproar and drama. Whether it was through his self-centered humor, or his incessant demands for the entire staff to do his work, Tony's style of operation was loud, fast, and guaranteed to bring all attention to him. Especially when he succumbed to 1980s fraternity pranks like this.

Tony's role as the top account manager was unique. To his credit, no one could match his account billings. No one, not even top management, would challenge him despite their proclaimed zero-tolerance policy and their attempts to move their company culture into the diverse and inclusive era. Tony's unruly behavior was endured by management and left the staff at their wits' end. Rosalind worked hard to avoid the man.

She needed that cup of coffee more than ever. She left the paper in the output tray, wanting nothing more to do with that embarrassing behavior. When she turned to her left, her breath caught in her throat.

Tony Findley was sprawled across the aisle lying face down in front of the men's restroom. His shoes shone as if he had just finished cleaning and polishing them while his feet pointed inward as if he was pigeon-toed. He was not.

She maintained her distance. "Tony, please get up. You need to clean your mess with the copier. I'm not doing it for you." Rosalind resolved to rise above his immature behavior this time.

Dead Reckoning

Breathe, Rosalind said to herself. Three slow breaths in, three slow breaths out just like your friend Issy Candella always suggested. Rosalind practiced her breathing, but patience was not her strong suit. She thought of Issy, a botanist, working at the Botanical Gardens in peaceful serenity. After counting to sixty, she walked two steps closer to Tony, stomping her feet on the carpet, so he had to hear her footsteps. She hoped it would be enough to stop his latest foolishness. She backed up and looked around the office hoping someone else was here. If this were not the only route to the breakroom and coffee, she would have taken a detour.

Tony did not respond. He lay still, not moving. Rosalind approached him cautiously, expecting Tony to wait until she was closer and then jump up with a screech to scare her. That's what he did two months ago from behind the file cabinets. His other recent antic was hiding behind a cubicle wall and waiting for her or some unlucky person to look around the corner and then throw a report or calendar at them. Both incidents embarrassed Rosalind when she screamed, which only caused Tony to laugh and mimic her surprise for hours, days and weeks afterward. So, she peered from a safe distance.

Rosalind took two small steps toward him. She was impressed with how determined Tony was to maintain his unmovable pose. Her resolve to rise above was waning.

She tapped her shoe against his heel. "Tony, you can't let anyone see you like this. You know, this is unacceptable behavior."

Tony's face remained smack down on the carpet. She bent over him when she saw a greenish brown discharge coming out of his mouth and pooling on the carpet. Her empty stomach churned, and acid rose up her esophagus. She dropped her energy bar and covered her mouth with her hand. Tony did not move. Tony did not laugh. Tony did not jump up to scare her. Horrified, Rosalind stood frozen in place.

She heard the side door swing open, and she saw the tops of Bob McMahon and Audra Lorenz's heads over the cubicle walls as they entered the office.

"Morning," Bob yelled.

"Morning," called Audra.

Rosalind could not utter a word.

"Rosalind?" said Bob. "Not had your coffee yet?"

When they rounded the cubicle wall and stopped cold in their tracks, Rosalind saw them exchange glances.

"Rosalind?" asked Bob.

Still frozen with her hand over her mouth, Rosalind turned to them. "He was lying there, the copier was running, I-I stopped it...I thought it was a trick, but he won't move."

Audra turned to Bob and directed him. "Call 911 now." Bob grabbed his cell phone as he walked away from where Tony lay.

Rosalind stared at Audra, then turned again to make sure Tony remained on the floor.

Audra Lorenz was Rosalind's best friend at work. Although commiseration was the basis of their friendship, a true affection existed between the two women. Audra always maintained her cool professional corporate ladder-climbing exterior. Her eyes were alert, her jaw in line with her chiseled smile, and her emotions were in check. Her raven hair gently nudged her shoulders, her suit was tailored to perfectly fit her well-toned body which towered at five feet eight inches. Her grace and charm was irresistible to potential clients and co-workers. She opened doors that other account executives were too intimidated to approach. Her life was dedicated to perfection. The perfect employee, the perfect mountain climber, the perfect friend, and she didn't fall short.

"Audra, I thought this was a prank, I don't know what is happening."

Audra knelt next to Tony and lightly touched his wrist. "I don't feel a pulse."

The stillness in the office was at odds with the typical hustle and bustle of the day, even though it was early. Rosalind opened her mouth as Bob returned to the hallway. "I was going to the break room for coff-_"

"Save it for the police," interrupted Bob.

Rosalind stepped back appalled at Bob's comment as if she was responsible for the man lying there. Her head began to pound. Her empty stomach churned. She breathed in deeply again. All she inhaled was the odor of the greenish brown discharge next to Tony's mouth.

She felt the floor begin to sway as if she was on the deck of a ship sailing in open water. She tried to stop the ebb and flow motion and the overwhelming sense of seasickness. Her nose wrinkled, her stomach churned, and her vision faded. She closed her eyes as the beige walls around her disappeared and consciousness slipped away.

Chapter Two

Rosalind awoke to sirens wailing outside the building, reverberating off the walls near the lobby. Her eyes flickered open to flashing lights reflecting through the glass entrance doors. She was on the floor eye to eye with Tony, his lids covering only half of his iris.

Audra extended her hand to Rosalind to help her to her feet then walked toward the front entrance. Police officers peered through the window and pulled the door handle, but the security system prevented entry to anyone without an ID badge. Audra reached the door and swung it open for them. Tall and muscular, the police hurried into the building making their presence hard to ignore.

The tallest man said, "Good morning, I'm Detective Hamilton. This is Officer Enders and Makowski." He pointed at the woman and man next to him. "We received a 911 call of a murder. What's going on here?"

"How did you get here so fast?" asked Bob. "I hung up the phone two minutes ago. I have no idea if this is a murder, we simply found Tony on the floor."

Detective Hamilton looked directly at Bob. "We received an anonymous call regarding a murder fourteen minutes ago. Now, what's going on?"

Bob shrugged. "We, that is, Audra and I, arrived a few minutes ago and found Rosalind here with Tony on the floor. Uh, that is, Tony was on the floor and Rosalind was standing next to him before she collapsed."

"I found him, and I must have passed out." Rosalind put her hand to her forehead hoping to steady the wobbly feeling in her knees.

"You ok now? Can you stand on your own?" Hamilton watched Rosalind nod yes as she held onto the wall to maintain her balance.

"Who called the police fourteen minutes ago?" asked Rosalind.

Officer Enders walked over to the body and put her index finger on Tony's wrist. She shook her head. "He's already cold, but EMS will be here soon."

"Who's in charge here?" Hamilton surveyed the entire office as if looking for his answer.

"I'm Bob McMahon, Vice President of Kelco Marketing." Bob extended his hand to the detective. Hamilton ignored Bob's outstretched arm and grabbed his tablet. Rosalind swallowed hard trying to compose herself.

Hamilton jotted notes then continued. "We need to control access to entrances and exits then secure and search the building." Hamilton turned. "Makowski, secure the parking lot entrance. If anyone tries to enter, tell them the office is closed for the day. Take their name and phone number. We will follow up with them as soon as we can. Wait out there until SOCI arrives and then barricade the parking lot."

"SOCI, what is SOCI?" asked Rosalind.

"Scene of Crime Investigators, you might recognize it as CSI."

As Makowski left through the front door to secure the parking lot, the side door flung open.

"What's going on with the police vehicles?" Josh Bartholomew, the first person through the door, was tall, dark, and not too handsome. He was the creative force behind Kelco's most successful marketing campaigns. His easy-going manner caused the staff to rely on him for support. He led most of the social activities for the Kelco employees.

Behind him, starting to build as good a reputation as Josh, was Graham Grayson, who at three years younger was Josh's shadow. Josh mentored Graham and they composed the artistic duo of the team.

Enders directed Josh and Graham away from the restroom hallway, motioning them toward the front lobby so they did not see Tony. At the same time, three SOCI technicians pushed past them and scrambled to where Hamilton stood.

"Enders," said Hamilton, "get all of these people into one room with you. No one leaves the building until I authorize it." He turned toward Rosalind and Audra and said loud enough for Graham and Josh to hear, "No talking about what you saw."

"We didn't see anything," mumbled Josh.

"McMahon, you stay with me." Hamilton walked to the widest aisle. He scrutinized every cubicle, file cabinet and chair he passed.

Enders led the group into the main conference room, away from any view of Tony.

Rosalind shuddered. This was certainly not a typical Tuesday. Finding a dead body was not on her calendar. So far, this was one of the worst Tuesdays of her life.

Chapter Three

Rosalind squirmed in her chair. Of the four employees gathered around the mahogany table in the conference room, only Rosalind and Audra had seen Tony's body. Josh and Graham had no idea what had happened. Officer Enders stood like a sentry outside the door letting no one in or out of the room.

Josh sat at the foot of the table with a puzzled look on his face. He looked over his shoulder occasionally to see if anyone else came near the door. Next to him, Graham focused exclusively on swiping left or right on his phone. His hair, the color of his namesake cracker, fell over his eyes. Graham looked carefree, as if he hadn't a concern in the world.

Every few minutes, Josh would glance at Rosalind, open his mouth to ask a question, then close it before any words escaped. When Enders moved a few feet away from the door, Josh whispered, "What happened out there? Is someone dead?"

Rosalind swallowed. "They said we can't talk about it."

She grabbed a sheet of paper from the center of the table and pulled her pen out of her pocket. She wrote, "What will happen to Kelco without Tony?" and slid the paper and pen to Audra.

Audra casually read the note then checked if Enders was still away from the door. She wrote, "We'll survive," and passed the note back. Rosalind nodded.

Enders turned and said, "No passing notes either."

Rosalind laid her head on the table. "I'm sorry, I'm not feeling well at the moment." She closed her eyes. If Tony was killed, a murderer was on the loose. She shivered thinking that someone she knew might have killed him. And, despite Audra's optimism about Kelco after Tony Findley, Rosalind's stomach twisted and turned again.

Rosalind imagined how the staff would react to his death hoping that her fainting would not be part of the conversation. Her only consolation was Tony would not ceaselessly tease her about it, then she regretted that thought, knowing he would never tease her again. Her concerns were not relevant given the circumstances. She realized how Tony's dear friend, Theresa Mars, would be devastated upon hearing the news.

Dead Reckoning

Detective Hamilton appeared at the door frame. He walked with a swagger of confidence and control. *He must be at least six feet three, no, four inches tall,* Rosalind thought. She gazed at his erect posture and her seasickness returned. She grabbed onto the edge of the table to stop the sensation.

Hamilton stood at the front of the room. His presence commanded attention as all eyes focused on him. His hat covered his dark short hair. *Why did he wear a fedora hat, and why did he leave his hat on indoors,* wondered Rosalind? *Was he concealing a bald head? His brown eyes could pierce through any lies he heard. Intimidating? Just a bit.*

He pointed at Rosalind. "Come with me."

Rosalind stood, her knees shaking as if she were trying to balance on board ship. Her left knee was her Achilles heel and it ached as it always did after her morning run. She steadied herself by tracing her hand along the table and put one foot in front of the other to walk toward him.

He led her past her own office to Bob's, which filled the southeast corner of the building. The autumn desert sun streamed through floor to ceiling blinds casting stripes across the room. Hamilton sat behind the desk. Officer Makowski was already in the room sitting in one of two side chairs.

"Please sit down." Hamilton extended his hand toward the open chair. As she sat, he said, "So, tell me your name. Your role with Kelco. And everything you saw since you arrived. Then tell me about your relationship with Tony Findley."

Chapter Four

After talking for more than an hour with Detective Hamilton, answering his questions three or four times, Rosalind was allowed to leave but stay close to home.

Frazzled and exhausted, she drove through Tempe past the Phoenix Zoo and Botanical Gardens to Aunt Ruth's half-acre property in a small neighborhood. She headed through the open gate toward the casita she rented behind the main house where her aunt lived.

As she parked her Volvo in her carport, the bright Arizona sun cast shadows and shimmered on her front door. The warm rays lit up the colors of emerald and turquoise on the elephant food, totem poles and cacti around her white stucco studio casita. Rosalind had chosen each plant and its location to create her peaceful "Adobe Hacienda." Rosalind filled her lungs with the calming air, sighed and unclenched her shoulders as she exhaled.

Combined with the sunshine and fresh air, the sounds of the mourning doves resonated through the neighborhood as she slid her key into the front door lock. She glanced up at her tile roof and saw the doves before they flew away. She heard "Honk, honk, honk" from above and tilted her head to see the exacting V formation of sixteen Canada Geese heading south. It could have been a glorious October day, except for Tony Findley.

She pushed the arched door open and Hercules, her three-year-old black Doberman, jumped up to greet her. He circled around her as she placed her bags on the entry table. She inhaled deeply and sighed. After closing the door, she braced her back against it, slid down to the stone floor, and allowed Hercules to lick her face. Up until now, this was the best part of her day.

"Baby, you have no idea how glad I am to be home. Saying it was a bad morning doesn't do it justice." She rubbed his ears until he settled his head onto her lap.

There was one main room divided into three functional living areas for cooking, sleeping, and entertaining. Spanish and Native American influences dominated the architecture. Wooden ceiling beams were accentuated by a built-in stone corner fireplace. Her walls were bare white, no shelves with mementos, no framed photographs, nor vacation getaway memories. The furniture was minimalist anchored by her modern couch and kitchen table. She stared across the room but only saw flashes of Tony lying on the floor. After a few minutes, she felt the cold tile seeping through to her legs, so she climbed to her feet and walked into the kitchen. She grabbed two pieces of bread, peanut butter, and strawberry jam out of the refrigerator.

"This is the extent of my cooking ability today, Hercules." She picked up his bowl, went to the pantry cabinet, and took out a tall container. Hercules' eyes followed Rosalind's every move. She plopped a dog treat into his bowl and set it on the floor next to his water basin. Hercules scarfed down the treat.

Rosalind kicked off her shoes and sat at the kitchen table. Yesterday Tony was alive and annoying staff members. Today he was dead in the hallway. Was it real? She bit into her sandwich and tried to focus on anything but him.

Across the kitchen table she looked at old family photographs, scattered as she had left them. Black and white images, ready for her to scan, research, and identify. She loved finding pictures of her dad as a young boy, especially since she lost both parents when she was so young. Aunt Ruth—her father's adopted younger sister and the only living connection to Rosalind's late parents—encouraged Rosalind to remember her family by researching and learning their shared history.

Only a few photos had notations on the back. Could these photos give her a sense of home? Or distract her from worrying about what happens to Kelco without Tony? She knew she was capable of finding a new job because any work would do, but she didn't want the discomfort to re-establish her routine and build new relationships. She preferred to stay in her cocoon.

If someone could kill Tony, could the murderer be a threat to her? She stepped back to her entrance and locked the door. Then she chuckled aloud at how her imagination ran wild. Time to change this train of thought.

If she found any of her ancestors, Ruth would be pleased with whatever she discovered. But, if she fell down the genealogy rabbit hole, would she be able to climb out to focus on the present?

The past invaded her thoughts more than she had imagined. If she allowed it, genealogy could usurp her life. Yet you only get so much time. How much of it can you spend on history? Now slipping into the past might help ease her concerns of Tony's death and foster a bond with Aunt Ruth. It was worth a try, almost a welcome distraction.

Rosalind knew from her family stories that her great-grandparents were born in Russia. They immigrated to the Americas in the early 1900s. She found three out of the four obituaries in her hometown newspaper in Wisconsin. Details of her grandfather Schmidt's death were unknown. She disliked feeling like a novice, but she meticulously logged her clues into a spreadsheet. She wished for a clear-cut path in front of her. There wasn't one.

Her thoughts were interrupted when her phone beeped. It was a text from Josh.

"Hey co-workers, let's meet up at the Daily Planet at 5:30 to discuss today."

Rosalind groaned. She wanted to hear what everyone had to say but dreaded the discussion would revolve around her. She deleted the text.

She held one of the photos up. "Do you see a family resemblance, Herc?" Hercules turned his head toward her.

These pictures were a massive project, not one she was ready to undertake today. The most she was inclined to do was grab a book and read in bed until exhaustion overcame her. But it was only early afternoon. She hoped her thoughts would not keep her awake all night.

Her phone buzzed. It was her friend Issy, a botanist at the Desert Botanical Gardens. Rosalind answered.

"Hey Roz, I just read your horoscope. Are you ok?"

"Not really. What did the horoscope say?"

"Today is a day you might prefer to miss and stay in bed. Tomorrow is a new day."

"I wish I had heard that before I went to work today. I found Anthony Findley dead."

"What? Oh, no, Roz. I'm so sorry."

"I know it happened, but it hasn't sunk in yet."

"If you want to talk to someone, I'm here for you."

Rosalind took another bite of her sandwich and thought the serenity of the Botanical Gardens might be what she needed. "Can I bring Hercules?"

"Of course. What time can you get here?"

"Give me an hour. See you soon."

Dead Reckoning

Rosalind ate the rest of her sandwich, and then turned to her laptop and saw ten new messages in her inbox.

She scanned through the promotional emails, and a new, unread message caught her eye. It was from Margaret Gardner.

Rosalind smiled. Perhaps today was not a total loss.

Chapter Five

When Rosalind opened Margaret's email, she scrolled through it checking for highlights. There were at least twenty paragraphs, more than three bulleted series, and multiple links. Margaret was certainly thorough, and based on the length of the email, it looked like there were no shortcuts or quick answers. Margaret volunteered and focused on one particular German Russian village: Mariental. She hunted for records and compiled family trees mapping original settlers and their descendants.

"Start with yourself, your parents, your grandparents and work backward from there," Margaret wrote." Your goal is to find out who crossed the pond."

But it wasn't just practical advice about discovering that potential ancestor, Christoph. Margaret also shared the basic history of the settlers who answered Catherine the Great's invitation to relocate to Russia. Rosalind had already read about Catherine, born Sophie of Anhalt-Zerbst, the daughter of an impoverished Prussian prince. After she ascended to the throne of Russia, she reached out to her Germanic homeland to help her settle and consolidate her Russian Empire. Her manifesto attracted residents from war-torn middle Europe to create a new start in a new land. As for Mariental, there were three hundred and sixty brave souls who left behind their lives in western Europe for the promises of land and freedoms of which they only dared to dream, and two families shared the last name of Schmidt so tracking the lines would be critical to determining the correct link.

Margaret agreed Christoph Schmidt could be her ancestor because her father's name was Christopher but there was no guarantee, since families named their children after fathers, uncles, grandfathers, great grandfathers and occasionally friends or cousins. Rosalind's eyes glazed over as Margaret cited a recent research project about a family whose father's name was Nikolaus Johannes. Nikolaus named his five sons Nikolaus—all with different middle names thank goodness. Then, each son named his sons the same way. Unbelievably confusing, tracking each line required the utmost patience.

"Oh great," said Rosalind while she considered the complexity of similar names. She absorbed what she could and realized she would have to review a bunch of records before confirming and connecting

Dead Reckoning

her family. US and Russian censuses were merely the beginning of research, there was much work ahead of her. Would knowing her background fill the hole in her heart, the hole created when she lost her parents and her home when still in high school? Would she ever confirm she was a descendant of Christoph Schmidt? Would she gain Aunt Ruth's approval? Not today. She had promised Issy she would visit.

Chapter Six

Once parked at the gardens, Rosalind grabbed her phone and called Issy.

"Hey, I'm in the parking lot. Meet you at the entrance?"

Hercules in tow, Rosalind walked through the Zen Garden and paused at the three beautiful Chihuly glass sculptures. The sight made her stop to breathe in. Why hadn't she come here after finding Tony dead? *Breathe it in, breathe it out.*

She caught sight of Issy, a botanist, who started working at the gardens a little over a year ago and was waved toward the greenhouse.

Rosalind and Issy met years earlier at a gardening class. Love of plants solidified their friendship, and although Rosalind never recorded her volunteer hours, her time here with Issy was always a pleasure. Issy had a unique perspective on life, formed from her studies of Feng Shui, reincarnation, Reiki healing, cleansing auras, astrology, or whatever the New Age crowd followed now.

Issy swept back the flap of the greenhouse. Five rows of tables were filled with plants, too many varieties for Rosalind to count.

"What are you working on today?" Rosalind asked.

Issy arched an eyebrow. "For the plants, we're transplanting these Lophoecereus Schottii Monstrosus into large pots. But for you, well, we need to take a moment for you to tell me how you're doing."

"I guess I'm stunned."

"What happened?"

"Well, he was on the floor in the hallway to the break room, while images of his bare butt spewed out of the copier by the hundreds."

"How awful." Issy's lips twitched.

"And then I fainted." Rosalind perched on a stool near the plant covered table. She grabbed a totem and settled the plant gently into a dirt filled clay pot with Navajo designs while she talked about the police officers, her co-workers, and Josh's text.

"Ok, so, you found Tony lying in the hallway. How was he killed?"

"Not certain. I didn't see wounds or a murder weapon. The police received two phone calls. The first was anonymous claiming someone was murdered at Kelco. The second call was Bob McMahon after he and Audra arrived and found me standing next to Tony's body. I'm afraid Tony's death shows all lives are too short. I didn't like Tony, but I'm horrified knowing he is gone."

"You've had a traumatic experience. I would worry if you didn't feel dreadful." Issy poured dirt around the cactus and steadied its column to upright in the container. "What you describe doesn't sound like murder. Can I offer a suggestion?"

"Can I stop you?" Rosalind laughed with a high-pitched nervous energy as she shook her head indicating no.

"There's that laugh." Issy told Rosalind months ago to control her breath so her laugh would be calmer and more relaxed.

Rosalind shrugged then focused on the totem in front of her. Hercules nudged her shin, and she bent down to scratch the top of his head.

Issy continued. "I know this just happened today and it was disturbing.. It will take time to adjust."

"I know, I focus too much on work and negative thoughts."

"Work is only part of your life, but you need balance. You need to feed your spirit, your soul, too."

"Ah, you are trying again to reach my soul. I appreciate your thoughts, Issy, but I thrive on work."

"Ok, I have an idea that could help you now. How would you feel about some magical protection?"

"Magical protection?" Rosalind pushed her hair off her face. She twirled the totem deeper into the pot. "Is this like your feng shui studies?"

"This is different. Feng Shui is about your environment. You need magical protection. Protection from your spirit animal, also known as your totem." Issy picked up another plant and gently stretched the roots before setting it into a new container. "Your totem in this context is not the plant. Rather, it is your spirit animal who guides and protects you. Is there an animal that is your go-to, an animal to which you relate?"

"I relate to Hercules."

"Hercules is family. A spirit animal is completely different, it's a being, like a sacred object. It is a huge part of the belief system of Indigenous tribes, and other cultures who believe each person connects with an animal spirit that accompanies you through life. Some think there are many animals who support you. It can be a boar at one stage of your life, or anything from a butterfly to a buffalo to an alligator at other stages. Each animal brings qualities to help you on your journey."

"Even a javelina?"

"Even a javelina."

"Issy, I don't believe in that stuff. All I can do is hope that they figure out what happened to Tony and keep Kelco operational so I can return to work. The longer I am away the more deadlines I miss." Rosalind grabbed another clay pot avoiding eye contact.

"I doubt returning to the office will help you through the trauma. Are you game for an experiment?"

"Probably not. Especially if it means trusting my instincts. I proved those were off kilter years ago. Remember Scott?" Rosalind shuddered. She was beyond vulnerable after her parents died. So, she married the boy next door to keep a sense of belonging, a sense of home. Not her best decision.

"No, not like that. It'll be fun. Let's try this…when you are going to bed, grab a notebook and pen. Sit with these two items and ask to see your totem animal in your dream. Actually, write your request." Issy eyed Rosalind to make sure she was paying attention. "It might take a few nights before you have results, but if you wake and remember the animal, it's your totem. If you can't remember your dreams after three nights, I promise to drop the subject forever."

Rosalind smiled. "You know, I came here to forget everything, not come away with an assignment. But I'm not worried. I never remember my dreams."

Issy grinned. "This will be a great exercise if, and only if, you follow the directions. Write your request before you fall asleep. Can you call me tomorrow and tell me what you remember? Deal?'

Rosalind looked directly into Issy's eyes. "You're on."

Chapter Seven

On her way out of the gardens Rosalind checked the time. In five minutes the Kelco team would meet at the Daily Planet. It was only ten minutes out of her way. The Planet was the watering hole of choice two blocks away from the office. Rosalind had heard rumors that more than one individual often would leave their car at the office, walk to the bar, overdo it, and walk back to their car to sleep it off. Reporters and editors from the newspaper across the street, and anyone who was anyone in marketing and advertising spent more time there than they'd admit.

Rosalind wasn't interested in reliving her morning -- much less socializing. But she wondered. *Was Tony murdered, and if so, would the murderer attend? And who else would show up? Were people ready to talk about what they knew?* Since she already had left the casita, maybe she needed to reconsider. If she saw the group on the patio, she and Hercules would join them. If they were inside, where Hercules could not go, she would head straight home. She steered her car toward the Planet parking lot and saw Josh at a round table nursing his beer, eyes glued to the supersize monitors which lit the entire outside bar. She parked and gave Hercules a snack for being such a good companion.

Except for the chairs at Josh's table, there were no empty seats in the place. She took a seat next to him.

"Are we the only ones here? I thought you would have drawn a huge crowd."

"Yeah, I wouldn't have predicted that you would have been the first one here." Josh held his hand out to Hercules who sniffed and then sat between them. "I texted everyone after talking to Detective Hamilton. Kelco hasn't experienced anything like this, so it's impossible to know how everyone will react." Josh waved to the proprietor, Ernie, who tended bar behind the open overhead garage door that was closed when the weather was bad. Today was warm and sunny, a perfect beautiful autumn day. "What would you like to drink?"

"Ah, the same thing you have." She noticed a strawberry blond-haired woman at the bar who turned to offer a sad smile to Josh.

Josh held up two fingers. "Ernie, two more Leinenkugel, please."

The drinks arrived just as the patio gate banged open. Graham Grayson strode to the table. He pulled out a chair and sat on the other side of Josh. When Rosalind turned back toward the entrance, she could not believe she saw Tony's ex-wife, Pamela Hanson Findley.

Pamela was stunning. Blond hair, piercing blue eyes. The exquisite scent of jasmine surrounded her.

She sat down next to Graham who immediately straightened his posture. His eyes brightened. "Pamela, what brings you here? I thought this was an employee only meeting."

"The invitation was wide open. Why would I miss this? My sources tell me everyone wants to be here, but who knows who will show. I need to know everything to protect my interests." Hercules set his head on Rosalind's lap. She gently scratched the top of his head.

"Your interests?"

"Tony and I are divorced but I'm the first ex-wife, so I have privileges which I plan to maintain."

"I bet you do." Josh whistled. "How did you find out about this get-together?"

"I have my contacts."

Josh sipped his beer. "So, what have you all heard?"

Graham raised an eyebrow and leaned forward. He looked around the bar to see who was near them. Josh and Rosalind leaned in close. "All I know is he is dead. Some said they can't believe he wasn't killed sooner."

Pamela leaned in, too. "Are you certain he was killed?"

"Nothing is certain," said Josh, "but Tony wasn't one to come into work early. It was quite the scene with the police and EMTs this morning."

"What did you see?" Pamela rotated a diamond ring back and forth on her right hand.

"Graham and I got to the office at the same time, we didn't see anything, and we were taken to the conference room straightaway. We couldn't talk until after we met with Detective Hamilton."

"Max was there?" asked Pamela. "Too bad he only earns a detective's salary."

Josh rolled his eyes. "The only others I saw were Audra and Rosalind." He gestured across the table. "Then we were questioned separately."

"What did you tell the police?" asked Pamela.

Dead Reckoning

"All I could tell them was what I knew about Tony before today…he's a top account manager, he knew how to create a scene, and Kelco would not have survived without him. Rosalind, you were there ahead of me. What did you see?"

Rosalind swallowed hard, then slowly took another sip of her beer. "It was awful. I never had such a horrible experience. I was headed to the break room for coffee, and Tony was on the floor, but he didn't move." There was no way Rosalind would tell them about the copier.

From the inside back of the restaurant, Theresa Mars walked toward their table. In one fluid motion, everyone sat back in their chairs.

Pamela turned to Josh. "When did she get here?"

"I don't know. I've been here since 5:15. She didn't come through this way."

"Hello co-workers. And Pamela." Theresa glanced at Pamela through swollen, red-rimmed eyes. "I'm glad to see you here alive and kicking."

The group nodded at Theresa and mumbled hellos. Theresa had been the Kelco receptionist for more than twenty-three years. She oversaw phone calls, meetings, mail, and dry-cleaning. She knew everything about everyone, and, if she didn't know, she found out. She took the chair next to Pamela.

"Theresa, you hear everything. What's everyone saying?" asked Josh.

"Lots of talk, but nothing concrete. The police left the office around 4 p.m. but they'll return tomorrow morning." She shifted in her chair and brushed her blonde bangs off her forehead. Her roots needed a touch up. "Anyway, who saw Tony?"

"I didn't, but I heard he was in a compromising position." Graham tipped his chair back on two legs.

"What is a compromising position for Tony?" asked Josh.

"Who knows? Bob said it was so sad to see him," said Graham.

"Bob saw him?" asked Pamela.

"Oh, yes, he found Tony and Rosalind together, and Tony was dead on the floor." Graham expected a gasp from the group, but it never came. He shrugged his shoulders, pressed his feet to the floor and tilted his chair back again.

Rosalind hooked her hair behind her ears and took another drink still cushioning Hercules' head. She cleared her throat to minimize irritation in her tone. "Graham, I need to set the record straight. I found Tony but we did not spend the evening together if that is what you mean by 'together.'"

The gate swung open again, and Audra Lorenz walked to the table and sat next to Rosalind. "Hello all, sorry to be late. Please don't let me interrupt. I'll catch up."

Pamela looked directly at Graham. "What do you mean together?"

"Well, I don't know exactly, I just know it was in the hallway." Graham tilted further back on his chair.

"That sounds a bit odd, don't you think?" Pamela squirmed her nose as if she smelled a skunk.

"It sure does," said Theresa. "Rosalind, you're such a workaholic. Getting to work so early every day."

Rosalind cringed at Theresa's remark but ignored it. Theresa was always rude to her, why should today be different?

Audra exchanged glances with Pamela. "When I arrived, Rosalind was standing next to him. By the time Bob called 911, Rosalind fainted. There was nothing odd about it from what I saw."

"That's correct, Audra," said Rosalind.

Pamela nodded. "I think Tony would be disappointed to have left this earth without creating more of a scene."

Graham cut in. "Did the police contact Cassandra?"

"No idea, I assume so, but who knows? Did you call her, Theresa?" Josh raised his glass to his lips and swallowed a quarter of his beer.

"I didn't call Cassandra." Ernie set a martini in front of Theresa, and she appeared grateful for the distraction.

"Cassandra? Who is Cassandra?" asked Pamela.

Josh's drink slipped through his fingers dropping on the table, beer foaming over the mug and spraying his neighbors. He apologized and offered napkins all around. "Tony has been dating Cassandra for more than six months."

"I...I didn't know." Pamela uncrossed her legs, then re-crossed them the opposite way. "Gosh, isn't it enough that Jennifer will be going after his estate? And now he had a steady girlfriend who could make trouble, too. Just how steady is...or was this relationship?"

"Going strong. She really has…well, had a connection with him. I heard they're engaged," said Audra.

"Enough. I must contact my attorney now." Pamela scooped up her Prada purse, sprang from her chair and bolted toward the exit.

"Dang." Graham's eyes followed her as she walked to her car. "I wish I were her attorney."

Rosalind shook her head. "I need to go. All this is irrelevant. Tony is dead, gone forever. To talk money and rumors, it's too much for me. Come on, Hercules. Good night y'all." She slowly pushed the gate open and gently closed it, but she really wanted to fling the gate open and slam it shut along with all the meaningless drama.

Chapter Eight

Despite a restless night, Rosalind started Wednesday attempting to follow her routine. She donned her left knee brace, grabbed a bottled water, then she and Hercules walked out of the door at 5:30 a.m. A long run was what she needed to shake the disconcerting mood she had since she left the Daily Planet.

Rosalind loved the outdoors, and the warm Arizona weather was the best tonic. She breathed in the orange, pink and yellow blossoms bursting open in her yard and through the entire Valley this autumn. Her neighbor's oleanders added stunning hues to the brown earthy landscape. The melancholy cooing of the mourning doves was music to her ears.

Hercules sniffed along the white lantana, barked at a gecko, and scattered stones on the sidewalk when a gecko scampered up and over the wall. Rosalind gently kicked the stones back into the yard. The morning was her favorite time of day. And it was a gorgeous day for a run.

They ran their usual jaunt around the subdivision and neighboring communities off Galvin Parkway. By 6:15 a.m. they had walked back through the gate and secured the latch. The sun edged above the horizon. The timers cut the lights in Aunt Ruth's house. Rosalind felt alone without the lights to comfort her especially when her aunt traveled for her job as a flight attendant. She should return home today. Rosalind jogged past the main house to her casita on the back half acre of the property.

She was grateful for her aunt's generosity despite the strain on their relationship caused by her early marriage. When Rosalind's parents died unexpectedly, Ruth offered the casita to Rosalind. Instead of accepting her aunt's offer, Rosalind married then divorced her high school sweetheart, delaying the move for a few years. She felt foolish for believing marriage would give her a sense of home and family again.

As Rosalind and Hercules entered the casita, her phone rang. She pulled it out of her pocket. "Hello?"

"Hey Rosalind, how are you?" asked Bob.

"Fine," she lied. "I was just getting ready to drive to the office."

"Well, that's why I'm calling. The office is closed for the day."

Dead Reckoning

Rosalind sighed, then pulled off Hercules' leash and harness. "Bob, is that necessary?" She paused. Maybe it was a blessing not to see where she found Tony. "Is it ok if I work from home? The bills and payroll are already a day behind." Rosalind put Bob on speaker so she could fill the dog's water bowl. Hercules slurped his fresh water and jumped on the couch which he covered almost entirely when stretched across it.

"The company prefers that we grieve in private today so no work in the office or at home. The police are still working on site. We should know when and where Tony's service will be later this afternoon."

Rosalind clenched her hands together. "Bob, please tell me I don't have to attend the service. I don't think I can bear it."

"Oh, we should all attend."

Rosalind switched the phone off speaker and back to her ear. She ran her fingers through her hair trying to find an excuse not to go. "Um, I'm not certain I can."

"Rosalind, you found him. You know your relationship with him was tempestuous at best. This is not the time to raise any suspicions."

"Suspicions? Who could suspect me?"

"Well, you found him. It automatically makes you a 'person of interest.' The company expects all employees to attend. No one should stand out by not being there. And the whole organization is in shock and has to regroup before we move forward without Tony."

Rosalind sighed. "He had the bulk of the billings but surely the company can survive."

"I'll text you with the time of the service. I have more people to call. Take care, Rosalind." Bob hung up.

She turned to Hercules. "It's you and me today, Herc. No work for me."

Hercules peered up at Rosalind. She heard the hum of a jet engine soar above the casita. Rosalind picked up her phone to check if she had service. No bars. Whenever planes flew over the property following the Sky Harbor airport flight path, service dropped. The bars reappeared after the plane moved past their neighborhood.

Rosalind pulled out a chair and sat down. She propped her elbows on the table, then rested her head in her hands. Her run helped, but Bob's call unsettled her. Bob didn't comment whether Kelco could survive without Tony.

Hercules jumped off the couch, walked to her, and set his chin in her lap. Rosalind crossed her arms and laid her head down.

Two hours later, the doorbell rang. Groggy from her unplanned nap, she looked through the peephole. She swung the door open.

"Aunt Ruth, thank goodness you're home."

"Rosie, why aren't you at work?" Ruth reached out and hugged her niece.

'Well, it's been an unusual 24 hours. Do you have time to talk?"

"Come over so I can unpack while we catch up. I bought the European coffee you like so much."

"I'm in." Rosalind grabbed her phone and walked out the door behind Ruth.

"Come on, Hercules." More coffee was just the antidote she needed to combat the suspicions that hung over her.

Chapter Nine

At five feet ten inches, Ruth Hoffman was difficult to miss in a crowd. She was a head taller than Rosalind with dark auburn hair and a graceful, ballerina walk. As a flight attendant, Ruth traveled the United States and Europe. She loved flying and had explored the world.

Rosalind looked up to her aunt in more ways than height. Even though Rosalind didn't move to Arizona when Christopher and Elizabeth Schmidt were killed, Ruth wrote her niece weekly until the time was right for the transition.

Once they entered the main house, Ruth pulled her suitcase into the laundry room then headed back to the kitchen. She opened the coffee bag, added the grounds to the filter basket, poured in water, and pressed the brew button.

"Something's upset you." Ruth, always multitasking, headed back to the laundry room and tossed clothes from her luggage straight into the washer.

Rosalind walked her aunt through everything from Tuesday morning until Bob's unnerving call. Hercules' ears perked up and his head turned side to side to watch whoever spoke. When Rosalind finished, she felt relieved.

"What a bizarre turn of events. How can I help?"

"Just listening to me helped. Beyond that I don't know what either of us can do. Because of my relationship with Tony, people might consider me a suspect. And I don't even know what caused his death."

Ruth poured laundry detergent into the washer tray, clicked the setting, and hit start. "That man made enemies at every turn." They headed back to the kitchen.

"You're right, but fortunately for them, I'm the one who found him laying lifeless on the floor." Rosalind shivered despite the beam of sunshine streaming through the window.

"The police will find the guilty party."

"Hopefully soon. But what can I do in the meantime?" She regretted the question as soon as she asked it.

"Steer clear of the commotion." Ruth zipped up her suitcase and stood it upright next to the washer. "If we need to, we'll find an attorney, but not yet. In the meantime, why don't you distract yourself with something? Did you have any luck figuring out how your grandfather came to the United States?"

Rosalind shrugged. She wanted to build a stronger bond with Aunt Ruth. Doing the legwork on their family tree would help to cement their relationship. Yet, Rosalind feared disappointing her. "I doubt I have the patience to focus right now."

"What better time is there?" Ruth raised an eyebrow when she grabbed coffee mugs, filling each to the brim with the fresh brew. She walked to the living room motioning Rosalind to follow.

Rosalind perched on the arm of the leather couch. The intricate hand painted teal and burgundy flowered tiles that surrounded the fireplace comforted her. The dark furniture suggested a hint of Native American overtones amid Spanish architecture.

Rosalind knew better than to disagree with her aunt. Ruth spent her free time trying to locate her birth parents to no avail. She embraced her adoptive family and loved them, of course, but she wanted to know more about her biological family.

"Well, I received an email yesterday about what to do next." Rosalind pulled a piece of paper out of her pocket and hit the highlights of Margaret Gardner's email.

"Sounds like a good start. It's the beginning of a journey."

Rosalind smiled. She loved to learn new things but filling in her family tree would require more than a lesson or two.

"She recommended a book written in German and Russian."

"Great, we can brush up our German and rejuvenate our brain cells. I can already hear the synapses firing." Ruth laughed.

"Speak for yourself." Rosalind knew a little of the language, but it had been years since she spoke it. Car tires crunched on the gravel driveway. Out the window, Rosalind saw a black car stop near the entrance. Detective Hamilton. Rosalind's heart sank to her feet.

"It's the police detective from yesterday. His name is Max Hamilton."

Before Aunt Ruth could respond, Hamilton knocked on the front door.

"Go to the back of the house and stay out of sight." Ruth motioned Rosalind into the kitchen. "I'll answer the door." Hercules followed Rosalind.

With her hand on the doorknob, Ruth looked back to ensure Rosalind was out of sight then opened the door.

Dead Reckoning

When her eyes met Detective Hamilton's gaze, she feigned surprise. "Oh, hello officer, may I help you?"

"Good morning, I'm Detective Hamilton. Is Rosalind Schmidt here?"

"No, Rosalind lives in the casita.."

"Oh, I see."

Ruth nodded. "I'm Ruth Hoffman." She extended her hand. Hamilton shook it.

"May I come in?"

"Is there a problem, officer?"

"Detective. Routine procedure. I need to ask you a few questions."

Ruth shrugged her shoulders and held out her hand toward the brown leather couch in the front room. She smiled, closed the door after he entered, then walked to the couch and motioned for him to sit on the opposite end. "How can I help you?"

"I have some questions about Rosalind Schmidt. What can you tell me about her?"

"What do you need to know?" Ruth smiled graciously.

"Do you know where she was last Monday night?"

"I don't. I was out of town. I'm a flight attendant. I was gone from Sunday until about two hours ago."

"What can you tell me about her?"

"Rosalind is a great tenant and a nice woman. Normally she's home on Monday nights."

"She found a co-worker dead at her office yesterday." Hamilton shifted his legs and straightened his posture, so his back did not touch the pillows on the couch.

Ruth raised her index finger and rested it against the side of her forehead. Rosalind could tell Ruth wanted to flirt with the detective. Her coy answers and gracious smile were her giveaways that Rosalind recognized. Ruth widened her eyes as if surprised to hear the news. "How unfortunate. What happened?"

"I can't say at this point as it is under investigation. Did you know Tony Findley?"

"No, detective, I didn't."

Hercules padded into the front room and looked apprehensively at Hamilton. He walked over to the detective, sniffed three times, and laid down at his feet.

Ruth cleared her throat. "May I ask you a question?"

"Of course."

"Why do you leave your hat on indoors?"

Hamilton coughed, then smiled. "You are one of only a few people bold enough to ask me about my hat. It's a long-standing tradition in my family.' He looked down at Hercules who nuzzled against his feet. "You are probably aware that the hat has been associated with law enforcement for decades. As a homicide detective, I wear it to honor all the detectives who came before me, in particular, my father who died in the line of duty." Hamilton stood up.

"I'm so sorry about your father. Obviously, the fedora is more of a tradition than I realized."

"If you find out anything you think may be important to the investigation, please give me a call." Hamilton stood up and carefully stepped around Hercules. He handed Ruth a business card and headed toward the door.

"I can assure you, Detective Hamilton, that Rosalind was not responsible in any way for the death of Tony Findley. She is one of the kindest, most considerate people in the world."

"Thank you for your time." Hamilton opened the door, then walked to his car. Through the window Rosalind could see him look back at Ruth still standing in the doorway. He gave her a slight smile and with his right hand he tipped his hat. He drove off without looking back.

When Ruth closed the door, Rosalind came out of hiding, her hands on her hips. "You were flirting with him!"

Aunt Ruth laughed. "Was I?"

Chapter Ten

After Ruth settled in for a morning nap, Rosalind returned to the casita. She had already finalized customer invoices despite Bob's instruction. But the sooner the invoices were mailed, the sooner Kelco would be paid. She would stop at the bank this afternoon to finalize the bills with notary signatures.

Perplexed about what to do next, she looked at the mess on her kitchen table. She was surrounded by photos, printed emails, and half a grilled cheese sandwich, from which Hercules never moved his eyes, hoping a morsel would drop to the floor.

Feeling stuck, Rosalind called Margaret Gardner. She assumed her call would go to voice mail and was caught off guard when she heard Margaret say, "Hello."

"Hi Margaret, this is Rosalind Schmidt. You answered my email about the Schmidt settlers in Mariental. Do you have a few minutes to talk?"

"Yes, I do."

"I have tracked most of my great-grandparents who were born in Russia, so I'm wondering how I can find out more about their parents and follow the line back?"

"Each Russian village had its own censuses, church records, and family lists. Most records are stored in archives in Saratov or Engels, Russia."

Rosalind imagined archive records accumulating dust on the shelves anticipating the day someone would pull the books away from where they landed decades ago. When the records were opened, dust flew, binding cracked, and pages split open to reveal the past. She almost sneezed at the thought.

"The society translates many records. The books I recommended can help you along with some of the current censuses. If you like, I can check my records and send you what I have for the Schmidt line."

"Thank you, Margaret. Yes, please send me what you have. I will investigate, too and compare what I find to your information."

"When you are ready, we can review it together."

"Great. I will contact you soon."

To Rosalind's delight, her father's village, Mariental, had published many census Lists and birth records. Her mother's village, Reinwald, had less censuses, but Rosalind would explore that village next. Ruth was curious about both lines of the family despite her non-existent blood lines. Family connections did not always equate to DNA connections.

Why not start a genealogical book collection to demonstrate her commitment to Aunt Ruth? Rosalind purchased Mariental census lists and books as she worked through the site's online store. Straying from her budget, she finalized her purchase which included *Einwanderung in das Wolgagebiet 1764-1767 Band 1, 3 and 4* by Igor Pleve, and *1798 Census of the German Colonies along the Volga Volume 1 and 2* by Brent Alan Mai. These books were investments to keep her busy until she could return to work. She paid extra for next day delivery.

Next task was the photographs still scattered across her table. This piece was not as easy as ordering books online. Rosalind propped her elbow on the table and rested her chin on her fist. She had counted at least two hundred loose photos and five photo albums.

"Hercules, here I go, guessing the decade of each photo. Perhaps fashion, cars, and houses will provide clues." Then her phone rang.

"Hey Issy."

"Hey Rosalind, how about a girl's get together tonight? Do you have snacks and wine at your place?"

"No, not much, maybe some potato chips."

"Ok, I'll pick-up a good pinot and snacks so we can chill this evening. Sound good?"

"That sounds great. I'll be here with open arms."

"Good. Oh, also I was curious which animal you discovered to be your totem. Remember our deal?"

"Oh, Issy, I'm sorry, I stopped at the Daily Planet after I saw you and I completely forgot."

"I knew I should've reminded you. Don't worry I'll bring you a new dream notebook, too. See ya later." Issy hung up before Rosalind could disagree.

How did she forget something so simple? She knew she would win the bet. All she had to do was accept the notebook, put it next to her bed, sleep, wake up and she would win the bet. Dreams? No way would she remember any dreams.

For the next hour, Rosalind guessed and separated the photos into piles of the 1920s, 30s, 40s, 50s, 60s and 70s. Once she identified her grandparents and great-grandparents, and estimated their age, she guessed the year. It may not be accurate, but it was a start.

She labeled by decade the blue archival storage boxes she had, then carefully tied the photos together with ribbon and stored them in the containers. As she picked up one of the packages Ruth had given her, she heard a thump.

Rosalind turned the box upside down to empty the contents and noticed a brown leather case stuck out between two photo albums near the top of the pile. She pulled it out.

The case was worn smooth and appeared handmade. Rosalind ran her fingers over the dry leather which had not been cared for in years and smelled of the prairie, a bit like manure. Hand-engraved etched lines of angels among magnificent clouds over a fertile land growing plants that Rosalind believed was tobacco, were darkened with time.

She undid the band and carefully slid the case open. An elegantly carved wooden handle transported Rosalind back in time, a time she could not recognize but felt her heart drawn to. She touched the decorative handle and a chill shuddered down her spine. Were the temperatures dropping to autumn norms? Or was she connecting with an ancestor's prized possession? She examined the swirls and twists in the wood then gently slipped the handle out to reveal a blackened, yet sharp knife. Why would this knife be in a box of photo albums? She grabbed her phone and photographed the knife with its case from all angles. Hercules eyed her, patiently waiting for Rosalind to notice.

Rosalind looked at Hercules and realized why he was staring at her. She lifted her plate. "It's all yours, Herc. Enjoy," and set her leftovers on the floor.

Hercules snapped up the grilled cheese as the plate touched the ground. He was happy.

"Hercules, I need to figure out how old this knife is. I also need to get a notary to sign these invoices. Can you guard the casita?" Hercules tipped his head to the right, and Rosalind accepted it as a yes.

She walked to her Volvo, jumped into the driver's seat, and drove to an antique shop she remembered passing in southern Scottsdale.

As she opened the door, a shopkeepers bell rang out. She stepped through the threshold and was transported back in time surrounded by antique clocks, estate furniture, and display cases of shiny jewelry. She inhaled the scent of ages past.

"Hello?" She walked further into the past then heard footsteps and to her right a man wearing a full apron over jeans and a Chicago Bears t-shirt emerged.

"Hello, can I help you find something?"

"Do you conduct antique appraisals?" asked Rosalind.

"Yes, I do. I'm James Simon. And to whom do I have the pleasure of talking?" He extended his hand to her.

Rosalind accepted his hand and shook it. "I'm Rosalind Schmidt, and I'd like to determine the age of this knife. I know nothing about its history. But I hoped you could date it and tell me what you can of its origin."

"Are you looking to sell the piece?"

"No, not at this time. I'm interested in the value, but I want to know how old it is and if it was made in the United States or elsewhere. I'm happy to pay for the appraisal." Rosalind pulled the knife case out of her purse and handed it to James.

Before he accepted it, he slipped on archival gloves from his apron pocket. James reached for the leather case, looked at it, and whistled. He unfastened the band and extracted the knife with the wood handle and the dark blade.

"The blade is iron, not the stainless steel used for knives today, so you are correct, it is old. To determine its age, I need to run some tests. I don't have the equipment here, but I have good, reliable contacts who can help."

"I can see you are a Chicago Bears fan. Can you assure me, despite that, that the knife will be safe and returned to me in the same condition?"

James laughed. "You must be a Packer fan." Rosalind nodded and he continued. "And, despite that, I can assure you the knife will be safe and returned you exactly as it is now. By the way, this wood is birch, incredibly old birch."

Rosalind drifted back and remembered the old birch tree next to the garage of her family home. Majestic, until lightning struck it causing it to split and crash to the ground narrowly missing the garage. Could her father have used some of that wood to have this knife made? Surely, he would have told the family about it if he had saved a piece of that history. "Ok, that would be great. Thank you."

Dead Reckoning

James provided Rosalind with an estimate, asked for a week or two to get some results, and wrapped the knife gently in cloth. After handing her a detailed receipt, she left the store, heady with thoughts of long-ago.

Chapter Eleven

Rosalind drove to the bank to utilize their notary service to finalize the Kelco customer invoices. As she walked into the waiting area, she saw Pamela Findley sitting and clicking her heel against the coffee table.

The bags sagging under Pamela's blue eyes made her look like she hadn't slept for days. Pamela's fingers were wrapped tightly into fists as Rosalind approached. The scent of jasmine permeated the air around her.

"Pamela..."

"Rosalind, service here is slow. I have already waited for five minutes."

"Did you have an appointment?"

"Why do I need an appointment to access my safety deposit box?"

Rosalind shrugged. "I'm sorry. And I am also sorry about Tony."

Pamela shuddered. "I never planned to work for a living again. I need to get to our deposit box to see his will and confirm I'm still his beneficiary. My attorney doesn't know who will inherit Tony's estate...his boat, his cabin, his apartment, his portfolio, and the nightclub. I thought my monthly maintenance payments would last forever. I was wrong." Pamela tried to open her fist, but her fingers were so tightly wrapped she had to pry each finger open with her other hand to reveal a key. When Pamela lifted the key, Rosalind saw a reddened replica of it embedded on her palm.

A bank attendant walked up to them. "Mrs. Findley, we are ready for you now."

Pamela exhaled a sigh of relief. She looped her bag on her arm and walked toward the vault.

"See you later, Pamela." Rosalind watched as Pamela walked into the vaulted room where a rectangular beige metal box was left on the center of the table. Pamela inserted the key into the lock, turned it to the right, and heard the lock disengage. As she lifted the lid, the bank attendant closed the vault door.

After waiting a few minutes, Rosalind was escorted to the notary's desk. As the last of the invoices were notarized, she heard sirens wailing in the distance reminding her of the police arriving at Kelco. Once her business was done, she walked to the front door. A fire truck with flashing lights blocked the bank entrance. In an instant,

Dead Reckoning

paramedics burst through running to the vault where the door was now open.

Rosalind froze, watching until the EMTs lifted Pamela onto the stretcher. Please don't be dead, she thought.

As the gurney passed Rosalind, she saw tears puddled in Pamela's eyes, her hand clasping two crushed envelopes hanging out of her purse. Pamela wasn't dead. Rosalind approached but the EMTs would not let her get close. She heard Pamela mumbling, "No...you told me I was the one... I hate you...none of this was worth it."

The bank attendant walked next to the stretcher until the EMTs quickly loaded her into the ambulance. When he came back inside, Rosalind approached him. "What happened?"

"She finished her business and was walking toward the vault door when she screamed and clutched her chest. We immediately called 911."

Rosalind thanked him and left the bank more confused than ever. As she turned back to look toward the vault, she noticed a crushed envelope on the ground similar to the ones in Pamela's bag. Rosalind bent to pick it up, planning to return it to the attendant. She grabbed it off the floor, but photographs and a CD dropped out of the envelope. Her mouth fell open. One of the pictures was of herself and Tony.

Chapter Twelve

After her bizarre encounter at the bank, Rosalind drove directly past the post office forgetting to mail the invoices that seemed so important earlier. Pamela's words --*None of this was worth it*-- cycled in Rosalind's mind. Could Pamela have killed Tony to get his money? And why did Tony have a photo of her in their safety deposit box?

Looking for distraction, Rosalind gathered up her photo boxes and took them to Ruth's house. When they settled at the kitchen table Rosalind convinced Ruth to review the semi-organized photographs together.

The blazing sun shone through the side window brightening the room as Rosalind leaned over the table. Twisting and turning from side to side, Ruth re-arranged the organized photos documenting who she recognized. Occasionally one of them picked up a photo, printed names and potential dates on a post it note, then stuck the note on the back of the picture.

"Ah, now this one brings back memories. Your dad loved the knife his grandfather gave to him. I remember the day this picture was taken. We had a picnic in the backyard, played badminton, and Mom made great side dishes to go with the barbequed pork." Ruth sighed as she handed the photo to Rosalind. "I wish I had her recipes."

Rosalind looked at the photograph. "I found this knife in one of the boxes. I'm getting it appraised. What do you know about it?"

"It's a family heirloom, I have no idea who had it before your great-grandfather."

"How old was dad when this was taken?"

"I'd say about ten years old. It was the 4th of July."

Rosalind attached a post-it to the back photo with the information. "Now this next photo has me curious. It's my Mom and it looks like she is standing in front of her high school. Who is the guy next to her?:

"Gosh, I can't remember his name. They were quite close in high school. We might need to find her yearbook to track down his name."

Rosalind made another note to find her mother's yearbooks, likely stored in one of Ruth's spare rooms.

"We're making progress." Ruth went to her kitchen desk and grabbed two small boxes. "You remember how my original birth certificate was impounded?"

Dead Reckoning

"If I remember correctly, the only version you can get is the amended birth certificate showing your adoptive parent's information."

"That's right. But, well, it's a longshot, but there might be a way for me to find out who my birth parents are." Ruth held out one of the kits to Rosalind.

"A DNA test?"

"It's my only chance to get any answers. Neither of us has any children we don't know about, so we won't open that can of worms." Rosalind nodded as Ruth opened her kit and then she followed suit. They read the directions carefully, giggling as they spit into the vials, filled in the forms, and smiled once the process was completed.

They were so preoccupied enclosing their samples that they did not notice a car pull into the driveway. They jumped when they heard a knock at the back door.

Rosalind said, "Audra, come in. We were just brewing some more coffee."

"Coffee this late in the day? Count me in," said Audra.

Hercules jumped up and down toward Audra until Rosalind said, "Good boy, Hercules. Sit." Her well-trained Doberman sat until Audra crossed the threshold and he followed behind her. He knew Audra was a soft touch and that she carried special treats.

Ruth sat with a steaming cup of coffee in front of her. Her eyebrows narrowed as she saw Audra enter and said, "Audra, you are the most impeccably dressed person I know?"

"Thank you, Aunt Ruth. How is business above the clouds?" asked Audra.

"Just wonderful. I have the best job in the world."

Audra sat in the chair next to Ruth. "So, these are the famous photos you told me about. You are right, there are a lot of pictures."

"These are from the 1940s. I have five more decades in the casita." Rosalind walked to the coffee pot and poured another cup. She set the hot mug in front of Audra who inhaled the aroma before sipping. She smiled and shrugged her shoulders with the relief only a good cup of coffee could provide.

"Any updates from the police?" asked Rosalind.

"Nothing new. I think the police have interviewed everyone in the company. Have you heard anything?"

"Nothing at all. I hope we can go to work tomorrow and put this behind us."

Audra shook her head. "I wish it was that easy." She took another sip of coffee then leaned forward in her chair. "Didn't Bob call you?"

"I haven't heard from him." Rosalind picked up her phone. No messages. No texts.

"I'm sure he'll call you soon. I heard from him about a half hour ago. The office will be open tomorrow for limited staff only."

"Which means?" Rosalind picked up her mug and peered over the rim.

Audra cleared her throat. "Well, corporate believes anyone who could be considered a party to the situation should not report to work."

"A party to the situation? Everyone knew Tony."

"Well, in other words, anyone who could be involved needs to remain off site. Pending the police investigation, of course." Audra sat back in her chair.

"Who is limited staff?"

"Me, Bob, Theresa, Josh, maybe a few others."

Rosalind shook her head slowly in disbelief. "Is Bob suspending me?"

"No, I don't think so." Audra crossed her arms with her elbows on the table. "Stay here, relax for a few days. Work on your hobbies, get some new plants for the yard."

Rosalind loved the flora of Arizona and rarely drove past a nursery without stopping to check on stock. She had completely revamped her yard over a year ago. Audra knew that. Rosalind shot her a look.

Audra shrugged. "Well perhaps it's time for a new hobby? Continue working through the photos?"

"Ok, I get it. Bob doesn't want me in the office. But it could be months before the police find Tony's killer. Who else needs to stay away from the office?"

"I'm not certain. He'll call you soon."

"Seriously, I need to get back to keep our finances afloat. That should be our top priority." Rosalind groaned. "Audra, does corporate think I killed Tony? Is my job at risk?"

"I don't know, Rosalind. Bob said those who can't come to the office will receive full pay." Audra stood up, grabbed her purse, and walked to the door. "I'll be in touch. Bob will call you soon. He'll share the funeral details when they're confirmed." She opened the door and stood with her hand on the knob like she wanted to run out of the house.

Rosalind's shoulders sank and her head rolled forward. "I dread attending funerals."

With a sympathetic look, Audra turned back. "I know it's not fair. However, everyone must attend his funeral. And on the bright side you have time. Better yet, time off with pay. You could go to a yoga class…" Audra's words hung in the air without closure. She stepped through the threshold and gently closed the door behind her.

Rosalind's stare stopped Ruth from saying a word. Stalling, Ruth picked up the pot and refilled their cups. "I know you want to work, but there could be a good reason for a break. We just don't know the reason yet."

"I feel betrayed. In this mood, I should start looking for a new job." She drank the fresh coffee, then set her cup on the table. "It's like I'm guilty, sentenced, and I didn't have a fair trial. Or any trial at all."

"I understand, and you need to acknowledge those feelings. Hopefully, you'll find something positive about staying home."

"Ah, I can think of one positive thing. The best part of not going to the office is I am not the one who has to clean the copier."

Chapter Thirteen

Rosalind returned to the casita after she delivered the DNA kits and invoices to the post office. She glanced out her window. Two hummingbirds fluttered around the red yuccas, diving into the dried flowers for their dinner.

As she waited for Issy to arrive, Rosalind drew a preliminary family tree with Christoph Schmidt at the top, followed by generations of question marks, until she wrote the names of her great-grandparents, grandparents, parents, and then hers. There were quite a few blank brackets spanning over 250 years that she needed to fill in.

Rosalind's phone chimed with a new email Bob sent to the entire staff.

"Update. The police have confirmed that Tony's death was murder. He was poisoned. We will update you when we hear more. Thank you for your cooperation during this challenging time. The memorial service will be Thursday at 5:30 p.m. See you there."

Poisoned. Well, that should clear my name. She didn't know anything about poisons. Hercules walked toward her with a small tennis ball in his mouth. She grabbed the ball and tossed it toward the living area. Hercules ran after it and jumped on the couch where the ball landed.

Poisoned. How could it be? She felt her throat tighten and wondered if any of her ancestors experienced days like yesterday and today.

Rosalind knew one thing. She deserved wine tonight more than ever.

Chapter Fourteen

Thursday morning when Rosalind awoke, something dug into her side. Her head throbbed from dehydration, but the item poking her was more annoying than her headache. It was not Hercules. He was resting near her feet at the bottom of the bed. From the edges of the window shutters, she saw the sun had already risen. They were usually out the door at dawn, but their regular run might not happen, at least not this morning. As she stretched, the digging in her side persisted and she rolled over to uncover the culprit.

Oh, yes, now she remembered. Issy, along with her wine and snacks, brought her a dream notebook. How did it move under her during the night? She pulled it out but couldn't find her pen which was clipped to it when she set it on her nightstand. How odd.

Rosalind looked at the page. What was she seeing? There was writing on the first page. Well, writing might be an exaggeration, more like scribbling. Actual scribbles. And to make it worse it looked like her scribbling, yet it was impossible to read. Did she dream during the night? Or did she just try to write something? In the back of her mind, a dream memory stirred, leaving a sensation of being on board a ship, swaying to the movement of water.

"Hercules, did you write this?" She giggled when Hercules lifted his head and dropped his jaw open as if he was going to laugh.

She wished Hercules would answer. She had no recollection of picking up the pen, much less opening the notebook, holding it, or writing. It gave her an out with Issy. Yes, she can tell Issy she tried but no one could possibly make out this illegible gibberish.

Rosalind slipped on a sweatshirt and jeans then walked to the kitchen carrying the notebook. She knew Issy would insist on seeing the evidence that her scheme did not work. She set the notebook on the kitchen table to remember to take it with her the next time she visited Issy. Rosalind grabbed a glass of water, an energy bar, two aspirin, and she downed all four.

Before she could feed Hercules, she heard tires crunch on the gravel in the driveway. She looked out the window and saw Hamilton's dark car approach her casita.

"Oh, no," sighed Rosalind. "I don't need to see the police today."

Hercules gazed at her wondering why there was no food in the bowl. As he waited patiently near his dish, Rosalind walked to the door and opened it just as Max Hamilton stepped on the welcome mat.

"Good morning. I'm sorry to drop in without an appointment, but Bob told me you might be here this morning. May I come in?" Hamilton smiled revealing dimples which creased his face. In a good way.

Rosalind waved her hand from the door towards the kitchen. Hamilton entered and she motioned for him to sit at the kitchen table.

"More questions for me, Detective?"

"I have additional information about the Anthony Findley case. Things are moving fast, so there are more questions."

"Ok. I guess it's not like I have much choice in the matter."

"I understand these are trying times." Hamilton sat in the chair opposite Rosalind. He pushed his hat farther back on his head. "First, I finished talking to Theresa Mars yesterday and she believes that you killed Anthony Findley. Why do you think she believes you could be a murderer?"

"How would I know why and what Theresa thinks?" Exasperated, Rosalind looked at Hamilton. His expression was firm as he demanded a better answer. And Rosalind realized she did not have one. She wasn't certain what made her more furious, the accusation or Hamilton's silence. She did her best to keep her voice even and calm.

"I wish I could answer that question. I honestly do. Theresa and I worked together for more than ten years. We had a good working relationship. Theresa knows everything, and I mean everything. About Kelco, about our co-workers, who spoke to which co-worker before they headed to the rest room. Tony was her favorite and I'm certain she is grieving. She knew Tony was always demanding, he played office pranks, and he was not my favorite. But I told you most of this the day we met. Hardly motives for murder. She is the only one who can answer your question." She stared at the Detective trying to exude confidence while she trembled inside.

Hamilton focused his brown eyes on Rosalind. He tilted his head slightly to the right. "Is your neighbor at home? I don't see any signs of activity at her house."

"No, Aunt Ruth left this morning until tomorrow night."

"Aunt Ruth? She didn't mention she was your aunt when I talked to her a few days ago."

"Did you ask her if we were related?"

Dead Reckoning

"Good point, I didn't. But I do have another question for you." Hamilton's eyes were drawn to the notebook at the edge of the table. "Were you trying to write your memories?"

Rosalind's cheeks blushed scarlet. Everything is open for the police to question. "No, it was a crazy little game a friend and I were trying."

"Game?"

"It's something personal, nothing to do with Tony Findley."

"How personal?"

"Do I have to answer that?"

"Well, you can tell me here, or I could have you come down to the station." He smiled, but Rosalind did not feel any warmth. Could she trust this man?

"That won't be necessary." Rosalind shifted her crossed legs. "It was just a game, like a challenge. I don't remember my dreams. My friend refuses to believe it. She insisted that if I put a notebook close at hand while I slept, when I woke, I would remember and record my dreams. As you can see, she was wrong. I have no recollection, and nothing was written, only unreadable scribbles."

Hamilton held the notebook bringing it close to his eyes, then moved it back slowly. "It is difficult to read, but I can see the word 'bear' right there." He motioned to the slanted gibberish in the middle of the page.

"What? It can't be."

"I see it, it is right there." Hamilton pointed to the center of the page.

Rosalind grabbed the notebook and carefully examined the scribbles again. Could the Detective have a point? It was a stretch, but in the right light she could see 'bear' but, there was no way she could have written it.

"Whatever your bet was, it's a tie at best. We may have more questions as this case unfolds especially since you are a 'person of interest.' I recommend you stay near your phone. We may need to contact you fast. We want to bring this case to a close as soon as possible." Hamilton rose from the table gathering his tablet. "Which friend did you have the deal with?"

"My friend, Issy, she is a botanist at the gardens." Rosalind was glad to think these questions were coming to an end.

"Well, that is quite interesting. Quite interesting indeed. And you volunteer at the Desert Botanical Gardens?"

"Wow, I did not see that question coming, but yes, I do. I love desert plants, everything that grows here in Arizona. I usually volunteer there once a week. Why do you ask?"

"Because the poison that killed Tony Findley was oleander." He let that detail hang in the air for a few moments before saying, "Thank you for your time."

Hamilton let himself out.

Rosalind mumbled to Hercules, "Is it common knowledge oleander is poisonous, or do only gardeners and botanists realize it?"

Hercules looked up at her from his bowl.

"Oh baby, I forgot to feed you. I'm sorry." She filled his bowl and added a little extra since he was so patient.

She watched him devour the food and said to herself, "Oleander, why oleander?" Her heart raced, and her lungs strained to inhale air, but she only wheezed. She coughed trying to exhale, and after punching her hand against her solar plexus she slowly regained breathing. She sat quietly trying to make sense of it. Was she being framed? Why would someone frame her? She shivered as she searched for answers that did not come. She would have to ask Aunt Ruth for the name of one of her lawyer contacts, just in case.

She only knew today would become more difficult. Tonight was Anthony Findley's funeral.

Chapter Fifteen

Rosalind wanted to be anywhere else. But she arrived early at the Bethany Lane Funeral Home wearing a beautiful black jacket with a pencil skirt. As she waited in line to enter the building, she saw a purple Lamborghini drive past, then a silver car passed twice. The silver car was not unusual, but she could have sworn Tony Findley was behind the wheel. A woman sat next to him in the passenger seat. If she was seeing visions or losing her mind, this was not the place to do it.

After signing the guest book, she saw Pamela was back on her feet. Whatever caused her to scream and be cared for by EMTs looked like it was in her distant past. Her stunning appearance and calm demeanor was back. Rosalind forgot to bring the photos and CD from the bank. She walked toward the casket standing near the front row of chairs. Theresa Mars and Pamela chatted quietly nearby. Suddenly Pamela turned and called, "Mother Leona, it is so good to see you. You look marvelous considering the circumstances." Despite Pamela's linen handkerchief wiping at invisible tears, she smiled slightly. "And, Ralph, after all these years, we need to catch up."

Rosalind turned to her left and saw Anthony Findley walking with an older woman on her arm. Oh, no, I'm losing it. Rosalind grabbed the closest open chair in the front row.

Before Leona could answer, the Tony look alike unhooked his arm from hers and he moved away from Pamela.

As Rosalind stared she realized the woman was Tony's mother and this man was not Anthony Findley. He had walked into the room with a solemn grace Tony never had. Tony stormed a room. This man glided between the furniture and small gatherings of people. Tony would have burst through, shaking hands, and meeting everyone as if they were old friends. This man was his opposite.

He walked up to the casket near where Theresa Mars stood. Rosalind observed Theresa eye this man closely. He clasped his hands together then he stared at Tony.

Theresa made the sign of the cross. Rosalind did not believe she was religious but maybe old instincts kicked in at a funeral. Then extended her hand. "You must be Ralph. I'm Theresa Mars, I worked with Tony for many years, and he mentioned he had a twin. Were you close?"

Ralph eyed her curiously. Despite his identical looks to the man in the coffin he asked, "Who are you?"

"Oh, I'm so sorry, I'm the director of first Impressions at Kelco Marketing, Theresa Mars. I have known Tony since he started working there. We have our share of secrets, the two of us." She turned to look him in the eye. "Please accept my condolences on the death of your brother."

He frowned and slowly put his hand in hers. "I haven't seen him in a long time. This is all quite a shock to me." Ralph turned back to the casket. Rosalind stood up to follow his gaze to Tony's immaculate deep navy-blue suit and red tie. Impeccably dressed as usual with each hair in perfect place. His ring, a beautiful black onyx stone encased in silver was perched on his middle finger. She noticed Ralph reach out and touch the ring and wondered what memories the ring evoked.

Theresa watched Ralph, too. "It was a shock to all of us. To know someone so full of life and then suddenly, nothing. Terribly sad." Theresa sounded sincere, yet her eyes were cold and deliberate.

Rosalind knew Theresa had guarded Tony during his life, and she would guard him in death. Theresa's dark blonde hair, whose roots were recently colored, was pulled back into a smooth chignon. In contrast, her black suit, black shoes, and diamond jewelry echoed a flashback to the 1980s. Her lips twitched as she watched Ralph.

"The Detective assured me Tony was dead, but I had to see it to believe it. Excuse me, but I see someone with whom I need to talk. Thank you for your condolences, Theresa." Ralph turned to walk in the opposite direction toward the main entrance. Rosalind watched as Detective Hamilton brushed against Ralph.

"So have you solved the mystery of Tony's last hours?" asked Ralph.

"Not yet, but I need you to come to the police station tomorrow."

"And you ask me this now? What reason do you need to speak to me again?"

"Let's discuss that tomorrow at 10 a.m." Hamilton quickly turned, nodded to Rosalind, and walked toward the front entrance. Rosalind watched as Ralph walked through the doorway to the outside. She had the feeling he may never return. She wished she had the nerve to follow him.

Now more than forty people were in the viewing room huddled in small groups, a few venturing to where Tony lay. Leona took Pamela's arm and walked to the casket. Leona held tight to her ex-daughter-in-law's arm as she leaned over Tony and gave him a kiss.

As the two walked away from the casket, Leona patted Pamela's hand. "I heard you had an issue at the bank, my dear."

"Oh, it was nothing, the bank staff overreacted. It was only a mild stress episode, which apparently has the same symptoms as a heart attack. My heart is fine, except for my grief over Tony."

Rosalind couldn't stay near them or Tony's body any longer and walked to the back of the room where she saw Josh and Graham as they stood to the right side keeping a wide perspective on the entire room. She walked toward them, and Josh said, "How are you doing?"

Rosalind looked up at Josh. "Hey, I'm doing ok. I'm here, I made it." She tried to smile. "Not feeling good about this whole thing. I have to admit this is one of the most stressful moments of my life."

"You're very brave. It must have been awful to find Tony at the office."

"It haunts me. I tried not to attend but was told I had to be here since I am a 'person of interest.'"

"Who said you had to attend?"

"Detective Hamilton, Bob, so, everyone."

"Did you sign the register?"

She nodded.

"Then you are covered. It's proof you were here. Come with us, we can grab a few chairs in the back and sit until the time is right to leave."

Josh led Rosalind to a back row of unoccupied chairs. Graham followed closely behind until he noticed Pamela at the front of the room. "Excuse me, guys, I'll be back soon. It's now or never for me to try to talk to Pamela."

Rosalind settled in the chair and finally let out a long breath. Audra and Bob sauntered into the room, scanning the crowd and noting people to whom they needed to connect. Audra saw Rosalind, mouthed "hello," and gave her a thumbs up. Rosalind waved back to her.

Graham stood next to Pamela talking to her and the older woman. Rosalind envied his ability to find camaraderie and conversation within moments.

"How does he do that? He walks up, joins a group, and immediately is part of the conversation. I could have stood there for ten minutes and not been noticed."

Josh chuckled. "I would have noticed you." Glancing across the room, he added, "Oh, it's not that hard once you figure out a few key things to say. I always thought you were too preoccupied with work to bother with much conversation."

"Well, that's true. I focus a lot on my work."

"You don't have to say too much. All you have to do is ask questions and listen."

Before Josh could continue, a priest stood at the podium and put up his hands for silence.

"Welcome everyone, if you could all please take a seat, we will start our service shortly."

Ralph re-appeared and sat in the front row with his mother, Leona, on one side and Theresa Mars on the other. Pamela Findley sat next to Leona. Graham chose the chair on the other side of Pamela.

In the row behind Ralph, Rosalind saw a young blond woman who looked vaguely familiar. She sat next to Ernie from the Daily Planet. Across the aisle, a red-haired young woman sat alone.

"Who is the red-haired woman in the front row?" asked Rosalind.

"That's Cassandra Starmer, Tony's fiancée."

Bob and Audra headed toward Cassandra and sat beside her. As they settled in, Leona nodded to Cassandra. Pamela and Ralph did not. To the left, Rosalind saw Detective Hamilton discreetly take a chair near the back.

Once everyone in the room was seated, the priest recited a short prayer, then said, "Welcome everyone to this memorial service. We are here to celebrate the life of Anthony Findley. We welcome his family," he glanced toward the red-haired woman and the older woman next to Pamela, "and all his friends and associates." He motioned to the redhead in the front row. "Cassandra Starmer, Tony's fiancé, has requested that tonight be a celebration of his life. We experienced sorrow at this sad turn of events. We experienced grief at the loss of this man. However, tonight we honor his memory. There are several people who would like to say a few words in honor of Anthony Findley. Mr. Jansen, would you like to begin?"

Dead Reckoning

Rosalind turned to Josh and whispered, "I doubt that priest ever met Tony."

"Probably not, I have a hard time picturing Tony hanging out with a man of the cloth."

Rosalind stifled a laugh. "Good point. But there must be two hundred people here. I hope they don't all want to talk."

Four people who neither worked at Kelco, nor perceived Tony as Rosalind did, shared anecdotes resulting in tears, laughter, and outright sobs. With each new speaker, the man who looked like Tony stiffened his back solidly against the chair. Pamela bowed her eyes into her handkerchief and held the older woman close. Cassandra stared forward focusing on each speaker.

"This could go on for hours," whispered Rosalind.

Josh shrugged. "We can make it through this, plus we will get to the exit first."

After a young man accompanied by his mother and brother spoke, no one else volunteered to speak. The priest asked if anyone else would like to share their memories. After a few moments, Theresa Mars stood up and walked to the podium.

"Hello everyone, I'm Theresa Mars, one of Tony's closest friends. Tony was a miracle in all our lives. Through his nightclub, he provided entertainment and an exciting lifestyle for his customers and his family. Through his marketing work, he provided lavish results and growing bottom lines. Through his friends, he brought lively and loving relationships, complete and total understanding, and care for everyone. He brought joy and exuberance and love to all who knew him." Theresa's eyes filled with tears. She looked directly into the crowd and repeated, "He brought joy and exuberance and love to all who knew him, except for one person."

The crowd shifted in their chairs and murmured as Theresa paused to gauge their reaction. Once the side conversation quieted, she said, "There is one person who did not love or receive the joy Tony intended for her. This one person tried to make his life a miserable hell until she could no longer tolerate his existence."

Rosalind whispered to Josh. "Who is she talking about?" Certainly, Theresa did not mean Rosalind. She disliked Tony, but Theresa's exaggerations were too much to push on her. There must be someone else that Theresa described.

"Maybe she's crazy?" said Josh.

All eyes were on Theresa. "Yes, there is someone here in this room who hated Anthony Findley. Hated him enough to make sure he did not live another day. The person I refer to is..." The crowd buzzed, and Theresa waited until the sound died and she had their full attention.

The words spat from Theresa's mouth. "The person I refer to is, should I tell you?

The crowd cried, "Yes."

"The person I refer to, the one who is responsible for the death of this great man is...Rosalind Schmidt."

A crowd gasped and every head in the room turned until all eyes were on Rosalind.

"Rosalind, please tell us why you killed Anthony Findley."

Rosalind felt her lungs freeze. Blush colored her cheeks bright red. Rosalind looked around, searching for a place to hide. Before she had a chance to figure out what to do, Josh grabbed hold of her elbow, brought her to her feet and pushed her through the aisle and out of the room. Once at the exit, he turned to the right and they both started to run. They never looked back.

Chapter Sixteen

When they reached the edge of Tempe Town Lake, Rosalind slowed her pace to a walk and Josh fell into step next to her. Both breathed heavily. When they made eye contact, Rosalind asked, "What was that?" She stopped talking to catch her breath, inhaling and exhaling as she bent over resting her hands on her thighs. When she could talk again she said, "What made Theresa lash out at me? I didn't want Tony dead."

"I didn't see that coming. And that crowd staring at you, it was downright frightening."

"All those people must hate me now, or maybe they hated me before she spoke? Since when was Tony this wonderful guy and not the self-centered, bullying, abrasive person trying to get everyone in the office to do his work? Am I the only one who sees him this way?"

"You're not alone. There is always a fear of speaking ill of the dead, a fear which overwhelmed the crowd and created herd mentality. It's impossible to logically comprehend."

"I certainly don't. I'm flabbergasted."

"We need to put our heads together and talk this through. How about we grab a cup of coffee, and give ourselves a chance to catch our breath?" asked Josh.

Rosalind hesitated. What was Josh's true intent? Could she trust him? Josh was always considerate, and he did get her out of an awful scene at the funeral.

"Ok, but I can't stay too long. Hercules is waiting for me."

"Ok, we won't keep Hercules waiting for long."

They walked into a small coffee shop off Mill Avenue. After ordering the coffee of the day, Josh brought the two drinks back to the table.

Josh tested his drink to gauge the temperature. "Ok, tell me about your relationship with Theresa."

"If you had asked me a few days ago, I would have said we were good co-workers. But now? I don't have a clue. I must have offended her or something. Unless…"

"Unless what?"

"Well, grief makes people act strange but why would she cast me in the role of a murderer? Unless she is trying to deflect attention off herself?"

"It's possible. Or she knows who did it and is throwing attention at you to make sure the attention stays off the real murderer."

"Could Detective Hamilton have known something like that would happen?"

"I'm sure he was there to check attendance, eavesdrop on a few conversations. He also needs to see how people react at the service. I guess he would assume the murderer would attend."

Josh rotated the cup in his hand. "Rosalind, Theresa is a bit of an enigma. She knows everyone and everything about Kelco. She knows about more skeletons in closets than I can imagine. I have known her for years, and yet I do not know her at all. She can be a different person depending on the setting, the people around her, or her mood. She thought the world of Tony, but this doesn't add up. We need to figure out how to clear your name."

"I'm not an investigator. The police are paid to figure out who killed Tony. I didn't kill him, and I don't want to invest more of my life being connected to him. I don't know how to investigate a murder."

"I hope you are right that the police should unravel it."

"It's difficult enough not being able to go into the office since I'm 'a party to the situation.' Whatever that means."

Josh tilted his head to the side. "So, if you can't go to work and you don't want to figure out why Theresa accused you of murder, what are you going to do?"

Rosalind shrugged. She struggled to talk to co-workers about what she did away from work. Could she confide in Josh? He did help her out of a tough confrontation.

"I started a project a few days ago. You might laugh."

Josh dropped his smile and put on his serious face. "I promise no matter what you tell me, I won't laugh. Try me."

"It's a huge project. There are no fixed deadlines, plus I have no idea what I can discover or what the result will be. I'm starting to build my family tree." Rosalind waited for the laughter she anticipated. There was none.

"Wow. Where do you even begin with something like that?"

"The best place to start is with yourself. I have a few clues, but I'm still an amateur. My aunt gave me old photographs to organize, you know, try to figure out who is in the picture, then scan and build a digital album. I've looked at some of the pictures, trying to date them by looking at cars, clothes, houses. Fashion is helpful so far. So, with my free time, I want to dig deeper."

"Well, if you learn how to explore family history, you'll learn some skills that could help solve Tony's murder. Hunting down facts, conducting interviews, that's what detectives do."

"I'm going to focus on genealogy alone, thank you. I will leave the police work to Detective Hamilton." She sipped her coffee. "What do you do in your free time?"

"I like to learn new things outside the office."

They both heard a siren wail outside and saw Detective Hamilton jogging toward the coffee shop.

"Let's go out the back door. I'll call a car. No time to waste, we need to go now." Josh rushed with Rosalind toward the exit.

As they slunk to the back parking lot, Josh said, "How about lunch at the Daily Planet tomorrow?"

Rosalind hesitated. She realized how much Josh helped her tonight. He also didn't fully answer her question. At least not yet. She nodded. "OK, text me tomorrow morning." The car arrived and they climbed in for the short drive to Rosalind's place.

She exited the car at her casita and the driver pulled away with Josh. What a relief to make it home in one piece. As she opened her door, she noticed a box. She hefted the package on her left hip, went inside, and hugged Hercules. She set the delivery on the table and tore it open. She pulled out the first book. This would be the perfect distraction from tonight's events. She peeled off the plastic wrap and ran her fingertips over the smooth hard cover binding and got started.

* * *

On Friday Rosalind drafted three texts to Josh with her regrets for lunch but every excuse she typed was lamer than the last. She gave up, got her keys out of her purse, hugged Hercules goodbye, and drove to the Daily Planet.

A few minutes later, Rosalind opened the restaurant's front door and spotted Josh. She smiled as she walked to his table. He stood and held out a chair for her. When was the last time that happened? Maybe when her dad was alive? Rosalind never considered it an important gesture, but it tugged at memories in her heart, nonetheless.

"I was afraid you might find an excuse to skip our lunch," said Josh.

Rosalind laughed. "Ah you know me that well? It did occur to me. I read late into the night and needed the morning to clear out the cobwebs, but I feel much better now."

"I'm glad you're here. I took the liberty of ordering wine since neither of us need to work this afternoon. I hope you like red."

"I love red. I loved it a bit too much Wednesday night, but today is a new day."

"How long has it been since you hung out with a co-worker just for fun?"

"No idea, a long time. Audra and I are friends, but our schedules don't mesh well. We get lunch on occasion. And today is an exception for me, because I do need to officially thank you for saving me from the crowd."

She drank her water. "I struggle to hang out with co-workers, so I make excuses, some real, some exaggerated. After a while, people forget to ask you because they assume you will say no." Rosalind crossed her hands on the table. The server brought a bottle of pinot noir and poured their glasses full, after Josh sampled it.

"How about you? Everyone at the office is your friend. The creative team cannot function without you. You mentor everyone. How do you do it?"

"Guess I just enjoy getting to know people. I'm a learning addict. I enroll in different courses to get exposed to new topics. That way, I always have something new to talk about." Josh smiled. "But enough about me. What have you heard about the investigation?"

"You won't believe the latest. This little tidbit has me beside myself and I need to bounce it off someone. Detective Hamilton visited me yesterday morning. What threw me for a loop is he asked me if I volunteered at the Desert Botanical Gardens."

"Do you?"

"I volunteer about once a week. I help my friend, Issy, one of the botanists."

"Why did Hamilton ask you about that?"

"That's what has me crazy. You received the text from Bob that Tony was poisoned, right?"

"Yes, I did."

"Hamilton told me the poison that killed Tony was oleander."

"Oleander?

"The leaves, flowers, stems, twigs and roots are all toxic."

"Why is that important?"

"Since Hamilton confirmed I volunteer at the botanical gardens, well you don't have to be a police officer to know that he has included me on his suspect list. Not only is Theresa accusing me, but the murderer knew enough to use oleander which implicates me."

The server came to the table, they ordered their lunches, and the menus were whisked away. The volume from the televisions became louder. Josh leaned in closer so Rosalind could hear him. She bent closer to him, too.

"This situation is going to require some investigation for us to clear your name."

"What would I do? Question people about where they were the morning Tony died? They aren't going to answer my questions. Whoever is guilty is happy to have me as a suspect."

"There has to be a way to uncover the truth."

The food arrived and Rosalind was delighted with her salmon salad with Meyer Lemon Dressing on a bed of organic baby kale with a side of quinoa topped with blueberries. Josh's Bison burger topped with Swiss cheese, bacon, and Worchester sauce was completed with a side of sweet potato fries.

"I never ate here, Josh. The wine is great, and the food looks amazing."

"I'm glad you like it. I know it's popular as a sports bar, but the menu is more sophisticated than typical sports bar fare."

Rosalind relaxed with Josh, which was an unfamiliar feeling.

After their plates were removed, Josh leaned closer again. "I have a thought and you don't have to answer immediately. Tomorrow's Saturday and I'm attending a workshop. Can you join me? It's a full day, we must leave early, and we will be back late. I think you could use a change of scenery, put this Findley business on the back burner. Broaden your perspective, and 'clear out the cobwebs.' It's the anecdote before you determine your next steps."

"Where is this workshop?"

"Sedona."

Chapter Seventeen

After lunch, Rosalind visited Issy at the gardens to face the music. She brought along the dream notebook with the vague scribblings. Rosalind was ready to defend her "I don't remember my dreams" stance. She hoped she would succeed.

As she walked into the greenhouse, Issy took control of the conversation before Rosalind could mutter hello.

"And good afternoon to you. I'm dying of curiosity. Tell me what happened at Tony's service last night."

"Oh, Issy, it was awful. Tony's dead body lying in a casket. I had to listen to people talk forever about Tony like he was this wonderful, caring man. And, then Theresa Mars got up and told the entire crowd that I killed Anthony Findley." As Rosalind said the words, tears pricked at her eyes, and she held back the rage that could erupt out of her.

"What? She accused you?"

"Yes, I was so embarrassed. Everyone stared at me. Josh thinks I have to play detective to clear my name and I refuse to do that."

"Who is Josh?" Issy set aside the plant she was trimming.

"Oh, he is this guy I work with. He did help me get out of the funeral home in one piece."

"I'm so sorry you had to endure that. Any idea why Theresa thinks you killed Tony?"

"She thinks I hated him. If I didn't enjoy my work at Kelco and Tony bothered me, wouldn't I have left for another job? He was annoying, arrogant, and obnoxious, but he was not the only person I worked with." Rosalind sat on one of the stools at the table where Issy trimmed yellow leaves off a small seedling. "Let's not talk about Tony. I came here with a real purpose to prove I don't remember my dreams. I did as you said before bed the last two nights, and there is no totem animal listed on the pages."

Rosalind handed the notebook to Issy who squinted at the pages. She sat down and pulled out her readers to have a closer look. After a few minutes of analysis Issy raised her eyebrows.

"I see the scratching of 'bear' written right here." She pointed at the same spot as Hamilton.

"No way." How could Issy and Detective Hamilton see the same word? Could Rosalind have written the word bear during the night?

Dead Reckoning

"Issy, I brought this to prove that I did not have any dreams and that I won the bet."

"Hey, even if I couldn't make out the word 'bear' in your writing...'

"Scribbling."

"The pen contacted paper which is enough for me to win this bet. Just because you want to block out your dreams does not mean that you won the bet. And that is final."

Rosalind dropped her shoulders. Issy had a point.

"And, since I 'won' our experiment, I can continue to talk to you about dreams, totem animals, feng shui, ancestral karma and whatever other topics I desire. Your next step is to look for bear symbols in your life and bring the strength of the bear into your thoughts and actions."

"Ok, so your torture continues." Rosalind conceded with a laugh. "And how is knowing that you think a bear is my totem animal supposed to help me find Tony's killer?"

"I see a change already. First, you thought you could wait until the police found his killer. Now you are looking for a way for your totem to help you find the murderer. This is progress, and your bear is helping you already, to give you a broader perspective on what you can do. You know a bear hibernates quite a few months out of the year. Could it be you are waking from years of hibernation now?"

Rosalind groaned.

"You could be waking from a social or spiritual hibernation. You are fortunate to have a bear to help you. Bears are strong, physically, of course, but also mentally. They represent fortitude. You have a dedicated support system with a bear."

"All right I give up. I'll try to remember my dreams and see if my bear totem provides support. But isn't it odd I don't remember writing this?"

"It doesn't seem odd to me at all. You deny you have dreams, and now your subconscious is alerting you to stop blocking it." Issy walked to the other side of the greenhouse and pulled a book out of her backpack. "Here, take this book. I brought it out of my library in the hope that you would connect with your totem."

Issy handed Rosalind a book with totem animals pictured on the cover. "This explains how to connect and even if you don't buy into it, it is enjoyable reading to distract you from Tony."

Rosalind shrugged in defeat. "Ok, I'm in. I will try anything to forget Tony Findley." Rosalind flipped the book over to the back. "And why did you mention ancestral karma? What is it?"

"Ancestral karma? Well, it's like the concept of karma, like a universal law in which your actions, good or bad, determine the outcomes of your future existence." Rosalind nodded at Issy. "Ancestral karma takes it a step further. Besides the genetics and DNA handed down to us from previous generations, ancestral karma can be patterns and beliefs, even traumas, passed to descendants which might require healing and release. You think you are making your own decisions, your own way in the world, but you could be acting out from issues ancestors had. I'm fortunate, I know the trials and tribulations my Hispanic ancestors faced the last three hundred years. I'm not named Isidora Candella just because it is a beautiful name. I am named for my great-grandmother. You, on the other hand, are at the beginning of understanding your genealogy and, hopefully, your ancestors, too."

"Whoa, I'm not certain I can comprehend that right now, between genealogy and Tony Findley and finding my totem, my life away from work is filling up fast."

"It will come in time. I have an ancestral karma book I'll lend it to you. It's fascinating stuff. It wouldn't hurt for you to request the most benevolent outcome for understanding your new studies. Actually you can make those requests anytime. You'd be surprised how much it helps," said Issy. "And, you have the whole weekend to read the totem book."

"Not if I go to Sedona."

"Sedona?"

"Yeah, Josh asked me to join him for a short trip to Sedona for a workshop."

"Josh? I'm beginning to like this Josh and I don't know him at all. You must go. I request a most benevolent outcome for your trip to Sedona."

"We'll see."

Chapter Eighteen

Rosalind arrived home to a happy Hercules who followed her around the casita until she relaxed at the kitchen. Then he laid under the table at her feet. Before diving into the book on spirit totems, Rosalind turned to the listings of the settlers of Mariental in the Pleve book. She located the Schmidt listing, opened her laptop and started to record the information into her genealogy software. She typed:

Schmidt, Christoph, 24, kath., Ackerbauer aus Ansbach
Frau: Anna Barbara, 24
Tochter: Kristina, 9
Sohne: Johann, 6
Schwägerin: Maria Schumacher, 32
In der Kolonie eingetroffen am 14.6.1766
Erhalten von der Kamzlei in Petersburg 12 Rbl., von der Voevodenkanzlei in Saratov 150 Rbl.
1768 gab es in der Wirtschaft 2 Pfd., 1 Kuh, gepflugt: ½ Des, gesät: 5 Cetverik Roggen

Rosalind knew enough German to determine Christoph Schmidt, age twenty-four, Catholic, was a farmer of crops from Ansbach. His wife, Anna Barbara, was twenty-three. Without a marriage date listed, she recorded a tentative marriage date of 1759 adding the note that this was a guess. They had two children, daughter Kristina, age 9 and son Johann age 6. It seemed unusual that they were both parents at the age of fifteen, but it was a different era. The family arrived in Mariental on June 16, 1766. Maria Schumacher was listed as Christoph's sister-in-law, so if the records were correct, she was Anna Barbara's sister. Her last name was Schumacher and not Schmidt. Could Schumacher be Maria and Anna Barbara's maiden name or was it Maria's married name? Rosalind wrote a note to follow up on the name later.

The rest of the entry detailed what rubles they were given in Saint Petersburg and Saratov and what they had in 1768. Kuh was cow, but she wasn't certain what Pfd. meant. Gepflugt translated to plowed and Roggen meant rye. She would do additional research and translation if she confirmed Christoph was her ancestor.

She searched for Ansbach on maps and discovered it was in Bavaria, about twenty-five miles southwest of Nuremburg and ninety miles north of Munich. She glanced through the history noting the area was developed in the eighth century as a Benedictine monastery and housed a castle known as Margrafen Schloss. Anna Barbara might also be from Ansbach. She noted it was an assumption which required follow-up.

Hoping to tie to the next generation, Rosalind jumped to the book entitled *1798 Census of the German Colonies along the Volga, Economy Population, and Agriculture*. She found the colony of Mariental and searched for the Schmidt family. She discovered the listing which read:

Christoph Schmidt, head of household, age 54

Walpurga Wächter, spouse, age 34

Rosalind didn't know these people, yet her heart ached as she imagined Christoph losing Anna Barbara. Rosalind knew first settlers struggled and death was common. Rosalind presumed that Anna Barbara died between 1766 and 1798, which was a thirty-two-year period but until she received further details it would have to suffice. Rosalind was concerned about the age difference between Christoph and Walpurga. A difference of twenty years was a significant gap. Couldn't there have been someone closer to Walpurga's age to marry? Was this age gap typical? Whatever the reasons, life changed immensely for Christoph between 1766 and 1798.

Rosalind read further and saw the first son listed was *Johannes, age 14*. Was Johannes the son of Anna Barbara or Walpurga? She glanced back to the Pleve book and realized by 1798 the Johann on the settler's list would have been 37 years old and may have established his own household. Another point for future research was to locate the original Johann Schmidt, Kristina Schmidt and sister-in-law Maria. The latter two would be ages thirty-nine and sixty-four by 1798.

The second son was *Nikolaus, age 11*, followed by *Mattias age 1*. The daughters were *Anna, age 15, Margaretha, age 5*, and then *Maria age 32*, with her spouse, Christoph's son-in-law, *Jakob Sander*. Maria must be the daughter of Anna Barbara, but the others could have either Anna Barbara or Walpurga as their mother.

Rosalind recorded her notes, jotting reminders to research these questions. She needed to read more about the colonies so she could understand why there was no reference to what happened to Anna Barbara and whether a twenty-year gap in marriage was common. She felt confident her family line would track back to Christoph Schmidt, but would the maternal line tie to Anna Barbara or Walpurga? Rosalind had merely scratched the surface of these two books and her head spun with questions. Genealogy research could boggle the brain.

Dead Reckoning

What if she was a descendant of Walpurga and not Anna Barbara? Rosalind checked back on the original settlers list from 1766 and found the Wächter family listed as:

Wächter, Joseph, 42, kath., Handwerker aus Bleifeld bei Hoffnungstal
Frau: Maria Magdalena, 34
Sohne: Henry, 15
    Jakob, 12
    Friedrich, 8
Tochter: Walpurga, 3

This meant Walpurga and her family were original settlers. Her father Joseph, age forty-two, was married to Maria Magdalena, age thirty-four. There was an eight-year age gap between husband and wife, which seemed a bit more reasonable to Rosalind. After three sons, Henry, Jakob and Friedrich, there was young Walpurga, age three who made the trek from the Germanic states to Russia with her family.

Then Rosalind returned to the 1798 census and found no trace of the Wächter family except for Walpurga's listing with the Schmidt family. After thirty-two years, the only remaining Wächter she could find was Walpurga.

Rosalind checked the clock and realized it was late and, if she did go to Sedona with Josh tomorrow, she needed to sleep now.

"Hercules, time for us to rest. There are too many questions which can't be answered tonight. Do you think I can dream of the answers?" With that thought, Rosalind climbed in bed and fell asleep as her head hit the pillow, with Hercules snuggling at her side.

Chapter Nineteen

The sun peeked out behind the Coconino National Forest as Josh steered his Jeep to exit I-17 onto Hwy 179. Ahead the red rocks of Sedona jutted out of the earth upward toward a crystal blue sky. The green foliage of pine and mesquite trees crept up trying to match the rocks' stature, standing in contrast to the rusted sandstone on the horizon and the cloudless sky. Sedona was a geologist's dream. The beauty, awe and tranquility of the area was the right tonic for Rosalind's worries.

They had been on the road for over two hours leaving the darkness of Phoenix behind them. She missed Hercules, of course, but Aunt Ruth invited him to her house since she was in town. She always spoiled him with special treats. And Rosalind did not mind at all.

"Josh, you still have not told me what this workshop covers. Since we are in Sedona you can let the secret out."

"There is a reason I haven't told you yet. I don't want you to have any qualms about the topic."

"I have qualms since I don't know."

"All will be revealed. We will be there in five minutes."

He circled the roundabout and exited onto the southern street. Rosalind inhaled deeply as the view of Cathedral Rock loomed large. It was awesome to her how the earth of Arizona changed in such short distances. The beauty was staggering, the colors divine.

Josh turned right, which led them into a sprawling and luxurious southwestern resort. Stone horse artwork, metal cacti, and towering saguaros greeted them at the entrance. In the center of the circular drive near the entry stood a seven-foot-tall metal sculpture.

Of a bear. This had to be a coincidence.

The bear was magnificent with minute metal fur hanging down and swaying in the breeze. The claws stretched out above its massive head. The bear's stance alone could have scared creatures to death before the claws and teeth reached its prey.

Josh located a parking spot and they walked to the entrance. Rosalind stopped for a moment to capture a picture of the bear, the horse, and the cacti. As they neared the sliding doors, the sign over the entrance read, "Sedona Genealogical Society Symposium."

"Genealogy. Are you interested in genealogy, too?" asked Rosalind.

"I told you I like to learn about new topics."

Dead Reckoning

She stopped and glanced around her to feel the beauty and energy of the earth. "What do you know about genealogy anyway?"

"Not much, that's why we're here. To find out more. We don't have to make it our life's calling, but we may hear some interesting stories along the way."

They registered, slipped on their name tags, and scanned the agenda. Rosalind's jaw dropped as she noticed a session on organizing family photographs. She had to attend that session. Some of the other workshops were: *Census Records and How to Locate Your Grandparents, Can Homestead Claims Uncover Your Family History, Tracking Social Security Records to Build your Case to Join Daughters of the American Revolution, How to make Cemetery Searches Part of your Vacation/Lifestyle, Tracking your German Roots, Immigration to the Americas-What if your Great Grandparents did not arrive at Ellis Island, Chasing your Ancestors from Eastern Europe, Discovering your Irish Roots* and *What Does Epigenetics Mean to You*. The list jam-packed over five pages.

"Do you have enough sessions to choose from?" asked Josh.

"Unbelievable. I had no idea this event existed. I must attend the photograph session, though I will learn from any of these speakers."

Josh and Rosalind walked through the vendor exhibit area outside of the meeting rooms. Books, videos, and software programmers filled the hall with more paraphernalia than Rosalind could absorb. She picked up flyers and tossed them in the seminar tote bag, then they headed to the Grand Canyon meeting room for *the How to Organize your Family Photographs and Explore your Family History*.

The time in the workshops flew past Rosalind like a jet zooming across the sky overhead. The next session started too soon. It moved fast, but Rosalind was grateful for her notes on websites, books, and contacts so she could learn more. There was more to family history than skimming through photographs and reviewing a few books. She felt herself edging further down the rabbit hole. Was Rosalind being carried away in the moment? Did she want to be a genealogist? Where does one begin?

"You look a million miles away," said Josh. "A penny for your thoughts."

"Ha. It might cost you more than a penny. How about we grab lunch? I'll tell you my thoughts, but my stomach is growling."

Josh laughed. "Lunch is this way." He motioned to the right, so they turned toward the line queuing to pick up their box lunch.

As they passed a double exhibit space, Rosalind glanced back and saw the sign, "Did your Ancestors come from Russia?" Rosalind stopped in her tracks causing Josh to bump into her.

She turned toward the exhibit. A small, dark-haired woman stood behind the table covered with brochures, books, and keychains. Rosalind looked to the woman's name tag which read Margaret.

"Margaret? I'm Rosalind Schmidt. Are you the Margaret who answered my email about Christoph Schmidt?"

"Rosalind? I didn't know you would be here. Yes, I'm Margaret Gardner. I remember your emails. It is so nice to meet you." Margaret extended her hand to Rosalind who shook it.

"I would love to talk to you. How long are you in Arizona?"

"I live in Arizona. Here's my card." Rosalind glanced at the card and noticed that Margaret resided in Apache Junction.

"Thank you, Margaret. I have so many questions for you about the books you recommended.

"I'm happy to help. What questions do you have?"

"I can't tell which of Christoph Schmidt's children tie to my line, but the surprising thing to me was that his second wife, Walpurga Wächter, was twenty years younger than he was. Wasn't there someone closer in age for her to marry?"

"I understand why the age difference causes concern. In those times and in such a remote location, their main goal was to survive, and it required a man and a woman to work together. From what you said, it appears Anna Barbara passed before 1798. The community of Mariental needed people to work the farms, build the village and care for the families. No matter what their age, men worked until they were no longer able. Christoph may have been the best match for Walpurga despite the age difference. Not all children survived the harsh life, and there may not have been a better match to Walpurga's age. As you read more of the history, you'll understand the challenges of these settlers."

Another couple came to the table, so Rosalind busied herself picking up brochures from the display. After the couple left, Rosalind said, "Margaret, this is my friend Josh. We were just heading to lunch. Would you like to join us?"

Dead Reckoning

"I would love to, but I need to stay at the booth. The workshop team already brought me my food."

"OK, I will follow up with you later."

"That would be fantastic."

Rosalind and Josh headed toward the pre-packaged boxes. They selected their sandwiches, walked through the entrance doors, and headed to their left around the hotel to a grotto of red rocks. Secluded and quiet, it was the peaceful setting Rosalind craved. The sessions sparked something inside her she had not felt in years. How could she explain this to Josh? She barely knew him. Well, she had known him for years, but these were personal feelings she was not used to sharing.

They chose a black iron café table with chairs facing the grotto and settled in for their lunch break. A trickling waterfall cascaded over the rocks into a small, limpid pool. A family of koi glided in the clear blue water. Bougainvillea wrapped around the outside courtyard and gold lantanas circled the pond's edge. Rosalind breathed in the sweet air and relaxed.

"All this information makes me hungry." Josh opened the box filled with chicken salad croissants, mini arugula salad, chips and a chocolate chip cookie. "Well, 'fess up, what is going on in that head of yours?"

"I was worried about falling down the rabbit hole, and now I'm sliding right down it. I'm drawn to each topic and want to dig deeper."

Josh nodded. "There are many paths to research. Each workshop highlights some aspect of genealogy, and it would be fun to putter in all of it."

"I want to try."

As they devoured the last bites of their lunch, a shadow crossed their path. They both looked up. In front of them stood Theresa Mars.

"Good afternoon," said Theresa. "Now you are a genealogy buff? Choosing to go back in time before you killed Tony?"

Rosalind squared her shoulders. "Theresa, I had nothing to do with his death. Why are you here?"

Theresa leaned in, her lunch container touching the café table. "Because I understand you. You are young, you are beautiful, and you were jealous of his life. He was wealthy, and he invested well with the nightclub, accumulated mountains of money, and you could not bear that he was not with you. Everyone knows you hated him for not pursuing you more."

Rosalind held back a laugh as she gazed into Theresa's squinting eyes. "Oh, Theresa, you are mistaken. Whatever vendetta you imagine has more to do with you than me."

Josh interjected, "Rosalind, let's go. Theresa needs to sort this out for herself." He picked up the empty lunch cartons and extended his hand to Rosalind. She put her hand in his without thinking twice. They walked away, leaving Theresa alone in the grotto.

"You will regret your actions, Rosalind. I will see you pay for what you did."

Rosalind and Josh sped past the exhibit tables heading to the exit. She stopped short at the Russian exhibit.

"Margaret, I wish I could stay but I must leave now. I'll call you soon."

"Of course, keep in touch." Margaret waved goodbye.

"Will do." Rosalind walked back to Josh, and they raced out of the hotel toward Josh's car. When she turned back, she saw Theresa heading toward Margaret's booth.

* * *

As Josh and Rosalind headed back to I-17, Rosalind turned to him.

"How did she know I would be there? Could she be stalking me? Did you tell anyone where we were going?"

Josh lowered his head. "The only person I told was Graham. I don't think he would have told Theresa, at least not directly." He paused as he navigated through the roundabout. "Perhaps Graham told Pamela? For some reason he is caught in her web. Could Pamela have told Theresa?"

"I guess that's possible." Rosalind pouted. She was upset and regretted missing the afternoon sessions.

"I'm sorry, Rosalind. I don't want the day to end early. I had hopes we could have a nice dinner and more conversation." He looked ahead, not ready to make eye contact with her yet. "I have an idea. I don't want Theresa to spoil today. I checked and she isn't following us. Let's stop ahead, take a break. We can hike around Bell Rock."

Dead Reckoning

"Normally I would love to hike, but I don't have the right shoes for these trails."

Josh nodded. They sat in silence for a few minutes.

"Ok, here's a risky suggestion." He remembered the signs they passed on their drive. "Are you game for something different? You know Sedona is the spiritualist capital of Arizona and the southwest."

"I'm game if it helps me to forget about Theresa. And Tony."

"How about we go see a psychic? Might lead us to who killed Tony. If they are wrong, no loss. But we can try."

Rosalind laughed. "Oh, I wish it were that easy. Drive up and get answers to murder."

"Hey, it will be my treat. Consider it entertainment. We might get a few clues. Are you up for it?'

Rosalind didn't want to visit a psychic. She also didn't want to mope on the drive back when Josh tried so hard to make the day enjoyable. She conceded. "Ok, we can try. But I won't believe any predictions."

Josh steered his car into the parking lot of a Southwestern style outdoor market. They located the storefront of "Madam Damara's Psychic and Healing Readings." He jerked the transmission into park, jumped out, ran around to the passenger side, and grabbed the handle swinging Rosalind's door open. Rosalind wondered how he tapped into such enthusiasm. She stepped out of the car. "Are you always this energetic?" He laughed and extended his arm. She looped her arm through his as they walked past stores called *Angel Therapy, Harmonic Resonance, Gloria's Massage Therapy* and *Reiki Healing*. Josh opened the door labeled *Madame Damara* and Rosalind walked in. At first they didn't see anyone. Then, they heard an office door squeak open, followed by soft footsteps and rustling from the back room.

Peering out from behind the door was a round, wrinkled face with heavily lidded brown eyes gazing at them.

"Hi," said Josh. "We saw your sign and hoped you could conduct a reading. Do we need an appointment, or can we get the reading now?'

"Do you have cash?" she asked.

"Yes," said Josh.

Rosalind asked, "Is there a restroom I can use?

"Yes," said Madame Damara, "down the hall and on the right."

Josh and Madame negotiated the terms, and he handed the cash to her. She accepted it and placed it in the hidden folds of her flowing orange and blue caftan. When Rosalind returned, Madame led them to a small private room. The walls were covered with pink and purple silk scarves. In the center was a round table covered with two cloths, again purple and pink, topped with cards, divination tools, and crystals. Alas, no crystal ball.

"Sit, sit." said Madam Damara. She sat in the high back chair and Josh and Rosalind settled on two of the stools. "Tell me what you seek."

Josh looked at Rosalind. "Just looking for a general reading, nothing in particular."

"Aha," said Madam. "Let us see what the cards tell us." She shuffled the stack of cards at least five times, then held out the deck for Rosalind to cut. Rosalind picked up the top two-thirds and Madam slid the sliced cards to the bottom of the deck.

Madam selected the top card and laid it on the table, then peeled another card and set it parallel to the first card. She did the maneuver three times.

"Ah ha," said Madam. "The first card is your past, the second card your present and the third card is your future."

"Ok," said Josh.

"This first card represents trauma not yet overcome. The second card says you are struggling to resolve issues. You fear you may not have the skill set to resolve, yet you cannot rely on others to solve this dilemma. Yes?"

"No," said Rosalind. Trauma? Who didn't have trauma and issues to resolve?

"You are a skeptic. Let's see what the future holds.'

Madam looked at the third card. "One must always analyze not just each card, but how each card balances with the others. Your past shows losses, emotional, and physical. Your present indicates strife, transition, and a new beginning only if you are open to change. But the last card..." Madam stopped.

She looked toward the ceiling. Josh and Rosalind glanced at each other, then Rosalind looked up, too.

"Someone is reaching out to me who wants to connect with you. From the other side." Madam's body shuddered. Her head dropped to

Dead Reckoning

her chest, and she was still for two minutes. Rosalind thought, I didn't expect theatrics, I thought Madame Damara did card readings not a stage show.

Madam inched her head upward, her eyes glazed. How does she manage to do that, wondered Rosalind.

Madam, in a deeper voice than what they had heard from her, said, "My name is Christoph." Her head rose higher with her chin jutting out from her chest, and she looked straight ahead, but she also appeared to look through them. "There is much to learn, Rosalind, and it is good you are seeking answers."

Rosalind mouthed to Josh, "Did you tell her our names?" Josh mouthed back, "No."

"I know more than you realize, you are in turmoil over current events. Your family on this side loves you. We watch out for you." Madam inhaled deeply. "You need to stop, reflect, and begin again. There are forces around you. Some of these forces will help, some can hurt. We are doing what we can. You need to do what you can from your side. Please meditate, contemplate, listen to your dreams. We will guide you as will your bear. Only you can clear this karma."

Madam's torso flopped forward onto the table.

"What the heck?" said Josh.

Rosalind's hands shook and she wasn't certain she knew how to pray anymore. "Please don't let her be dead."

"No way can she be dead. I hope she just gave us our money's worth."

"Is this what happens in card readings? This doesn't seem normal from what I have seen in movies."

After a few more minutes, Madam's back trembled. She breathed in and out loud enough for them to hear. Her head lifted off the table, her eyes still closed. Sitting upright, she adjusted her hair and necklaces, then she opened her eyes.

"That hasn't happened in a long time. You, my dear, must have powerful connections in the universe. This message came from your ancestors. Do you know Christoph? Or did you know Christoph?"

Rosalind volunteered nothing. "Maybe."

"He forced his way into this session. Do you have any idea how rare that type of intervention is? No, I'm sure you don't. It is extraordinary. I know of one other instance where a spirit interrupted a reading."

"What happened in that interruption?" asked Josh.

"It was for a famous client who demanded confidentiality. I'm not at liberty to discuss."

"What does it mean? Why did they interrupt for me?" asked Rosalind.

"They want your attention. An intervention must be heeded. Do you remember his instructions?"

"Something about meditation," said Rosalind.

"Christoph took over my reading without my permission. This was not to be a channeling session. Channeling sessions cost more because of the demands on the channeler. It is an emergency for him to step forth as he did. There is concern for you, and you must heed what he said. When I channel, I hear these words as an echo, but I know he said 'You need to stop, reflect, and begin again'...and 'Please meditate, contemplate, listen to your dreams, and re-evaluate everything. Do this daily.' You need to write this down, follow it. It is critical to your life." Madam stood up, walked to a small desk, and grabbed a pad of paper and pen. "Write it down."

Rosalind wrote the words on the pad. Madam supervised to make sure she did not miss a syllable.

"Good, now you need more guidance." Madam walked to a small bookcase. She chose three books and walked back to Rosalind. "You need to study these books. Since meditation, dreams, contemplation, and re-evaluation are not mainstays of your lifestyle, you need to focus on these practices."

"What do I owe you for the books?" asked Rosalind.

"Nothing. I have these books memorized and you need support during this time. Besides, it's good karma for me."

Rosalind and Josh shook her hand and offered their thanks for her support. Josh laid an extra twenty dollars on the table before they headed to the door. As they walked to the car, Rosalind searched her purse for her phone. She pulled it out of her bag, checking for messages. "And my battery is dead."

Once in the car, Josh turned to Rosalind. "Here, plug your phone in. It should get charged before we get back to Phoenix." Rosalind connected the phone. "Well, we got more than we bargained for. You never answered Madam's question about knowing the spirit who interrupted. Did you know a Christoph?"

Dead Reckoning

"My father's name was Christopher."

* * *

Monsoon season ended on September 30, but the October calendar didn't mean anything to the dark clouds over Camelback Mountain. As the haboob crossed over the mountains, rain pelted the windshield and Josh slowed the Jeep to a crawl for the last ten miles to Rosalind's casita.

The dust and wind stopped as they reached her home, but the dark clouds hovered above. Rosalind squinted her eyes not certain what she saw. Something was out of place, but the darkness made it hard to focus.

Josh jumped out. A thick mesquite branch had plunged through the sidelight of the casita. As Rosalind unlocked the door, he dragged the branch away from the shattered remains of glass in the windowpane. Shards of glass had burst all over the foyer inside.

Rosalind sighed. "Looks like lightning split it off the tree next door. I have some cardboard and tape we can use to cover the window for tonight. I'll call for repairs tomorrow or Monday."

"Sounds like a plan. Let's make sure nothing else was disturbed." They looked through her rooms and the backyard and nothing was out of place. After securing the opening and reassuring Josh that she would be all right, Rosalind thanked Josh and said good night.

She walked to Ruth's house to pick up Hercules, and once he was with her, she breathed a sigh of relief. "Hercules, these days are getting stranger and stranger. Let's go home.."

Chapter Twenty

Sunday Rosalind eyed Hercules as he tried to look out the window next to the front door. He seemed unsettled. Was he out of sorts due to missing her yesterday? He sniffed along the baseboards and circled the couch like a border collie.

She unfolded her note from Madam Damara and reread the words. The folded edges creased lines onto the paper. The books on her kitchen table would require discipline to study as Madam Damara recommended. She ran her fingers through her hair to stall the inevitable. Before she could open the book, her phone rang.

"Hello Issy, what's up?"

"That's what I was going to ask you. How was Sedona?"

"It was fascinating and frustrating."

"Wow, tell me more."

Rosalind had not planned to leave her casita today, but this was a chance to delay her studies. And she could justify talking to Issy because there was no one who understood these matters better than she did.

"How about if I come to the gardens and help you? I can explain it better if I talk to you in person. It will be another hour before I can head out. I'm waiting for the window replacement service to fix a broken window from the storm yesterday." Rosalind heard Hercules whine. "If I enter the back way, would it be ok if I sneak Hercules in with me?"

"That sounds good. Would love to see him again, too."

"Ok, we will be there in an hour, an hour and a half max. With coffee. The repairperson is less than five minutes away."

In less than an hour, the glass was replaced. Rosalind gathered up her notes and new books. She grabbed Hercules' leash from the hook. "C'mon boy, we are off to see Issy."

Hercules loved car rides. He looked out the window at the Buttes which reminded Rosalind of giant potatoes sprouting out of the earth. The crevices in the rock mimicked the eyes on the skin. She checked her rear-view mirror repeatedly to make sure Theresa wasn't following her.

Rosalind chose a parking space close to the greenhouse and made sure no one saw her when she let Hercules jump out of the car. As they hurried to the building, careful not to spill any coffee, Rosalind was certain they arrived undetected. She opened the greenhouse door, released Hercules from his leash, and yelled to Issy, "We're here."

Dead Reckoning

Issy was bent over a group of pots, filled with mini saguaros, golden barrels, and Old Man of the Andes. She walked toward them, but Hercules arrived at her side first, looking for attention, and a treat. Issy bent on one knee and greeted Hercules, scratching between his ears. "Hello Hercules, you're such a good boy."

She reached into her pocket, pulled out a dog biscuit, and held it above Hercules. "Sit." Hercules immediately sat, then she rewarded him with the treat. "Hey Rosalind, I can't wait to hear about your journey to Sedona. And Josh."

They sat in two old wooden chairs drinking their lattes, Hercules nestled at their feet. Rosalind explained the Sedona trip from the genealogy conference, to Theresa, to Madam Damara and the intervention of Christoph. When she finished the story, she looked into Issy's eyes. "What do you make of all of this?"

Issy smiled. "First things first. Do you have any idea how much Josh cares about you? He helps you, understands you, and he goes out on a limb visiting a psychic."

"Yes, he was kind to me. That doesn't mean I trust him yet."

"Don't sabotage this, Rosalind. He gets you. He has demonstrated loyalty. You need to stay open to him, and to this synchronicity."

"Synchronicity?"

"Nothing happens randomly. Why did I ask you to write your dreams and focus on your totem animal? Why did you write 'bear' on the notepad? Why did you see a bear as you entered the conference center? Why did you visit a psychic who channeled a Christoph who wanted to give you a message and confirmed your totem? Do you have a connection to Christoph?"

"Perhaps. My father's name was Christopher. It's a common name in my family. My earliest ancestor in Russia was named Christoph."

"Rosalind, that's incredible. Why did she give you books to help you to work on dreams, reflect, and meditate? She was generous and concerned enough to help you. And why did you need to discuss these events with me? Because I believe in dreams, meditation, and reflection which you need in your life right now."

"You truly believe the universe is trying to get me to change?"

"There is no doubt in my mind. You have some special guides helping you now. It is time for change. Change by going with the flow of genealogy, spirituality, and this Tony Findley investigation. Theresa is not going to stop her accusations. It is a grieving outlet for her. Or else she killed Tony and is trying to shift the blame. Can you see it was necessary that she appeared yesterday because without her actions, you would not have stopped at the psychic? You are being guided."

Rosalind downed the last of her coffee. "I'm skeptical. What if I try without success?"

"People go their entire lives searching for guidance. If you track your dreams, meditate, read the books which have fallen into your lap, imagine what you could discover. This is not happenstance. It is clear guidance."

Rosalind stood up. "And I'm a suspect in Tony's murder because he was killed by oleander, and as a volunteer here, the police know I know that."

"Lots of people know oleander is poisonous, but it does seem an odd choice for murder. I agree with you, it's a lot to take in. You could ignore it. You could give it a try. If you give it a try, you will never regret not doing it."

"I could fail."

"Fail? If you don't try it, you immediately fail." Issy took the reusable coffee cups and set them on her desk.. "Tell me, Rosalind, what are you afraid of?"

Tears welled up in Rosalind's eyes. Memories flooded back to her, and tightness spread throughout her chest. Her heart ached as images flashed through her mind like it happened yesterday. The bad choices, the horror of her loss, her worst decision. She sat down and held her face in her hands.

Issy sat next to her. "It might not clear the pain, but it could help to resolve this reluctance you have about living life, everything except being a workaholic."

Rosalind swallowed hard. "It's difficult to discuss."

"Try me," said Issy. "If you don't tell me, I'll never understand."

Rosalind gripped her hands onto the sides of the seat of the chair. She held herself firmly and stretched her back to sit as erectly as she could. "Ok, you know my parents died when I was in high school, right?"

"I remember."

"Two nights before they died, I had a horrible dream. I saw them in a car accident in River Falls. I dreamt of the accident, the aftermath, the whole thing." She stopped to catch her breath. "It was a terrible dream, and I didn't tell anyone, not even my parents, because I knew they looked forward to their weekend away. I thought it was a dream with no meaning." Tears streamed down her cheeks.

"Two days later, when the police arrived at my doorstep and told me what happened, I became numb. I foresaw this in my dream, didn't know what to do with it, and if I had told them, would they have believed it and changed their plans? Do you know what that does to you?" Rosalind wiped her eyes.

"Oh, Rosalind, I'm so sorry." Issy leaned over and wrapped her arms around her not releasing the embrace until she could feel Rosalind's tense muscles relax.

"I fell into such a deep depression. I lost my home and my parents." She sobbed again. "At that point I swore off dreams for the rest of my life."

Issy held Rosalind until the waterworks subsided. "Rosalind, your fear is completely understandable." Issy waited while Rosalind caught her breath. "This happened more than fifteen years ago. You were so young, and it was not your responsibility to change your parent's choice. Your parents know that, and they sympathize with you carrying a burden that isn't yours to bear."

"What if I don't understand the meaning of my dreams? How will I know what is important and what isn't?"

"I can't answer all of those questions though it seems to me that the universe wants you to try."

After sharing her story, relief flowed through Rosalind. From where she stood now, could it hurt to attempt a new way?

Issy added, "If you try, I will be here to support you every day, every night, every moment that you need me."

Rosalind grabbed a tissue to wipe her face and blow her nose. She had reached a turning point. "Ok, you will be my sounding board as I work through it?"

"We can talk every day and compare notes."

Rosalind breathed a sigh of relief. "And, perhaps, after fifteen years of embarrassment, I can rid myself of the hyena laugh."

Issy chuckled. "I am looking forward to hearing a new laugh."

Anna Dalhaimer Bartkowski

Rosalind understood this change was inevitable and her new path was set. She would have to be disciplined to follow a new course. What did she have to lose?

Chapter Twenty-One

Rosalind sat at her kitchen table Monday morning, dream notebook in hand. She looked at the page and saw more scribbles, something she had written during the night. She didn't remember picking up the pen or paper. She closed her eyes, as one of the books from Madam Damara suggested, and tried to re-envision the memory. Dark images blurred in front of her eyes. Trying to focus, she breathed in and breathed out to a count of eight. After a few minutes, she opened her eyes. Hercules watched her with interest.

"Herc, this dream and meditation stuff sounds fluffy, but it takes attention and time." Rosalind recorded what she recalled. Blurry images resembled a ship's mast with sails open on a rolling sea. Hercules walked to her side and lay on the floor, content to be near her.

Rosalind jumped when her phone rang. She saw it was Audra.

"Hello?"

"Hey Rosalind. How are you?'

"Doing fine. How about you?"

"I'm doing great. I wonder if you've heard anything more from Detective Hamilton?" asked Audra.

"No, I haven't heard anything new. What's going on?"

"There's nothing new. Have you recuperated from the funeral?"

"Doing as well as can be expected."

"I'm so sorry that you experienced the wrath of Theresa. She has been out of sorts at the office, too. I knew they were friends, but her actions were bizarre."

Rosalind breathed a sigh of relief. She realized how much she missed Audra's empathy. "Thank you, that means a lot to me. I have felt like an outcast since Tuesday, I missed talking to you."

Rosalind heard a soft knock at the door. It was Aunt Ruth. "Come in."

"You must have a guest, I'll let you go. This week is jam packed with meetings, but can we get lunch early next week?"

"That would be wonderful. Let me know what day works well for you. I haven't heard when I can come back to work."

"It's best to steer clear of Theresa. I'll call you soon." Audra hung up.

As Rosalind set her phone on the table, she checked for messages. There were none. She looked up and smiled at Aunt Ruth. "I'm so glad you are here. Let's make grilled cheese sandwiches, soup, and commiserate."

"Who could resist that?" Aunt Ruth opened a cabinet and pulled out a can of clam chowder. Hercules walked to her, and Ruth rubbed his ears. "I missed you, too. What trouble is Rosalind in now?

As the soup warmed and Rosalind grilled the sandwiches, she told Aunt Ruth about the challenges of remembering her dreams.

She held out the dream notebook with her scribbled writing. "Look at this."

"You wrote this, yet you don't remember doing it. I don't understand dreams, but I do want to meet Josh. Anyone who gets you to a genealogy conference is ok in my book."

"We'll see."

When Rosalind finished grilling the sandwiches, Ruth ladled and served the clam chowder. The meal hit the spot. "Theresa Mars, what does she have to gain by accusing you of murder?"

"That's a great question. She and Tony were good friends. She would do everything he wanted without question."

"Maybe it's time for us to ask her. What time does she get off of work?" Ruth sat back in her chair and tilted her head to the right.

"Sometime between four and five."

Hercules eyed the last bite of Rosalind's grilled cheese sandwich. Confronting Theresa was scary but perhaps with Aunt Ruth by her side she could find the courage. Her chest felt heavy and clearing the air might lessen that feeling. "You might be onto something. I can text her and ask her to meet me. If she shows up, we can talk. If she doesn't show, well, at least I tried. I'll ask her to meet me at the Daily Planet at 5:30." She gave the tidbit to Hercules, and he devoured it.

"Good plan. I will come back at 5 and we can go."

She drafted the text to Theresa. Rosalind took a deep breath. Was there anything she could add or change to get Theresa on board? She sat for a few minutes. Nothing came to her, so she hit send.

"Hercules, 5:30 tonight could change my life."

Chapter Twenty-Two

Rosalind and Ruth opened the door to a packed Daily Planet at 5:15 p.m. Every bar stool was occupied, tables were filled, and happy hour was in full swing.

"It's Monday, isn't it?" asked Aunt Ruth.

"Yeah, what have we been missing?"

Rosalind watched as Ernie served up two chocolate martinis to the strawberry blond-haired girl and her friend at the end of the bar. He looked up as Rosalind and Ruth entered the restaurant and maneuvered through the crowd. Ernie picked up the phone near the back of the bar, still observing the two newcomers by looking into the mirror behind the bar. Rosalind watched his eyes scan everything in his place.

Ruth spotted an empty table near the back. They sat down and surveyed the scene again. Rosalind sat with her back to the wall, to have a full view of the restaurant.

"Do you see Theresa?" asked Ruth.

"No, not yet, but I'm glad we got here when we did."

"Hi, can I get you something to drink?" asked a dark-haired server.

"Yes, I would like a glass of cabernet," said Ruth.

"Same for me, plus a glass of water."

"Water for me, too, please," said Ruth.

"No problem, I'll be right back."

Rosalind moved her head from left to right and left again, hoping she would see Theresa.

"Are you watching a tennis match?" joked Ruth. "That ball is moving across the court with professional speed."

"I want to see Theresa before she sees me. It gives me a subtle advantage."

Rosalind glanced toward the front door as Josh and Graham swung the doors open. Josh saw Rosalind and motioned Graham to follow him.

"Rosalind, it's great to see you."

"Good to see you, too." After the introductions, everyone shook hands. Rosalind said, "I'm meeting Theresa here."

"Oh, that's good to hear. Best to get to the bottom of the situation. We'll stay out of the way so you can talk to her when she gets here. We're your backup if needed. Would it be ok if we check back with you after Theresa leaves?"

"Of course, but I don't know if she will show up. I texted her and I didn't get a response."

"I don't know what Theresa looks like," said Ruth, "but the woman walking in from the back of the restaurant has a look on her face that could kill."

Graham faced the back of the room. "Yeah, that's her. Josh, let's grab those two stools that opened at the bar."

"Ok," said Josh. "We'll talk later."

Rosalind watched as Graham sat next to the woman with the chocolate martini and Josh sat next to him.

As Theresa approached Rosalind and Ruth, she nodded to Ernie behind the bar and to the blond-haired woman with the chocolate martini. Then she stood, hand on her right hip staring at the two women when she reached the table.

"Did you bring your mother to defend you?" asked Theresa.

"Theresa, I'm happy you could join me. This is my aunt, Ruth Hoffmann. I didn't know if you would be here, so she accompanied me. Please join us." Rosalind waved her hand to the two open seats. Theresa sat in the chair farthest from Rosalind. Theresa tucked her blond hair behind her ears. She scrutinized Ruth from head to toe.

"I hope we can talk, Theresa." Rosalind wanted Theresa to look her way, yet Theresa continued to look at Ruth. Rosalind tried again. "Why do you think I killed Tony?"

"Because I know you did. You were there in the morning, you secretly loved him, and you were upset he never asked you on a second date. You refused to fulfill his requests at work. Whenever he talked to you, you were angry. I heard you have a vision board which shows how you planned to kill him."

"I'm not a vision board person and I never went on a date with Tony. If I secretly loved him, which isn't true, why would I want him dead?"

"You were jealous of Jennifer and Cassandra. You could not accept competition anymore."

Theresa was in everyone's business, but this train of thought was ludicrous. Rosalind glanced at Ruth, uncertain what to ask next.

Ruth asked, "Theresa, you knew Tony a long time, is that correct?"

"Yes, I knew him since he started working at Kelco."

"You cared about him very much, didn't you?"

Theresa teared up. She put her hand to her forehead and cast her eyes to the floor. Her shoulders trembled.

"It's ok to admit it. We love our friends, and we want the best for them. When something like this happens, it's hard to comprehend, isn't it?"

Theresa nodded. Her eyes remained focused on the ground.

"Tell me about you and Tony."

Theresa looked directly at Ruth. "I can barely remember a time without him. We were pals through thick and thin. We were always there for each other, no matter who he dated or married. We had a stronger bond than his marriages. We were partners in life and business. Without me, Tony would never have had the funds to create the nightclub. And now he will never walk through those doors again."

Rosalind knew they had been close, but Theresa's story made her recall a picture she had seen in the Kelco archives. Tony, with his arm around a beautiful, blond-haired woman in her late thirties. The photograph celebrated Tony's first sales award. When she saw the picture, she didn't recognize the woman. Now she realized it had been Theresa. The image tugged at Rosalind's heart. Theresa, now closer to retirement, barely resembled her younger appearance. This was a grieving woman who lost a part of her life when Tony died. Yet no one considered her loss or consoled her. Theresa had been Tony's mainstay, and now she was alone.

"Theresa, I'm so sorry for your loss. I'm deeply sorry." As Rosalind uttered the words, she suddenly felt cold since all the reasons that were given for Rosalind to kill Tony could be applied to Theresa. What if Theresa could not tolerate one more girlfriend, wife, or alliance?

Ruth offered her condolences, too. "What has you so convinced about Rosalind being a murderer?"

"I talked to Pamela. She went to Tony's safety deposit box after he died. She found a photograph of you and Tony among his most sacred items. Rosalind, why did Tony keep a picture of you?"

Caught off guard she remembered she forgot to give Pamela the envelope she dropped at the bank. Rosalind straightened her shoulders. "There is only one person who can answer that question. And unless you have a way to communicate with those who have passed, I'm afraid we'll never know."

Chapter Twenty-Three

When Theresa left, Josh spun on his barstool and nudged Graham toward Rosalind and Ruth. They sat in the open chairs forming a small circle.

"Well, I'm exhausted," said Rosalind.

"Did she explain herself?" asked Josh.

"She believes I killed Tony for all the wrong reasons."

After explaining Theresa's side of the conversation, Josh and Graham shook their heads. As Rosalind finished, she saw Issy Candella walking to their table. Tall and radiant, her long dark hair swayed around her shoulders.

"Well, if it isn't my friend Isidora Candella. I didn't know you hung out here," said Rosalind.

"I don't usually. A group from work decided on a last-minute get-together."

After Rosalind introduced everyone, she asked Issy to pull up another chair and join them.

"I would love to, but I need to go back to the team. I'm certain they're plotting plant swap outs behind my back. I need to maintain some order. It was great to meet you all."

After Issy left, Graham asked, "What does she do?"

"She is a botanist. She works behind the scenes at Desert Botanical Gardens, propagating succulents, training new hires. Basically, she is a plant wizard," said Rosalind. "But getting back to Theresa, what frightens me is why Theresa thinks I murdered him. Is she blaming me to deflect attention because she killed Tony?"

Ruth nodded. "I agree. Her thoughts are distorted due to her overwhelming grief. Until Rosalind expressed her sympathies to Theresa, I don't know that anyone truly acknowledged her loss. She lost her best friend."

Josh nodded. "Where do we go from here?"

Rosalind set down her glass of wine. "I've no idea what to do next. My job is gone temporarily, and I'm a prime suspect. I need to retreat and recoup."

Ruth wrapped her arm around Rosalind's shoulders. "It's complicated. But you are surrounded by friends." She looked at Josh and Graham and they nodded in agreement. "And it has been a long day. I have an early flight tomorrow and I need my rest. Our best bet is to go home and sleep on it. Hopefully, we will wake with new ideas on how to discover Tony's murderer."

Rosalind raised her glass and toasted. "To tomorrow."

Everyone said, "To tomorrow."

* * *

Tomorrow came too soon for Rosalind. She didn't want to move a muscle to get out of bed. Hercules had other ideas. He nuzzled his nose against her shin for at least ten minutes before Rosalind stirred. She awoke with no new ideas to solve Findley's murder.

As she opened the casita door after their morning run, Rosalind heard honking and looked above to see one lone Canada Goose flying overhead. She waited to see the V formation, but none appeared. The goose honked louder and louder sending its position to the flock. No flock came into sight. Tears formed as she said a quick prayer for the lone goose to find his family.

A half hour later after two cups of coffee, Rosalind sat at the kitchen table, elbows propped on the wood and her chin resting in her palms. Photographs scattered across the table reminded her of an easier time, when her main concerns were running, working, and playing with Hercules.

Seeking distraction, she flipped open her laptop and composed an email to Margaret. She asked for help following up on Kristina and Johann Schmidt, who weren't in the 1798 census. And she suggested a few potential dates for lunch. She hit send and crossed her fingers.

She returned to her search for her maternal grandfather's port of entry. Having exhausted searches for other ports, she clicked on the immigration records for the port of Philadelphia. After typing his name, she found a link matching his birth year and point of origin in Russia. She saved the search and clicked into the original document when her phone rang. It was Bob.

"Hello."

"Rosalind, are you sitting down?"

"Yes, I am."

"Have you heard the news?"

"No, what news?"

"There has been another death."

"What?" Rosalind stood up. "What's going on?"

"Another Kelco employee has died."

"Who?"

"It's Theresa, Theresa Mars."

"What happened? Oh my God, I just saw her yesterday."

"You saw her yesterday? Why?"

"Well, I needed to talk to her. Tell me what happened."

"I don't know, but Detective Hamilton called me. He said Ernie from the Daily Planet found her."

"What does Ernie have to do with Theresa?"

"I don't know. Theresa lived in the upstairs flat above the Daily Planet. He went to check on her and she was dead."

"She wasn't murdered, was she?"

"The police aren't saying much, but Detective Hamilton led me to believe it was suicide."

Chapter Twenty-Four

"Rosalind, I have a warrant to search your home." Detective Hamilton entered and walked around Rosalind's kitchen table. As always, his presence intimidated her. Rosalind tried to control her emotions. Could she find out more from him than he would from her? Enders stood behind Hamilton surveying Rosalind's home.

"Why do you need to do that?" Rosalind fidgeted in her chair.

"It's a routine search. Theresa accused you of murder and now she is dead. We have to follow up on every angle." Hamilton nodded to Enders who started opening drawers and peering behind furniture. "And, just for the record, you have the right to remain silent. Anything you say or do can and will be held against you in a court of law. You have the right to speak to an attorney. If you cannot afford an attorney, one will be appointed for you."

"That's going a bit far, isn't it?"

"Why did you not return my phone call from the weekend?"

"I did not receive a phone call from you."

"Where were you last weekend?"

"I went to Sedona on Saturday but was right here most of the time."

"After I told you to stay close to home?"

"I didn't leave the state, I simply went to Sedona. Sedona is close to home. I was back the same day." She noticed Enders was now looking through drawers and looked under couch pillows.

"Alone?"

"No, I went to a conference with Josh Bartholomew. During the conference, my phone battery died. The phone wasn't fully charged until I was back in Phoenix. I had no messages."

"Perhaps my message was spirited away by a vortex?" He raised his eyebrows as he cracked half a smile.

"I didn't visit vortexes, I attended a conference," said Rosalind without disguising her exasperation. "I don't know why your message didn't show on my phone, I didn't get a message to call you. Check for yourself." She held her phone out to him. He glanced at it but shook his head.

"Sir, take a look at this," said Enders as she pulled a closed cardboard trifold presentation board and a huge Ziploc bag out from under the couch. When she opened the triptychs, Rosalind saw cut-out magazine images of oleander plants, photos of Tony with Jennifer and Pamela, and in the center the photo of Rosalind with Tony.

Her eyes widened. She groaned and clapped her hand over her mouth as she cried, "I've never seen that before. Someone must have put that here. They're obviously trying to frame me."

Hamilton sighed. "We need to bag this up and go to the station for questioning."

Rosalind remembered last night's toast. She would never do that again. "I don't want to go to the police station. What you are bagging does not belong to me. It's a set up. You know this is ridiculous." Hercules came to her side and nudged her leg.

Hamilton opened the door for Enders. "Shall we go?"

"Can I feed Hercules first?"

* * *

The police station smelled of bleach. The atmosphere sterile. White. Cold. Frightening. Rosalind hadn't been to a police station since she toured one as a child on a field trip.

Hamilton led her to a square room with a mirror on one wall. She did as she was told and sat in the metal folding chair, saw her frustrated face reflected in the glass, and closed her eyes.

Enders and Hamilton sat directly across from her. Making her wait must be part of the intimidation process. Rosalind would keep her eyes closed until they spoke.

"Rosalind," said Hamilton, "for the record we are filming this session."

Great, thought Rosalind as she opened her eyes. More intimidation.

He asked, "Where were you last night?"

"I went to the Daily Planet with Aunt Ruth."

"Aunt Ruth?"

"Yes, the flight attendant who lives next door. You questioned her after Tony died."

"Yes, I did. But back to last night. You were with Aunt Ruth; did you meet anyone?"

"Yes, the place was crowded. I talked with Josh Bartholomew and Graham Grayson. They walked in after we sat down."

"What time did you arrive?"

"5:15."

"What time did Bartholomew and Grayson arrive?"

"A few minutes later, around 5:20."
"Who else did you meet?"
"Theresa Mars."
"Did you know she was going to be there?"
"I wasn't certain if she would come. I texted her and asked her to meet me."
"Why?"
"Because she accused me of murder, not only at Tony's funeral, but in Sedona, too."
"Theresa was also in Sedona?
"Yes."
"Why was she there?"
"I have no idea. I thought she was following me, but I don't know. I had to talk to her to find out why she believes, or believed, that I killed Tony."
"Did you find out why?"
"Not really. She was delusional about me."
"Why?"
"She thought I was jealous of all his relationships, which I was not. It made me wonder if she had killed Tony."
"You don't expect us to believe she killed Tony?" asked Enders.
"I don't know. I was left with that feeling. Why did she blame me when I barely knew the man? She was grieving his loss. She lost her best friend."
"How long were you at the Daily Planet?" asked Hamilton.
"We left around 8."
"What time did Theresa leave?"
"It was close to 7:30."
"Was she upset after talking to you?"
"She was grieving before and after talking to me. That best describes her state of mind."
"Did she mention doing harm to herself? Not wanting to go on anymore?" asked Enders.
"No, she was sad, but I did not think she was suicidal. She was upset with me, but at least I tried to understand why she accused me."
"Did you want Theresa dead?" asked Enders.
"No, I don't want anyone dead."

"It seems odd that you find Anthony Findley dead. Then you meet Theresa Mars the night before she dies. When we searched your casita this morning, we found a presentation board that Theresa told us you had. It outlined how to kill Findley and had a plastic bag full of oleander stapled to it."

"Why would I do this? And why would Theresa tell you I had it? Someone must have planted the board to implicate me. I never saw that board until Enders discovered it."

Hamilton stood up inhaling deeply. "Rosalind, we are placing you under arrest for the murder of Anthony Findley. Enders, please take Rosalind to the custody suite."

"You know I didn't kill him! This is not fair, Detective."

Enders walked around the table and gently reached out to Rosalind's elbow to lead her away.

"Can I make a phone call first? I need to have someone care for my dog while I'm here. And I want an attorney." Tears pricked Rosalind's eyes. She had been in the wrong place twice. Now she feared she might not see Hercules again for a long, long time.

* * *

After appearing before the judge and being formally charged with murder, Rosalind was grateful her fingerprints were taken electronically rather than with ink. Unfortunately, horrible mug shots were taken and would be part of her records. She felt completely alone in the world.

Enders led her to the detention area where Rosalind walked into a windowless, square room. She forced back tears from the edges of her eyes. Enders locked the door behind Rosalind.

Aunt Ruth was flying today, so she used her one call to contact Audra, telling her where to find the spare key and begging her to check on Hercules until further notice. Thank goodness Audra agreed to help her.

Please let them find the murderer and release me as soon as possible, she prayed. There was no way she could prove her innocence locked in this white-washed box. She sat on a metal bench designed to be as uncomfortable as possible. No phone, no laptop, no life. She held her head in her hands and sobbed. After five minutes, she wiped her tears on her sleeve, hiccupped twice, and straightened her shoulders.

Rosalind had spoken to more police officers in the last week than she had in her entire life. Police dramas on television weren't her kind of entertainment.

Rosalind needed to use the time in custody to solve Tony's murder and to figure out a new career if she ever got out. She looked up at the ceiling, hoping answers would appear. Near tears again, the message from Madam Damara crept into her thoughts. What was that message again? Rosalind focused and remembered.

We are doing what we can. We need you to do what you can from your side. Please meditate, contemplate, listen to your dreams, and re-evaluate everything now. Do this every day. We will help and guide you as will your bear, your totem spirit animal. Reach out to us. Ask us for help.

What do I have to lose? This was not the ideal place to meditate, but, then again, she was here now, and she needed help. And there was nothing else she could do.

Alone and sorrowful, Rosalind said aloud, "I'm asking for help. I need help to get out of here and to solve Anthony Findley's murder. I am desperate. This is not my fate and I need assistance. Please hear my request. Please guide me, spirit guides, totem animal, ancestors, whoever can help. Please look favorably on my request and help."

As she finished, she envisioned the bear, like the metal sculpture outside the conference center. She laid down on the bench. She continued to murmur, please help, until she fell asleep.

Part Two

"Red sky at night, sailor's delight.
Red sky at morning, sailors take warning."

Ageless Mariner's Rhyme

Chapter Twenty-Five, December 1765, Büdingen, Hesse

Christoph plunged his right foot into the mud as he walked toward the city square. He heaved his left foot up, stepped forward and squished it back into the mushy ground. Of course, he thought, once he decided to leave Ansbach, the October clouds painted gray strokes across the sunless sky and the rains descended, soaking him to the skin. After years of drought and war and ravaged land, rain collided with the earth today. Yet, he would not go back, and onward he trudged toward his new life. The rain pounded on his frayed hat, cascaded to the brim, and bounced off his cheeks. The local priest in Ansbach, Father Trier, told him Büdingen was a wet and muddy valley. It was so wet that the castle and the town were built on old oak planks.

The corner of the advertisement LeRoy and Pietet circulated hung out of his back pocket. The paper creases were worn, formed from constant folding, and unfolding. Christoph read the advertisement every morning and evening. His one hope for the future was tied to the promises of Catherine II, Empress of Russia.

When he first saw the flyer, he could not read all of it, but Father Trier read it to him again and again. Now he could read the words on his own. As he scanned it, he daydreamed about a new life. The offer included freedoms of which he wanted to dream but dared not.

Of all these freedoms, he could not choose one that was more valuable than the others. Together these promises created a surge of emotion from his stomach to his throat. Inside he trembled.

He mouthed the words he memorized, "Freedom of religion." He would no longer have to pretend to change his faith based on the latest victory of one duchy prince over another. Being forced to change allegiance from Catholic to Lutheran and back again would remain in his past.

Every time he opened and closed the paper, he wondered, were the promises true? Exemption from military service for all settlers guaranteed that he would never have to bear arms. And this exemption applied to all descendants, too. He knew he would not have children again, because his heart could not bear any further losses, but it was a great offer even if it only applied to him.

Thirty years of freedom from taxation. Government interest-free loans with ten-year repayments. Guarantee of self-rule within the colonies. Free transportation to Russia. If even half of the promises panned out, he would be better off in the land of the Czarina.

Ahead he saw a line of people circling around the buildings near the square. Twenty people stood in front of a small table, behind which sat three men, asking questions, and writing notes. Christoph believed the men were the agents of the LeRoy and Pietet Company. He slowed his pace as he breathed in to gather his nerves. Exhaling he walked toward the end of the line. He tried to stomp the mud off his boots, thinking it best to create a good impression. The mud stuck. He hoped it was not a bad omen.

These men could change Christoph's life of sorrow and regret to one of survival and, he hoped, joy. He was ready to create a new life. Prepared to go it alone, he would make the best of his future in a country far away. As he stood in line, he imagined broad green fields and the glorious blue skies of Russia.

After twenty minutes of fidgeting in line, Christoph realized he was next. He listened to what the men asked the family in front of him. He also tried to hear how the family answered. He did not want to be denied this opportunity.

"Come forward, please," said the man seated in the middle behind the table. Christoph stepped forward. The man raised his eyes and stared at Christoph's worn clothing.

"Name?" the man asked.

"Christoph Schmidt." He shuffled his feet to gain his bearings on the soggy ground.

"Age, year, and place of birth?"

"I am twenty-four years old, born in 1741 in Ansbach," said Christoph.

"And your family?"

"I don't have any family…they are gone." He lowered his head to hide his eyes. He noticed the rain slowed to a light drizzle.

"No family? Go over to the line outside the blacksmith's shop."

Dead Reckoning

Christoph hesitated. He always did as he was told, but he was concerned he may have lost his chance. He raised his hat, so his eyes looked at the man who would determine his future.

Christoph breathed in and summoned his strength to stay calm.

"Why?" he asked.

"You will need support to begin your life in Russia."

Christoph exhaled. "And what happens outside the blacksmith's shop?"

"Every few hours we match people together to build families. In other words, before you board the ship to Russia, you must be married."

Christoph gasped. His eyes nearly bulged out of their sockets. He had sworn to be alone for the rest of his days. He knew he should not swear, but he had given his heart to Margaretha and their two children. When he returned to their home after the war, to the burnt fields, the war-ravaged land, he found the three of them deserted in the house without food to eat, and his heart collapsed. The children were already in heaven. Margaretha was two days away from joining them. He did everything he could, but it was too late. She could not eat and barely recognized him. All joy was gone, and his future did not matter. After burying them all on the land they had called home, he decided then and there he could not endure a loss like that again. And he could not stay on the land that had taken his family from him. After roaming the countryside aimlessly, doing odd jobs for farmers and tradesfolk, he saw the flyer and made his choice for Russia, alone.

"Is there a problem, Herr Schmidt?"

"No," Christoph whispered. His plans now changed. To have a chance at his dreamed future, he must marry today.

Chapter Twenty-Six

Outside of the blacksmith's shop, two lines wrapped around the cream brick building, men on the left, women on the right. Anna Barbara Kälberin stood in line behind twenty-six other women. Her golden hair was twisted into a braid, covered by a beige scarf. Her blue eyes darted from the front of the line to the church across the street, to her children and then back to the line. Her right hand clasped the left hand of her daughter, Kristina. Her left arm wrapped around the shoulders of her son, Johann. Each held a small bag with all of their earthly belongings. Anna Barbara shivered. She was scared and had never felt more alone in her life.

I must be brave. I need to hide the fear on my face, so the children are not frightened. As she looked down at Kristina, Anna Barbara projected calm on her face, but she felt Kristina's inner energy swirl. The survival of her children drove her to uproot their lives.

Johann was restless. Tired of standing in one place, he shifted from one foot to the other, then back again. His dark hair sprouted out from under his hat despite how often Anna Barbara licked her fingers and flattened it to his forehead.

The tall woman in front of Anna Barbara moved forward. She was at least six inches taller than Anna Barbara, with plain brown hair, a strong back and a small sack in her right hand. Anna pulled her children to follow as the tall woman stepped forward.

Anna Barbara could see the line of men but could not bring herself to look at their faces again. When she had looked earlier, the men wore haggard and wrinkled expressions. Others looked far too young for her to marry. She swore she would not look until after they told her who her future husband would be.

The line of men had not extended as long as the women's line when she arrived. Would there be a match for her? If she prayed hard enough, the man would not be horrible to look at, and dare she dream, that he have a heart of gold.

Her stomach growled. It had been four days since she had eaten. The final scraps of food she had salvaged had been divided between Kristina and Johann this morning. If she were matched today and given temporary housing, there might be a meal before the end of the day. She let go of Kristina's hand and softly covered her stomach. She thought of her home and moved her head from side to side to shake the images out of her mind. Not worth thinking about now, she thought, there is no going back. She and her children needed a new place to live. Russia was as good a place as any.

Scraping of shoes against the wood planks snapped Anna Barbara out of her daydream and she looked up and saw two men. The first was lanky, fair, and tall, at least six feet, with squinty brown eyes. The second was shorter, taller than her, but he was muscular with dark hair and soft blue eyes. She looked down, hoping they did not notice her glance.

The line moved faster now, due to the lateness of the day, and hunger in the bellies. Anna Barbara held Kristina and Johann's hands as she stepped to her future.

As the woman in front of her reached the table, she said, "Maria Herrmann." The tall man was also at the front of the line. He said, "Martin Schumacher."

The man behind the table looked up at Martin. "Herr Schumacher, please meet Maria Herrmann. She is assigned to be your wife."

Schumacher turned to his right and scanned Maria Herrman from head to toe. He eyed the sack in her right hand, her thin frame and well-worn outfit. Maria looked at him and offered a smile.

Schumacher, wearing clothing without signs of age or overuse, raised the brim of his felt hat over his forehead then snapped back to the men at the table. "No, she is too thin. And tall. And plain. How do I know she can bear children? She has none with her." He glanced back at Maria and shook his head. "No, I need a son. I need assurance that my wife can produce my heir. There are plenty of women here who brought children with them. No, I will not marry her."

The man behind the table gasped. No one dared to question the agent's authority.

Schumacher turned and pointed at Anna Barbara. "I want her."

Chapter Twenty-Seven

Maria Herrmann inhaled sharply and stepped back directly into Anna Barbara. Anna stumbled back and Kristina caught her. Maria's shoulders shook, and she placed her hands over her face. Anna Barbara steadied herself, and reached out to Maria, a woman she did not know, but empathized with. Anna Barbara embraced Maria. Maria sobbed.

Schumacher stood with his hands on his hips. He glared at the agents behind the table. The men met his look and kept their eyes steady.

"Herr Schumacher," said the agent who permeated an air of ultimate control. One look from him and it was apparent he made the final decisions. "This behavior is unacceptable. Part of the agreement for your relocation is that you bring your family with you. Your family has been chosen for you. Your family is Maria Herrmann. Either you marry Maria Herrmann, or your passage to Russia is jeopardized. If you do not marry her, her journey is delayed."

Schumacher shrugged as if the air was knocked out of him. He needed a new beginning. Russia was the way to put his massive gambling debts behind him. This woman, Maria Herrmann, was not at all what he expected for his wife. Her face was not pleasant, it was long and sad. Her lips were thin, and her pallor indicated poor health. The woman behind her was far more pleasant to look at, accompanied by two children which meant she could produce an heir for him. And the ready-made family she provided would help with chores and building a new life. He saw that she possessed an inner drive to survive. The desire shone through her.

'What is your decision, Herr Schumacher?" said the agent in charge.

The dark-haired man behind Schumacher nodded at Maria Herrmann, then stepped forward to Schumacher. He covered his mouth near Schumacher's ear and said, "She is a kind woman. She needs a new life, too. Give it a chance. You may grow to love her."

Schumacher was deflated. He must go to Russia, there were too many people here whom he owed money and could never repay. He reckoned if he stayed, he would be dead within the week. Would something change during their travels? Today was but one step toward a lifetime of change. Traveling to Russia would cover weeks, months of their lives. Changes will occur along the way before this journey is over. Maria Herrmann was not the person with whom he envisioned the rest of his life. Yet, this was simply one day. And one day does not dictate the rest of a new life.

He chose his words carefully. "I did not know how these decisions are made. Now I understand how this works. I will marry Maria Herrmann."

Anna Barbara released Maria who wiped her eyes and patted her hair. She turned to Schumacher who did not look at her.

The agent said, "Here are your papers, go over to Marienkirche and there will be another group wedding ceremony in an hour. Wait in the church foyer, your names will be called."

Chapter Twenty-Eight

Rays of sunshine broke through the silvery clouds as Martin Schumacher and Maria Herrmann walked away from the table toward the church. Anna Barbara moved to the front of the line, her children behind her. She, too, had no idea exactly how this arrangement was decided.

She looked to her left and saw the muscular dark-haired man again. This time she lifted her gaze and saw the bluest eyes she had ever seen looking at her. He nodded then also stepped forward.

He shifted his gaze to the agents at the table. "Christoph Schmidt."

"Anna Barbara Kälberin," she said, "and Kristina and Johann Kälberin."

"Ja, your papers are in order. Take these with you to the church, you should be able to join the next ceremony. And avoid Schumacher, we do not want any issues or confusion. There is a Lutheran marriage service being conducted now. Go there, let the man at the door know you are Catholic. Then, get married in the next Catholic ceremony by the priest. No delays."

Christoph took the paper and nodded. He put his right arm on his hip, then motioned for Anna Barbara to link her arm through his. Anna Barbara hesitated at first. How quickly our lives changed, she thought. Then she straightened her shoulders, stood taller than before and slid her right arm through his. Johann clasped her left hand and then in turn, he clasped Kristina's hand. The four walked through the mud. The bright sun shone upon them.

As they entered the building, Christoph searched for the top of Martin Schumacher's head, which would be visible above the crowd gathered inside the beautiful wooden cathedral. He saw the back of Schumacher's head two-thirds of the way toward the front on the right.

Christoph spotted an empty pew near the back on the left side and led his newfound family there. He offered Kristina his hand and then Johann as they genuflected and sat down on the wooden bench. He paused for Anna Barbara to enter before him. He offered her a crooked smile as his heart pounded in his ears and he thought of how he wanted to go alone. She smiled cautiously at him in return. He turned his gaze to the front of the church.

Chapter Twenty-Nine

Anna Barbara saw Christoph swallow hard as he and his new family climbed the steps to their assigned room. This journey was a new beginning, but he never thought he would be married today.

After the ceremony in the Marienkirche, they learned they would stay in a boarding house until there were enough settlers to transport to Lübeck. After Lübeck they would sail on the Baltic Sea to Kronstadt, then to Oranienbaum, then south to the Volga region to their Catholic village. Anna Barbara arranged the children on one of the two beds in the room.

"You rest," she directed. "We have walked long and far. You can rest now."

Christoph looked at his new family. He held the allotments for food so they could eat during their time here.

"Are you hungry?" he asked.

The children looked toward their mother who said, "Yes, we would like to eat."

"Good. I will fetch food for us and bring it back here. You three can rest. I will be back soon."

"Thank you, that is very kind of you."

As Christoph closed the door behind him, Anna Barbara sat down gently on the bed. She wanted to lay down and cry tears of happiness, yet she restrained herself as she did not want to confuse the children. How could she explain the relief she felt for her unborn child? Would she ever be more grateful than she was now for the food that was on its way? She thought not.

Two weeks later, Anna Barbara and Christoph had created a daily routine. They walked through the town, checking the best prices for food, to maximize their daily rations. They talked politely to each other, but neither had discussed their pasts. Anna Barbara was curious about Christoph. She sensed a sorrow within him that could take years to uncover. To ask now seemed premature. She believed he should initiate the discussion as he was the husband, the leader of the household, setting the course of their new life.

She did not have years to consummate their marriage. Granted the single room was not conducive to a wedding bed, however by her best calculations, she was nearly two months with child. Her food intake had increased, and it was not her imagination that she felt the child growing within her.

Anna Barbara considered that it would be nice for Christoph to believe this child was his own. Or was it a lie not to explain the truth? Would anyone know or care when this child was conceived? Thoughts of how children were essential to building a new settlement raced through Anna Barbara's mind. The entire family's help was needed along the way.

How this child was conceived was one thought Anna Barbara worked to avoid. Much had changed but Anna Barbara would protect this child as it was part of her. Which is why she had to leave. She wondered how long it would be before her condition showed. How long before Christoph guessed.

She saw Maria and Martin a few times and when she talked to Maria, she indicated that the marriage was formal, the actions were there, the emotions undemonstrated. Maria felt there would never be love, but she had a life, and she had food. There was a path for them to be together.

Anna Barbara prayed silently. "Christoph is a kind man. He is a lonely man. I am his new partner. Please guide me to help him settle in a brand-new country. We want to leave the past behind. Please guide this man to reach out to me in love. It does not have to be the deepest love he has to offer. I need only a small segment of his heart to help this child become a part of his family."

Christoph opened the door. "I have news. We leave for Lübeck in two days. The second part of our travels begins. We will be in a new land within a few weeks."

Anna Barbara went to him. She reached her arms toward him, hopeful that this good news would end in a hug. Christoph looked down at his hands then slid past her to sit on one of the chairs at the small table. Anna Barbara sat on the chair next to him. "How long does it take to get to Lübeck? Will the sea be frozen, and will we sail for Kronstadt? Will we arrive in Russia in spring?"

"I am not certain, although I know we are fortunate to be moving to Lübeck now. It is late January and spring is coming. It is best that we travel as early as possible so we can get settled before winter. It will take from eight to twelve days to get to Lübeck, depending on the weather and the number of people traveling."

"How long will we be in Lübeck before we sail?"

Dead Reckoning

"It depends on the weather and how well the agents work with the shipping lines. I hope we will not be there long, but we will need to be patient before we get full answers. There are stories about families who have been in Denmark for more than a year who have not yet been transported to Russia."

"Oh, my goodness, that's a long time."

"It's true. I heard much today from the agents and other travelers. All I know is that we leave in two days. We need to pray for clear weather as that will determine when we sail for Kronstadt. Then we will need to work through the formalities of entering Russia. After that, we will travel inland to the area where we will settle. Momentous changes are happening soon." He stood up and walked to the bed. He laid down. "The news has exhausted me. I need to rest, to clear my head."

Anna Barbara sat at the foot of the bed, biding her time to connect with her husband. That news was the longest consecutive conversation she and Christoph had had.

She kissed her children good night and laid on the bed facing Christoph. He rolled from his right side to his left, away from Anna Barbara. Every night Anna Barbara prayed for Christoph and her family on what was exclusively her side of the bed.

Chapter Thirty

Carriages lined the square as Christoph, Anna Barbara, Kristina, and Johann carried their bags to start their trek to Russia together. Anna Barbara had no idea what to expect on the journey. Would it be uncomfortable riding in a carriage for eight to ten hours a day? Would they see the terrain or would most of the view be blocked by fellow passengers? Most of all, would they have any privacy?

"We go to carriage number seventeen." Christoph led them to the vehicle where they would sit for the next ten or more days. When they reached the carriage, Christoph lifted their bags to the top and tied them securely with the ropes. He opened the door and extended his hand to Anna Barbara to help her ascend to the carriage. Kristina and Johann followed, and then Christoph joined them.

"There will be four other people in this carriage, so Johann will need to sit on our laps. I will rotate turns with the other men riding on the outside of the coach."

Anna Barbara thought the carriage looked small for eight people. She hoped there would be more children making the space more tolerable. Carriage seventeen was scheduled to depart in half an hour. She did not mind the wait since they could sit. Kristina was near the window, Anna Barbara next to her, Johann on Anna's lap. Christoph sat next to her. They fit comfortably on the back side of the coach.

The driver checked on them and crossed their names off the list. Another couple climbed in the coach and sat opposite the Schmidts. They introduced themselves as Peter and Katharina Asselborn. Peter shook hands with Christoph and greeted each member of the Schmidt family. They were younger than Christoph and Anna Barbara. She saw that they had not yet experienced the sorrow through which she and Christoph had survived.

About five minutes before departure, two more people approached the coach. Anna Barbara's heart sank when she saw Martin Schumacher and Maria Herrmann, that is, Mr. and Mrs. Martin Schumacher. She smiled at Maria. Christoph nodded to Maria before Martin and Christoph locked eyes.

Martin looked as dapper as ever. His boots shone, his pants and shirt defied wrinkles, his hair was neatly combed straight back from his forehead. "This is going to be a longer journey than I imagined." Martin backed away and walked over to the driver. The driver said,

"If you do not travel in that coach, you forfeit your trip to Lübeck." Martin hung his head.

"There are no changes allowed. We will have to travel in this coach," said Martin to Maria as she entered the carriage. As Martin climbed into the coach, his jacket slipped back, and Anna Barbara saw a long, brown knife case tied to his waist. Inside the case a wooden handle with elaborate engraving extended out.

"All we have to do is ride together for a few days. There is no need for concern. I am Christoph Schmidt." He extended his right hand in greeting. Martin ignored his hand. "This is my wife, Anna Barbara and our children, Kristina and Johann. We can make this travel arrangement work. We all want new homes in Russia."

Martin looked away. Maria glanced at Anna Barbara who smiled, hoping her eyes shone with warmth. Maria's brown hair was pulled back tightly away from her face. Her scarf was tied securely under her chin. Her clothes matched most peasant women, simple and plain. She appeared sad and discouraged. Anna Barbara nodded to Maria and looked at her children for distraction. Inside her heart raced as Christoph acknowledged her and her children as part of one family. It was a small step which she was grateful to hear. Were her prayers being answered?

Peter and Katharina's excitement for the journey negated Martin's behavior. The Schmidt family felt at ease with at least half of their traveling companions.

"Last call," shouted the driver. He pulled himself up to the buckboard and checked with his partner. They reviewed the list one last time. Then he flicked the reins, and the four horses started to trot.

Johann bounced up and down in Anna Barbara's lap. Yes, she agreed with Martin, it would be a longer journey than anticipated.

The convoy passed many towns, and Anna Barbara could not remember half of the villages they passed. Christoph rotated riding outside, and at other times he took Johann on his lap, to give Anna Barbara more room. Peter rotated often. Martin did not take a turn. Spring was ready to burst forth early in the first few villages they drove through, but by the third day a chill possessed the air.

The sleeping arrangements were not ideal, as they bedded in barns, one stall berth to a family. Most of the travelers were comfortable enough since they had a roof over their heads.

"Anna Barbara, you look a bit pale tonight. Is the jostling and bumping in the carriage too much? Johann can sit in my lap for the remainder of the ride, and I will sit outside more often to give you more room." Christoph looked to Johann who nodded at him.

"Thank you." Anna Barbara was grateful for this small change.

By the tenth day, everyone was exhausted. Despite the rest stops for the horses, and the village tavern's fresh food, the travelers envisioned staying in one place without the rocking and rolling of the carriage and the ruts in the road as a constant companion. They dreamed of clean beds in a private room in Lübeck.

The scowl lines on Martin Schumacher's face deepened each day. He rarely spoke except to criticize Maria. He stared at Anna Barbara throughout most of the drive, letting Maria sit next to the window so he would be directly across from Anna Barbara.

As dusk descended on the twelfth day of travel, the carriage entered the town limits of Lübeck. The town bustled unlike any of the previous villages through which they had driven. Horses trotted past the carriage, as wagon wheels heading in the opposite direction plunged through manure covering much of the roadway.

Anna Barbara saw Martin's expression perked up as they drove around the city square. She thought his spirit was revived as market owners shouted their wares, the clip clop of hooves sounded everywhere, and the wooden wheel rims pounded the brick road.

"Are we going to stay in this town?" asked Johann.

Christoph nodded. "We are heading to the warehouse district near the docks for our living quarters until we sail."

"This is my kind of scenery." Martin smiled.

Christoph watched as Martin eyed the taverns, hotels, and businesses. "Here I will find card games and earn money for our travel. It will ease the transition to Russia, both on the land and ship." Martin cleared his throat and looked directly at Christoph and Anna Barbara. "Christoph, I am energized by the change in this new town. Yet I have watched you and your wife for quite a few days now. I get a sense that you are married in name only. You have a beautiful wife. And you do not hold her hand or offer words of comfort to her. How can that be?"

Christoph looked into Martin's eyes. "I could say the same for you, Herr Schumacher. You have demonstrated disdain for your beautiful wife. And my marriage is none of your business."

"Actually, it is. And my wife knows the joy of the marriage bed. However, she is not as strong as yours and will not withstand the rigors of sea travel, and the additional wagon travel through Russia could cut our marriage short. God willing, if she is already with child, she has more rigors to endure." Martin turned to look at Maria who gazed at her lap. He turned back to Christoph. "You, on the other hand, may also not survive the travels. Accidents happen all the time during sea travel. Either way, I may need a new wife and your wife may need a new husband soon."

Christoph's blood rose turning his face from tanned to beet red. His arms trembled with rage and Anna Barbara put her hand on his arm to prevent him from swinging at Martin. She kept her face placid, never to reveal or admit to the truth Martin had spoken.

Christoph and Martin stared at each other until the driver stopped the carriage, dropped from the buckboard, and opened the door. The driver took Kristina's hand first, helped her down, then did the same for Johann and Maria.

Anna Barbara placed her hand in the drivers for support. She turned slightly to the side and her shawl dropped off her shoulder. She saw Christoph's eyes linger while looking at the roundness across her middle. They had eaten better over the last few weeks and did not walk as much. She watched his eyes search her arms and legs and his expression changed. She believed he now understood as there had not been a change to her limbs or her face. As she stepped down, Martin stood to follow her.

Christoph stood and pushed Martin back into his seat. He descended to join his family, took Anna Barbara's hand, and moved them forward to be assigned living quarters. She prayed their room would be far, far away from Martin Schumacher.

Anna Barbara did not believe Christoph was a vengeful man, simply that he preferred to let people live their lives and leave him in peace. But she also knew that words were prophetic. Martin should never have spoken as he did. In her bones, she knew Christoph would not allow Martin to intrude on their lives no matter what he had to do.

Chapter Thirty-One

The warehouse district, built of adjoining cream-colored buildings, lined the entire waterfront. Triangular peaks with square stepped facades topped the warehouse rooflines to accentuate the building's height. Christoph had never been in a big port city, only small harbors on riverbanks. Huge buildings amazed him and aroused his curiosity as to how the structure was built.

Again, they waited in line for their assigned living space. They did not expect much. Christoph learned the warehouses were previously used for storage and had been converted into temporary living quarters. But a single room with minimal furniture would be a palace to the weary travelers after sleeping in barn stalls or on the carriage during their trip. He checked behind them often to ensure that Martin and Maria were not close behind.

Christoph wrapped his arm around Anna Barbara's waist to keep her close to him. She was grateful for the support. An hour passed before they reached the table and were assigned their room. They hurried to the second floor of the warehouse at the end of the hallway. Once inside, they looked out the window and saw refreshing blue water. Was it the Bay of Lübeck, the straights of the Baltic Sea or a waterway that led to the sea? Anna Barbara did not know and did not care. She looked at their assigned room. The furniture was minimal, a trundle bed, and a table with six chairs. There were six plates and utensils in a small cupboard. On a sideboard, a pitcher and bowl were set for them. She was so grateful. She did not think heaven could provide a better home for her family.

"This looks wonderful." Anna Barbara set her bag on the floor. She immediately laid down on the bed, finally able to breathe and relax without Martin staring at her. The children pulled out the trundle and unpacked their belongings.

Christoph headed back toward the door. "I will get our meals. You three rest. I will be back soon."

Anna Barbara thought she could lay on this bed for the rest of her life. It was so comfortable compared to their travels for the last eleven or was it twelve days. A real bed, not a barnyard stall filled with old hay. Her body sunk into the mattress, and she sighed with happiness. Her bones finally relaxed, and she put her hands in prayer position. Dear Lord, please guide us through this journey, lead us to the way to becoming a true family. She closed her eyes and listened as her children enjoyed their temporary home.

Christoph was back in the room after a half hour with bread, soup, two pieces of chicken, milk, and beer. After setting plates on the table, he arranged the food at each place. He split two quarter pieces of chicken between Kristina and Johann. He took the remaining half for himself giving Anna Barbara one whole piece.

She glanced at him. "Christoph, you should have the larger piece, I can eat the half."

"No. You look pale after our journey. You need the sustenance."

Anna Barbara was ravenous and wanted to accept it. Yet, the head of the household always received the largest portions.

"Christoph, you are the man of the family, you are entitled to the largest share. You need it for your strength, too."

He turned and looked into her eyes. He did not waver for an instant. "I insist. The journey was long and hard. At this moment, you need it more than I do." His eyes remained locked with hers until she looked away. She did not want to quarrel with him.

She nodded. "Thank you." She prayed he did not realize that she needed to eat for two. Not that she would lie about her condition if he asked. *But if he does not ask, is it a lie?*

The children ate so fast, they did not talk at all. Anna Barbara waited for Christoph to finish eating. "How far did you have to walk to get the food?"

"About three blocks."

"Was there a long line?"

"About fifteen people. I never thought how much time I would wait in lines on the way to Russia."

"I never thought about it either."

Christoph looked at her. "Why do you want to go to Russia?"

Anna Barbara tried to keep the surprise from showing on her face. Christoph had asked her a question.

"My parents died soon after I married. I never had an extended family, no cousins, no aunts, or uncles. My husband was killed during the war, so it was just me and my children. We did our best to maintain our plot of land. When the marauders came and ransacked the house, and burned it to the ground, I could not stay, could not look at it any longer. Our hopes, our dreams. All gone, faded in one horrible evening."

"How long ago did your husband die?"

"A year ago." The moment she said it she wished she had bitten her tongue. *Why was she always so honest? What if this marriage does not consummate? What will he think of her?*

"That is a long time to be alone."

"We walked for days, not knowing what to do. We stopped at a church. I saw the flyer and decided it was the best way to make a clean start." She set her fork on the plate. "What about you? Why do you want to go to Russia?"

"Oh, there are many reasons. I served in the military the last eight years. It was hard to be away from home so often, changing sides, changing religions. The last time I returned home, I returned to a family that had perished. I arrived in time to bury them. I roamed the surrounding areas for weeks, uncertain what to do next, hoping to find something to make a difference." Christoph wiped his brow with his sleeve. "The entire countryside was starved. The victor took whatever rations and grains they found, like any army would. It was meaningless to the army, but my family was in their path of destruction. When I found the flyer, Russia offered the promise of never serving in the army again. It was the best thing I could imagine."

They finished eating in silence, the children were exhausted and slid without a whimper onto the trundle bed. Anna Barbara wiped the dishes and stored them back in the cupboard.

Christoph sat on the bed. She walked over and sat next to him.

"A fresh start for both of us, ja? I loved my wife, and I miss her dearly. Before this journey I swore I would never marry again. But I want this dream of a new life to work."

He turned and his knees met her knees. He held both of her hands.

"It is an odd situation we have gotten ourselves into with this arrangement. My heart was closed to it. But I do want our family to flourish."

Anna Barbara tried to remember to breathe. *Where was he going with this conversation?*

"Anna Barbara, you are now my wife. I know I have been slow to come to this, and I can't promise love or riches or a happy ending, but I am willing to try." He gazed into her eyes.

Dead Reckoning

"With your permission, I would like to make this marriage a real one." He tilted his head to the side, and let his lips touch hers. He kissed her. He moved to his side of the bed, still holding her hand, bringing her with him. "The children are sound asleep. Shall we make this a true marriage?"

Anna Barbara nodded. They both lay on the bed. This time facing each other.

Chapter Thirty-Two

Three weeks in Lübeck passed blissfully as Christoph and Anna Barbara settled into the routine of a stable household and built a foundation for the rest of their lives. Neither could remember a time when they felt so calm and content. No wars, no crop failures, no marauders. Anna Barbara trusted Kristina and Johann to play with other children waiting for passage to Russia without fear of harm. Soon enough Lübeck would be a memory as their journey continued.

At the end of February their tranquil world was upended as they waited in line to board the Ursa Major, the ship that would sail the Baltic Sea for about nine days to their new homeland. The ship harbored at the dock about five hundred feet from the table where the passengers checked in.

"What does Ursa Major mean?" asked Johann.

Christoph bent down to Johann. "Ursa Major is a constellation. It means Great Bear. Near it is Ursa Minor which represents the smaller bear, and it includes the North Star, also called Polaris. Since it is the brightest star, sailors use it to navigate travel. It is a point of reference for ships to determine where they are and the direction they want to move. The shipping company named this craft after an important constellation."

Ursa Major was built of long oak planks, its hull extended beyond their vision as some warehouses blocked their view of the stern. They eyed three tall masts on the vessel, sails hugged the poles as many ropes hung from the top of the post to the sides of the ship. Other ropes secured the vessel quayside. The water around it shimmered in the early daylight as it rocked in the water.

Christoph reached for Anna Barbara's hand when he saw Martin Schumacher and his wife walk from the housing area to the end of the line. Schumacher frowned as he realized his place in the line. He murmured something to Maria. She nodded but her expression of sadness never changed.

Within fifteen minutes, Christoph, Anna Barbara, Kristina, and Johann walked up the gangplank to board Ursa Major. The ship transported cargo, so loading fifty passengers instead of boxes of salt and foodstuffs would be a challenge for the travelers and seafarers alike.

"Christoph, have you ever been on a ship?" asked Anna Barbara as they strode through the gangway.

"Yes, a few times during the war. It was for river travel, not on the sea."

"How long will we sail on the Baltic?"

"It could be as short as nine days, as long as the weather remains clear and calm." Christoph led his family onto the deck. The ship swayed back and forth, and Anna Barbara's stomach cringed. Most of the seafarers on the deck ignored them, a couple nodded to them, and one introduced himself.

"Welcome to the Ursa Major. I am First Mate Hertzinger. Come along the deck to the companionway. It will lead you to your assigned area below." He motioned the family from mid ship toward the stern. He gazed longer than needed at Kristina who dropped her eyes and turned to her mother.

They navigated down a steep narrow set of stairs to head below deck. The light faded as they descended and after a moment their eyes adjusted to being below deck. Lit lanterns hung at the entrance to each stall. In contrast to the open air on the deck, Christoph's head was the same height as the passenger level ceiling. He led their way to the right and located berth fourteen. Straw on the floor and a small bucket in the corner inhabited the stall.

"The bucket is for fresh water, one bucket per day per family. You can fill your bucket from the wooden casks located near the stern of the ship." Hertzinger pointed back to the widest end of the vessel. He turned back to gaze at Kristina then he pointed in the opposite direction. "When you need to relieve yourselves, you must go to the head of the ship. There is a hole in the floor where you need to straddle and let the debris fall out of the ship. No exceptions, everyone must use it."

"Let's make ourselves comfortable." Christoph set their bags on the straw against the far wall. "We sleep here for nine nights, maybe a few more. We can make the best of it. This is better than the stagecoach jostling."

"And, we have more room to stretch our legs than we did on the wagon." Anna Barbara sat on their bags. "Join me. We can tell stories to each other to pass the time." Johann sneezed. "Gesundheit, Johann."

Kristina and Johann adapted to their quarters. Anna Barbara hoped they would sleep for most of the journey. The darkness on the passenger level would make it difficult to distinguish day from night.

Anna Dalhaimer Bartkowski

Boots stomped in the stall next to them. Slats spaced out every foot or more were the only wall between them. They saw the Schumachers enter stall thirteen through the gaps and look around at their home for the voyage. Martin held his nose in the air, despite having to duck to avoid his head hitting the ceiling. His usual sour expression remained on his face. He turned and saw Christoph and Anna Barbara. "We keep running into each other. It must be fate we are together again."

Christoph nodded. "We are starting our new lives. We can make this journey peaceful for all our sakes."

Another family, consisting of a man and woman, three boys and a young girl, approached from the entry way, walked past the Schmidts, and entered stall fifteen. They set their bags near the back wall. The head of the household looked over and stepped out to talk to Christoph.

"Hello, I am Joseph Wächter." He extended his hand to Christoph. Christoph shook it, and introduced his family, grateful for the distraction from Martin.

"It is nice to meet you." Joseph, in turn, introduced his family. "This is my wife Magdalena, my sons Henry, Jakob, and Friedrich, and my daughter Walpurga. Looks like we will be neighbors for the duration of the trip."

"Yes, it is good to meet you, too."

Anna Barbara, Magdalena, and their children greeted each other.

Martin stood up and extended his hand to Joseph. "I am Martin Schumacher, and this," he motioned back to his stall, "this is Maria."

Maria remained sitting on her bag Anna Barbara glanced to her and smiled. Maria smiled back and nodded to the Wächter family.

"Will you join me in a game of cards later, Joseph? It will help pass time below deck," asked Martin.

Joseph smiled. "I haven't played cards often, but it sounds like a good way to pass time."

Anna Barbara noticed that Peter and Katherina Asselborn were four stalls away from the Schumachers.

A massive crank churned as the crew started to pull up anchor through the chock. The ship swayed back and forth as water lapped up and down the sides. The oars slapped to maneuver the ship out of the dock and into the sea. Soon they would learn to ignore these sounds.

Dead Reckoning

The passengers retreated to their individual berths. There would be time for conversation during the long days and nights that they sailed. Anna Barbara prayed for their safety and serenity. She assumed Christoph prayed for calm, clear weather, and the Wächters prayed for beautiful farmland in Russia. She prayed that Martin would forget his thoughts of her as his wife. And she said a silent prayer for Maria hoping that her glorious dream of a new life would still come true.

Chapter Thirty-Three, October 2014, Arizona

Rosalind's eyes popped open, and she shook herself to bring her back to the present. Images of Christoph, Anna Barbara, a ship, and travels to Russia remained as blurry visions. She sensed strong emotions, and she regretted that she did not have paper or pen to record those images. She had none of those amenities in her jail cell. But what could she write? She was left with fantasies of a journey, movement, caring, and concern. Details were foggy, her emotions unraveled.

Had all her research wreaked havoc in her brain? Had she lost her mind? Had she experienced the hallucination of a lifetime? It all seemed real, too accurate to be a dream. Was she connecting with her ancestors' lives? Or was she experiencing a past life? And the name Christoph. She was certain it was in her dreams. Could the Christoph the psychic referred to be her five or six-time great grandfather? She had assumed Madam's Christoph connected to her father Christopher. How could the Christoph from centuries ago help her? She had a murder to solve if she could get out of here.

She sat upright on the cold, firm bench. She shivered, her neck ached, her back throbbed and she stretched to loosen her muscles and bones.

The guard talked outside, but the sounds were too muffled to understand a word. The door was solid, not a sliver of light shone through.

Despite the uncomfortable conditions, her eyelids drooped again. There was no way she could keep herself awake. She put her arm under her head for a pillow and said, "Please guide me on how to get out of here and find Tony's killer."

Chapter Thirty-Four, 1766, Baltic Sea

Christoph watched Martin as he stared across the stalls pacing and fidgeting with his knife. He occasionally looked up and frowned at Maria who sat across the stall from him. She looked down at her hands clasped in prayer, deep in thought.

"Christoph, will you walk up to the deck with me?" asked Martin with a smile.

Christoph was surprised. Martin appeared genuine in his request, so Christoph nodded.

Henry Wächter and Kristina descended the steps as the two men headed up to the deck. Christoph was grateful Kristina had a good friend to share the journey. Henry was fifteen, Kristina only nine, but when Christoph looked into her eyes, he saw an old soul.

* * *

Below, after the men had left, Maria entered the Schmidt's stall and sat near Anna Barbara. Maria greeted her. "How are you doing?"

"I am doing well, how are you?"

"I am fine. I apologize for my husband's lack of decorum. I do my best to tolerate him."

Anna Barbara nodded. "I understand. There are few options for us.'

Maria pointed toward Anna Barbara's middle. "How are you faring? How do the ship movements affect you?"

Anna Barbara sighed. "I thought I was disguising it. How did you know?"

"I sensed your energy, and the energy of your child. I helped women in my village when their time came. If you need help, I can assist."

"Thank you. I appreciate it. Please don't tell anyone. I need to wait a bit longer before I tell the children. There are many months and miles ahead."

"If you need to go on deck, I can stay with your children. I will check on Martin in a bit and get some fresh air in a few minutes. Let me know when you need a break. I am happy to help."

***

Once on deck Martin said, "I know we did not meet under the best of circumstances. You are fortunate to have an attractive wife and I apologize for my behavior earlier."

Christoph looked into Martin's eyes. He wanted to believe Martin, but his demeanor did not match his words. After a moment, Christoph said, "It is a huge step to marry a woman the first day you meet. It can be awkward at best. You have a very pleasant wife, and she deserves happiness with you. Are you working toward making her happy?"

Martin let out a long sigh. "I have not looked at it that way." The ship rose high on the waves and the sails pushed open wider as the wind kicked up. Both men grabbed a nearby pole to balance and maintain standing upright. A seafarer accustomed to the movement of the ship walked past and laughed.

"The fresh air is good, is it not?" the sailor said.

"The air is energizing. We've been below deck for only a few hours, yet it is nice to breathe fresh air." Christoph inhaled until his lungs were full and slowly exhaled.

Puffy steel gray clouds dotted the horizon in the east contrasting with the red sky of the sun setting in the west. Cool sea winds lifted their spirits. The land to the south shrunk farther and farther away. They would never again see Lübeck, a city both men enjoyed. Christoph due to the time to get to know his family and relax. Martin for the time to fatten his wallet with gambling gold in a seaport town where the card players came and went as often as the ships sailed into and out of the harbor.

Martin said, "We need to come up for fresh air often."

The sailor chuckled. "Just be sure you do not stay too long and let yourself get blown overboard. We mariners know when it is dangerous up here. You may not recognize the signs so be careful. At the pace we will be sailing, we wouldn't notice you were gone for days."

Christoph said, "If you see one of those treacherous motions coming, please let me know." He turned. "I am going back to my family."

"Thank you for coming here with me. I am going to stay a few more minutes and get my bearings up here. Good night."

Dead Reckoning

"Good night to you both." Christoph climbed down the stairs. He turned and saw Martin walking the bow to the stern.

* * *

Maria walked to the middle of the boat, climbed the stairs, and met Christoph descending to steerage when she was halfway up. They nodded at each other as they each moved to the outer edges of the steps so not to bump into each other.

Maria came out on the deck and was surprised as the glowing red sun set in the west. She had not realized how much time passed since they arrived. The waves shimmered with shades of reds, yellows, and dark blues behind the stern.

"Maria," said Martin. She turned and saw Martin near the bow of the ship.

"Yes?"

"Why are you up here?"

"I wondered where you went. I wanted to make sure everything was fine with you."

"Of course, I am fine. Let us return below, this is no place to be after dark and the sun is edging below the horizon.

Maria looked around and tried to memorize every curve and angle of the deck believing it was imperative. Despite not knowing why.

Chapter Thirty-Five

Anna Barbara was grateful that Christoph gathered fresh water every day for the family. She lost track of the days as she left the stall only to venture to the head when needed. Nausea troubled her and it abated slightly after the fifth day. Although she felt better, she preferred to remain in the stall near her children. She sat near the back wall deep in her own thoughts.

Thank goodness for the Wächter children. They entertained and played with Kristina and Johann as much as was possible. They traded stories and had a small ball that they bounced for hours creating new rules playing within the stalls and the narrow walkway. Knowing the children were safe helped Anna Barbara to rest as she feigned seasickness.

Maria became a good friend and resource. Anna Barbara learned that before immigrating to Russia, Maria was engaged to a soldier, and he went to war before they could be married. He did not want to restrict her future, not knowing whether he would return. He did not. Maria was heartbroken and there was no one in her village of an appropriate age. She cared for her parents until their deaths but discovered she could not farm the land or pay the rent alone. When she saw the flyer for Russia and the chance to make a new start, she walked miles and miles to Büdingen and was happy to stand in line. Meeting Martin? Not the best part of her journey but she would do what she needed to survive and make a new life.

"I'm going to talk to the Asselborns. After that I will stop by a few others to check how they are doing," said Maria to Martin. As she stood, she looked at Anna Barbara and smiled.

Anna Barbara watched Maria leave and twinged with regret that she was not as sociable as Maria was. With her queasiness, she did not trust herself to walk alone on the ship. She stood up as often as she could, holding tight to the timbers separating the berths. She did not take unnecessary steps since she struggled to maintain her balance. Walking to the head once or twice each day and balancing was enough exertion without additional jaunts.

Anna Barbara peeked at Martin discreetly, only for a second or two at a time, as he wielded his knife around the edges of a small piece of wood. Whittling was an art in which Martin was skilled. He focused on his knife and held it with tender respect. Anna Barbara looked away often so no one would notice. Martin was obviously proud of the knife, as he safely stored it in a leather case he guarded carefully under his jacket. *Where did he learn the art? Did he carve out his own handle and sharpen his own blade? Anna Barbara knew she would never ask him. He didn't just hold the knife, he caressed it. How she wished he treated Maria at least as well.*

Johann walked over to Martin. "Can you show me how to do that?"

Martin looked up, surprised that Johann had spoken to him. Martin smiled.

"Of course, sit next to me and I will train you to be the best whittler in the world." Johann sat on the floor as Martin demonstrated how to hold the knife, maneuver fingers away from the blade, and make safe contact with the wood.

Anna Barbara looked up from her reverie and saw Christoph watching her. She smiled, thinking about how happy she was with him. It was a simple thing, but so marvelous to be developing a bond with this man she met less than a few months ago on the day they wed. He moved to sit next to her and wrap his arm around her so her back no longer rested on the wood wall. She eased next to him grateful for the change of position.

"I know the ship ride is a challenge. How are you feeling?" he asked.

"Better. I am getting better every day. The seasickness is fading bit by bit."

"Good. You are not as pale as before. Are you hungry? I saved some portions for you."

"No, I am fine right now. Save it, you may need it later."

Christoph glanced at the Schumacher's stall. Martin looked up from his whittling and caught Christoph's eye. Martin held the knife and wood out for Johann to try. Johann carefully accepted it. He held the knife as instructed, edging the blade through the wood as Martin had demonstrated.

"Good work, Johann. You are doing well, keep at it."

Joseph Wächter and Peter Asselborn walked up the aisle and stopped at the Schumacher's stall. Although Peter was a newlywed and Joseph had been married for nearly 20 years, the two had a lot in common.

"Martin," said Joseph. "You have won our money at cards. How did you learn to play?"

"My father taught me to play cards, as his father taught him."

Wächter smiled. "I understand. Peter and I know what it is like to lose a bit of money to a trained card player, but from what I hear on deck, the sailors are not used to losing quite so much of their hard-earned pay."

Peter nodded. "We thought you should know the crew wants to win their money back tonight."

"We will see if I am up for a game tonight. Right now, I prefer to whittle and share my skills with young Johann."

"Well, tread carefully." Wächter walked back to his family's stall where Henry and Kristina sat talking quietly while Walpurga played with the ball. Magdalena and Katharina conversed quietly in the far corner.

Martin turned back to Johann who had added three new lines to the wood carving.

"Good work, Johann. You have demonstrated great skill as a whittler."

"Thank you, Herr Schumacher. I enjoyed the chance to learn to whittle. You have a beautiful knife and I hope to whittle again with you." Johann walked to the Wächter's stall and asked Kristina and Henry. "Did you see what I did?"

Kristina and Henry nodded as Johann sat on the floor next to them.

Martin said a few words to Maria when she returned, then he walked to the Schmidt's stall where Christoph and Anna Barbara were resting.

"Christoph let's go walk on the deck. I think we could both use some fresh air."

Christoph turned to Anna Barbara who said, "Go ahead." She hoped Martin's desire to spend time with Christoph would have a positive influence on Martin's behavior. She wished he would change overnight for Maria's sake.

Chapter Thirty-Six

Christoph saw First mate Hertzinger pace back and forth from stern to bow, keeping watch, and checking the horizon.

"There you are Schumacher. I intend to earn back my losses from gambling. You cannot win every hand, every night. The crew is ready for a new game. Are we on schedule for another round of card playing tonight?" asked Hertzinger. and wanted to see if Schumacher resumed the card game tonight.

Martin shook his head. "I do not know. Depends on getting players."

"Keep me posted, I want to win my money back from you." Hertzinger laughed. "You need to take care on deck, especially at night. It is dangerous for you. Though it appears calm now we often need to clear the deck in case of a quick weather change. We adjust course frequently. Your dark clothes make you rather difficult to see during the evening hours."

"My apologies, First Mate. Is there a spot where we can chat for a few minutes, catch some fresh air, and be out of your way?" asked Christoph. "We can't tell night from day from being below for so long,"

"If you must risk your life, stay on the port side closer to the stern, to be out of immediate danger. Since I oversee passengers and cargo, your safe arrival at port is on my head. In the future, limit your visits to the daytime. Stay near the grab rails. We anticipate a stormy night." Hertzinger headed toward the bow.

"We will," said Martin. "The fresh air is too tempting to stay away. We will only be here a few minutes tonight." He pulled a paper from his jacket, filled it with tobacco, and rolled the edges together gently with his fingers. Then he placed the newly formed cigar in his mouth and bent down to connect the tip to the lantern's fire.

"How did you manage to bring along tobacco and papers with you?" asked Christoph.

"I won it in a card game in Lübeck. Luck was with me, the winning hand at poker. I am grateful as I enjoy a good smoke."

Christoph smiled. "Well, I am glad you enjoy it. I have never smoked, could never afford the habit."

"I learned to roll cigars as a child, did it for my grandfather." He inhaled savoring every bit of the smoke. He exhaled and the billowing wisps floated to the stern dissolving into a long circular trail. "The sailors enjoy their cards. With little opportunity for entertainment on board ship, they need the distraction. Losing a bit of their money is just a pastime. Same for the passengers Asselborn and Michael Sanders. Did you hear that Michael Sanders' wife passed this morning?"

"No, I didn't." Christoph shook his head. "I am sorry to hear that."

"It is a hazard of the journey. Some people do not have the stamina for sea life." He inhaled from his cigar again as he cocked his head to the left. "But I must look to the future. I enjoy winning and I will make a fortune in Russia. I can grow tobacco, roll cigars, and sell them in the town. That is why I need your son. I need strong boys to build this business."

Not only did Martin not offer to share a cigar with him, but focusing on Johann was absurd. There were plenty of other boys on the ship. Then he realized his son was only a piece of the package. Martin wanted Anna Barbara.

"Martin, my son is staying with me and my wife. You and your wife can build your business, have your own children to help you, but I ask respectfully that you never mention this again. I am taking my leave now." Christoph turned away heading back to the stairs.

"Christoph," shouted Martin. "We need to change families. I have a great plan. You have nothing, no plans, no idea how to create wealth. I do. I insist that we change families immediately. No one will even be aware. We can exchange names if we have to."

As Christoph grabbed Martin's collar he saw Hertzinger come near, but the first mate backed up quickly but still peered around the corner at the two men.

Christoph pulled Martin toward him until they were nose to nose. "No, you stay away from me, my wife and my children. Do not make me take further action and destroy you. You need to remain far, far away from me if you want to be safe. This is enough." With his last word, he tossed Martin to the ground, and watched his cigar drop and its embers flicker across the deck. When the ship veered to the port side. Martin and his cigar tumbled over toward the edge of the ship.

"Did you see that?" Martin screamed to no one in particular. "Christoph tried to kill me."

He trudged away heading toward the stairs, yet he turned back and saw Hertzinger smile from around the corner. Christoph glanced back at Schumacher lying flat on the deck until he stood up, brushed himself off, stamped out the sizzling embers, picked up his cigar and inhaled.

Christoph stomped down the stairs. *I am not a killer, but I should have ended it then and there. The man is trouble no matter how kind he acts to Johann. The real Martin Schumacher is the cruel husband who ignores his wife.*

Christoph walked back and forth in the steerage aisle to dissipate his rage toward Martin. He monitored the stairs to be certain to avoid Martin if he returned. Soft snoring resonated through the cabin as he paced. Christoph hoped no one headed on deck for a card game tonight and it appeared everyone was asleep. When he had calmed himself enough to rest, he passed the Schumacher's stall. Maria, like everyone else except her husband, had already retired for the night, wrapped tightly in blankets to avoid the cold. He walked softly as he entered his family's stall not to disturb Anna Barbara or the children who were fast asleep.

He lay down next to his wife who shifted toward him. "I got tired and couldn't wait up."

"I am glad you are resting. I shouldn't have accepted Martin's invitation. That man has upset me for the last time. He is truly evil, acting like a friend and then turning on me. Well, he will never do that again."

"Turning on you?"

"Well, turning on us. He thinks he can have you and Johann. He talked about his plans and wanted to exchange places and names, to be with you and the children. I told him I would have none of it and he had to stop."

"Poor Maria. To be married to that awful man."

"Let us put it behind us. Sleep well, my love. Every day we are getting closer and closer to our new home." Christoph looked at Maria in the next stall jealous of her ability to rest.

* * *

At sunrise, First Mate Hertzinger followed his morning routine. He surveyed the starboard side of the ship and checked rope knots for tightness. He had a nagging suspicion that something was off kilter.

He couldn't put his finger on it, but he checked and doublechecked every step.

He walked to the stern and checked that the rudder stayed steady as the captain ordered. Weather was on their side on this journey and speed was the result as they started the seventh day on the sea. The sun shone bright in the east as they sailed toward the beautiful reddish orange orb.

Before he turned to his checkpoints on the port side, he saw a puddle of red seeping toward the back of the ship. He stopped in his tracks. This was not a pirate ship nor a war ship, but he could swear he saw blood on the floorboards of the deck.

He circled round the outer edge of the ship wondering what lay ahead of him. He wanted to give it as much berth as possible. Then he saw it, near the spot where Christoph and Martin were talking last night.

Martin Schumacher lay in a pool of red blood, which trickled from a two-inch gap in his neck where it was slashed wide open. A bloody knife lay next to him. Hertzinger ran quickly to the bell to sound the alarm. Hertzinger smiled to himself. Apparently he wasn't the only one who thought Schumacher deserved some retribution.

* * *

Anna Barbara woke first that morning. She sat upright and watched her family rest. She could sew today. If she felt up to it, she might walk to the Wächters stall and visit to pass the time. It was a short walk, and she could hold onto the wall if needed.

Suddenly loud banging footsteps on the stairs startled everyone. If someone was not awake yet, they were now. Anna Barbara saw three sailors run down the steps headed directly toward stall fourteen. Without any explanation, they grabbed Christoph under the shoulders and dragged him toward the stairs.

"What is happening?" asked Anna Barbara.

None of the men replied. She watched in horror as they took her husband away without explanation. Anna Barbara looked over to Maria's stall. Maria was awake, too, but Anna Barbara did not see Martin.

Dead Reckoning

The sailors pulled Christoph up the stairs, bouncing his heels against each step. Anna Barbara asked, "Where is Martin? Did they take him away, too?"

Maria studied the inside of her stall inspecting it like she was seeing it for the first time.

"I fell asleep. I thought he was playing another card game all night. I don't remember him returning here."

Anna Barbara had a sinking feeling envelop her. What did Christoph say last night? "He is truly evil, acting like a friend and then turning on me. Well, he will never do that again."

Anna Barbara hugged her children close and silently wept into Kristina's shoulder.

Chapter Thirty-Seven

Anna Barbara watched Maria sit alone in her stall after First Mate Hertzinger exited.

Maria walked to the Schmidt's stall and sat near Anna Barbara on Christoph's baggage. Anna Barbara directed her children to visit the Wächters and stay there for the morning. After the children left, Maria cleared her throat then whispered, "Martin was murdered. Hertzinger told me he found him on the deck."

"What happened?"

"They told me he was found with his beloved knife next to his body. I assume he was stabbed, but I am not certain, he would not share any details with me. I am the only one who knows and the only one who cares. When he told me martin was dead, I mourned for the loss of the life I envisioned in Russia. I did not mourn the loss of Martin. Will I be allowed to continue the journey as a widowed woman? I don't want to lose my chance to settle in a new land if I am alone."

Anna Barbara nodded. Her insides churned as she worried what Christoph might know about Martin's murder. No one wants to lose their chance for a better life. Could her brand-new husband be a murderer? Christoph was a good man, if for some reason he had to kill Martin, was it to stop him from some awful act?

"Maria, you will not be denied a new life in a new land. I will make sure of it. Things will change, we will meet other families. You will have your opportunity in Russia." Anna Barbara hesitated, but then asked, "Did the First Mate say who murdered Martin?"

"He did not. I am worried for Christoph as he was on deck with him last night. I had no idea why they came for him this morning, hopefully they are only questioning him. I do not know how these matters are investigated at sea."

"I pray Christoph will be cleared of any wrongdoing. They must be interrogating witnesses, undoubtably they needed to find out what Christoph knew." Anna Barbara held Maria's gaze searching for agreement in her eyes. "Was there a card game last night?"

"I assumed there was, since Martin was out so late, but I don't know."

"Christoph was not the only one who struggled with Martin's behavior. Both Herr Asselborn and Herr Wächter exchanged words with him, and the sailors, including Hertzinger, wanted a chance to earn back their losses. We must wait until Hertzinger tells us more. We only have a few more days on this ship before we arrive at Kronstadt. Let us pray together for our safe arrival and better lives ahead. With Christoph."

Chapter Thirty-Eight

Christoph had no idea why he was hauled out of bed and into a cell. His wrists were sheathed in chains behind his back, his head and neck curved below the ceiling of the cell. He sat at the bottom of the seafaring vessel, and his feelings matched these lower depths. Christoph knew he was guilty of many things. Sometimes he avoided the consequences, other times he paid for his transgressions. At those times he knew if he had done right or wrong. This time he had no idea. He re-traced his steps from last night fearing the worst. He heard someone descending the steps to the prisoner area.

First Mate Hertzinger walked toward the cell and rested his arms between the bars. Christoph expected to hear whatever charges would be pressed against him. Hertzinger gazed at Christoph, pity in his eyes.

"Why did you do it?" Hertzinger asked.

"Do what?"

"You know."

"I wish I did."

"Martin Schumacher," said Hertzinger.

"What about him?"

"I believe you already know he was murdered."

Christoph closed his eyes and bowed his head. Now he understood and Martin's last words to him echoed in his mind, "Christoph tried to kill me." Christoph's heart sank and for the first time on this journey, his last-ditch effort to re-create a life, fear surged through his bones. By walking on deck with Martin Schumacher, he was now suspected of murder. And he had no idea how Martin died. By joining Martin on deck, he had jeopardized his family's future.

"I do not know what happened to Schumacher. He was alive when I left him. I returned to my wife and assumed he did the same."

"Tell it to the captain. He will decide your fate."

* * *

Captain Van Doorn commanded the Ursa Major since its inaugural sail five years ago. Experienced in moving cargo from port to port, he navigated the troublesome fights among crew members from time to time as needed. Quarrels were infrequent, and those matters were old hat to him now. He solved these disputes using the eyes and ears of

Dead Reckoning

his mates and trusted sailors. Death and murder could happen, but most sailors wanted to earn wages, see the world, or seek safe harbor.

He never expected a murder on his first sail with passengers. He talked to LeRoy who had vouched for them as poor folk searching for a resurgence of life in Russia.

LeRoy had mentioned Schumacher wanted to marry another woman, not the woman assigned to him. He accepted Maria Herrmann as his wife when the man behind him, Schmidt, encouraged him to accept her. Oddly, the last man seen on deck with Schumacher was Schmidt, the man in chains in the bowels of the galleon.

Van Doorn walked past the body wrapped in cloth from head to toe. He held the knife which was discovered next to Schumacher. Hertzinger had cleaned it and Van Doorn admired the beautiful wood carvings on the handle, seraphic angels among the majestic clouds covering fertile land growing tobacco. Whoever whittled the handle had artistic talent. Hertzinger also handed Van Doorn the leather case in which the knife had been stored. Hertzinger laid money, Schumacher's winnings from cards, on the table, as the Captain examined the knife and case.

"Sir, I have the results of the dead reckoning you requested," said Hertzinger.

"How soon will we be in Kronstadt?"

"Based on the report, with the same wind and current speed, we should arrive in port early tomorrow morning."

"Good, I will be happy to deliver these passengers. People are not as easy to transport as cargo. But, I admit, I am grateful for their passage because their fares are a good source of income. I hope that if immigrants will be our future business, there are no more murders. What have you found out about this Schumacher?" Van Doorn kicked his foot in the direction of the corpse.

"No one liked him. His wife tolerated him because she wanted to go to Russia. He was described as arrogant and rude by the passengers. Seaman Jake in the crow's nest claims he heard nothing during his watch, but he has been known to doze off while on duty, especially overnight. Last night when I was on deck, Schumacher and Schmidt talked. The conversation turned angry at one point. I heard steps which I assume were Schmidt's walking away and then Schumacher yelled, "Christoph tried to kill me."

"Schmidt walked away. Yet, Schumacher yelled at the same time. Then what did you do?"

"I saw Schumacher on the ground alone. He was exaggerating so I moved forward on the starboard side to continue my watch. I needed to light the lanterns and went to the helm to finish my duties. Schumacher would not have been able to scream after his throat was cut."

"Could Schmidt have returned and then killed him?"

"Anything is possible. Someone else could have been on deck. Schumacher guarded his knife in a leather case under his jacket. I doubt that Schmidt would have been able to get to it without a struggle. I heard nothing more and gave it no further thought until I found Schumacher this morning."

"What about the rest of the crew?"

"I checked with them, and no one will say a word about it. Either they did not see anything, or they are holding their secrets close."

"What about Schmidt's wife? Did she confirm he stayed below deck after he returned?"

"Of course, for what it is worth. She would not say anything other than he was there for the night."

"Can the other travelers confirm he did not leave again?"

"Not that they would say, Maria Schumacher was the closest and she claims to have been in a sound sleep and did not hear Schmidt return."

"Bring the prisoner to my quarters at 1500 hours," said Van Doorn. "We will have a small service before we dispose of Schumacher. Would anyone but the crew and his wife attend?"

"Doubtful, but I will ask his wife."

The captain returned to his quarters and surveyed the maps of the port of Kronstadt, determining the best approach to instruct the crew to glide into the port and be towed into the harbor. It was the favorite part of his work. He loved maps, and he lived by them.

A few hours later Hertzinger knocked on the Captain's door.

"Come in," said Van Doorn. Hertzinger led Schmidt into the captain's quarters.

"Hertzinger, you can leave us. Come back to retrieve your prisoner in thirty minutes."

Dead Reckoning

Captain Van Doorn turned directly to Christoph. "Why did you do it?"

"Do what, sir?"

"Kill Schumacher."

"I did not kill him, Captain."

Van Doorn eyed the prisoner closely. Despite the chains, Schmidt remained calm. Was he delusional or innocent? Van Doorn tossed the knife in the leather case on the tabletop. "Did you want his beautifully carved knife? Or his money?"

"No, sir, I did not want the knife nor the money."

Not a talkative person, thought Van Doorn. Many people with their life on the line would be chattering like blue jays. This man is a different sort. "Why were you on deck with Schumacher?"

"He asked me to join him for some fresh air. It sounded good after hours below deck. And I wanted to check on my daughter Kristina. First Mate Hertzinger tends to follow her, and I wanted to make sure she was well."

"Were you friends with Schumacher?"

"Not really, we saw each other when we signed up for the journey. We were on the same coach from Büdingen to Lübeck. I did not see him again until we boarded the Ursa Major."

"You could have gone on deck without him. Why did you go with him?"

"He asked me to accompany him, and it was easier to say yes than to try to explain no."

"Who would have wanted him dead?"

"I have no idea."

"The crew said you argued with him. Schumacher yelled that you tried to kill him."

"He did shout that at me, but I was already walking away from him. I told him to stay away from me."

"Why did you tell him that?"

"It is quite personal."

"Is it worth walking the plank to keep it secret?"

"You are all powerful on the sea. You can hang me, force me to walk the plank, or send me to a prison on land. I believe that you will remove these chains and free me because the future of five people rests on your decision. So I will tell you everything."

Christoph explained every interaction and conversation with Martin from waiting in line, to the carriage ride, to getting on the ship. It was the longest he had spoken at one time in the last four years.

When he finished the story, he said, "I would never say such awful things about a man, but, Captain, my wife is with child, and she needs me in our new land. I share these things in the hope that you know I did not take Martin Schumacher's life. It is unfair for my wife to travel alone with our two other children."

Van Doorn listened carefully to every word, and he let Christoph stand silent for a few minutes. "You will now return to the cell. We cannot let accused murderers roam the ship. Get comfortable there." Then he called Hertzinger who was outside the door. "Take him away."

Christoph's head dropped forward as if he were a broken man.

* * *

Anna Barbara sat with Kristina and Johann. Fear gripped their throats making every word they uttered sound hoarse. Since Christoph was no longer in the berth, the short-lived sense of family evaporated. Although Maria Schumacher stayed in the stall with them, their safety was flung out to the upper deck trailing in the spray as the ship pushed onward to Kronstadt. The Wächters encouraged them to play and talk but mostly there was an odd silence in their vicinity as the other travelers distanced themselves from the Schmidts. They overheard whispers.

"How was he killed?"

"No one knows, or if they do, they aren't saying."

"He was a disagreeable man."

"True but he could whittle with the best of them."

"What happens to his wife?"

"Quiet, she might hear us."

"Do you think Schmidt is still alive?"

"Who knows? He might as well be dead if they have him locked up in the cell."

When folks asked Maria how Martin died, she explained that the crew had not told her, but she believed he was murdered.

Dead Reckoning

First Mate Hertzinger had told Anna Barbara her husband was locked in a cell on the lower level. When she asked if she could visit him, Hertzinger denied the request. "Too dangerous."

"Will I ever see him again?"

"It is up to the captain."

"Sir, how many more days until we reach Russia?"

"We are already in Russian waters. We will dock at Kronstadt today."

"What happens in Kronstadt?" asked Anna Barbara.

"Everyone disembarks. Passenger documents must be verified there. Most travelers from Kronstadt are taken in boats by Russian sailors to Oranienbaum."

"What happens to Martin Schumacher's body?"

"He has already been buried at sea per his wife's instructions."

Anna Barbara turned to confirm with Maria, who nodded.

"My sympathies, Frau Schumacher," said Hertzinger. "The captain sends his sympathies again and requested that I return this to you." He reached into his pocket and pulled out the beautifully carved knife. Hertzinger extended the knife out to her with his right hand. In his other hand, he offered her a small, netted purse which jingled with a stash of gold coins.

"Why are you giving these items to me?" Maria accepted the small purse and stared at the knife, not moving toward it.

"These were his only possessions. Since you were his wife, both belong to you."

Maria opened the purse and counted the money. "This is only half of what he had when he went up on deck. Where is the rest?"

"This was all we found. Could he have lost money in a card game before he died?"

"Perhaps."

Maria swallowed deeply before reaching out for the knife, clasping the hilt, and pulling it toward her. Her expression showed unbearable grief. She nodded to Hertzinger. "Thank you, he loved this knife very much, it brings me sorrow to see it without him."

As Hertzinger turned to leave and climb the stairs, Maria asked, "And the Captain will free Herr Schmidt?"

"His verdict is pending. It should be determined soon."

"You will tell us the verdict before we disembark?"

"Yes." Hertzinger nodded and bid her goodbye. Anna Barbara heard a jingle as he climbed the stairs and saw him hold his left hand over his pocket to stop the noise.

Once Hertzinger was on deck, Anna Barbara asked, "Did you hear the jingle, Maria? I think he kept the other half of Martin's money in his pocket."

Maria signed. "He could have won it, or he could have stolen it. I have no way to prove it. Either way, the crew wouldn't believe me." Maria held the knife out to Johann. "It is too much for me to bear to keep Herr Schumacher's knife. I do not know how to whittle, and this tool belongs in the hands of someone who can use it. When your father returns, I will ask him to train you on how to use this knife."

Johann's eyes gleamed with happiness as he accepted the blade. "Danke Schön."

Chapter Thirty-Nine, October 2014, Arizona

Rosalind awoke and realized her surroundings were pleasant compared to the cell of the Ursa Major. Christoph being imprisoned for murder resonated in her.

Images and visions vanished fast. She wished she had paper to record what she saw. Would she be able to prove the Ursa Major was a real ship?

The angst of their journey to Russia rang true based on what she had read about the Germanic settlers so far. Was this why she feared trusting others? Perhaps these sensations had been passed down to her DNA, become part of her karma.

The challenge remained to determine if her line connected back to Christoph Schmidt. If these insights were verified, Christoph was the stepfather of Kristina and Johann, and Anna Barbara's unborn child's father would be unknown. Did her Schmidt ancestor biologically descend from Christoph or from one of these stepchildren?

Rosalind sat up on the bench for a few minutes certain it would take weeks to work out the kinks in her neck and back. Please, she thought, help me to get out of here.

After stretching in downward dog and proud warrior poses, Rosalind lay flat on her back and tried to rest again.

Chapter Forty, 1766, Kronstadt

The sharp rattle of chains against wood awakened Christoph. It had to be the anchor. It was a rough, grinding sound louder than before. He sensed the vessel slowing. They must be close to Kronstadt. Within fifteen minutes the ship was still in the water. Whatever his fate, he knew it would be resolved one way or the other when they docked.

Hearing footsteps on the passenger level, he realized preparations had started to disembark. Please, dear God, let me be re-united with Anna Barbara and her children, for her sake and for mine, he pleaded.

Hertzinger bounded down the steps, keys jingling in his hand. He unlocked the door. "Come on. The captain needs to see you."

Christoph shuddered. Now he would learn the verdict for the rest of his life.

* * *

Anna Barbara, Maria, and the children stood in line waiting to go ashore to Kronstadt. Between the two women, they carried all their bags, including Christoph's and Martin's, with Kristina and Johann's help. Anna Barbara wanted to wait for Christoph, but Hertzinger said she must go with the group to enter Russia, or she would lose her opportunity to gain entry to her new country.

She was frightened. Once on land, it would be difficult to re-connect with Christoph unless he was freed soon. Kronstadt was the port to their new home. Neither she nor Maria had a husband, which, according to the agents, was required. Would she ever know the fate of Christoph? Not that she was envious, but at least Maria knew her husband was gone. Her greatest fear was that perhaps she would be forced to marry again today.

* * *

As Christoph walked on deck toward the plank next to Hertzinger and followed by Captain Van Doorn, he saw Anna Barbara in line on the port side to disembark. She did not see him. That is for the best, he thought. She can start anew again. He prayed for her and the children's safety.

Van Doorn stopped where the plank railway was open on the starboard side. Hertzinger pushed the opening wider as they escorted

Christoph to the plank. Not the gangplank that led to land, but the one leading to water.

"Remove the chains," directed Van Doorn. Hertzinger unlocked the shackles, yanked them off Christoph's arms, holding them so they did not fall to the deck.

Christoph saw Anna Barbara frantically search the deck. When she saw him, he nodded. She was pushed ahead on the ramp, but the line stopped. She said nothing to the children. He imagined she was afraid they would turn and see his demise.

With the strong wind carrying his words, Captain Van Doorn address Christoph. "I admit I am not certain who killed Martin Schumacher. But murder on board a ship must be punished. To not record a punishment leaves the crew and future travelers concerned for their safety. Without punishment, a Captain loses respect. And respect is paramount to maintaining a ship's order. This murder cannot be unresolved. Passengers expect resolution. So, I have determined you will walk the plank. If you are innocent, you will float and get to shore, then you are Russia's problem. If you are guilty you will sink, your punishment justly executed. You must jump now. This is your chance for survival.

"You force me to jump into freezing water to determine my fate?" asked Christoph.

"Yes, it is the best decision. I can record your punishment, and if you are a survivor, you have a fair chance of making it to shore. Jump now, or Hertzinger will push you."

Christoph looked in the man's eyes. "While I do not envy the commander's position, without witnesses to Schumacher's murder, this decision is unjust. It leaves another woman a widow and an unborn child without a father." Christoph took off his hat and tied it to a loop on his jacket. He checked his surroundings, noting the length of the ship, the distance to shore, hoping beyond hope he did not immediately sink to the bottom of the water. He stepped on the plank, turned around to look Van Doorn and Hertzinger in the eye. "You know I did not kill him. This decision creates bad fortune for both of you."

He saw Anna Barbara turn one last time before stepping onto Russian soil. Christoph jumped backwards from the end of the plank and splashed into the sea.

Chapter Forty-One

Anna Barbara stepped off the gangplank onto the land of Russia. She entered her new country without her husband, and she fought to contain her tears. *Distraction, I need distraction.*

Her plea was answered as Johann tripped and fell at the edge of the gangplank landing hard on his knees and his hands. He cried as Anna Barbara helped him to his feet. She wrapped her arms around him holding him longer than necessary to hide her own tears. Maria and Kristina stopped to help.

"Anna Barbara, I have no idea why Hertzinger would not tell us about Christoph's verdict. Now we are on land, and we must look for him. He must be here."

Anna Barbara breathed in and exhaled much slower to remain calm. She whispered to Maria, "I don't think we will see Christoph again."

"No that cannot be. We must go back and get him."

"There is no reason to go back, I will tell you what I saw later. We must go on. I do not want to, but we have no choice but to move forward. There is no going back. Let us join hands and say a prayer silently."

They stood with hands clasped together and eyes closed. Anna Barbara prayed, *please help us at this urgent time in our need. We do not know where we are going. We do not know what you expect us to do but we will do our best to survive. I request a most benevolent outcome, despite this dire situation in which we find ourselves.*

* * *

Christoph prayed for the most benevolent outcome and for courage while in the freezing water. As he jumped he immediately split his legs to prevent dropping too deep into the water. With full boots and clothing, he knew he would be lucky if he reached the water's surface quickly.

He hit the water hard. The Gulf of Finland was cold and dark, yet he was still alive and could not give up hope. Despite the heavy boots, he broke through to the surface. As he breathed in air, he shook his hair out of his face and focused on the side of the ship. If he could grab onto the boat and work his way to the port side of the ship, he hoped he could maneuver to land.

Dead Reckoning

He wanted to kick off his boots, but he knew going barefoot in Russia was another death sentence, even if it was spring. Slow and steady movements in the water should help, he had to remember his progress was not a race. This was his chance to survive, and he could see the ship so close to him. He feared the wood was slick, but it was better than trying to swim around the vessel on his own and wasting all his strength at once. It was difficult to tell how deep the water was, but he hoped to reach the boat and hang onto the vessel. Perhaps, he could work his way around it. Look forward, he told himself, not down.

He stretched out and swam toward a cracked uneven edge where the ship's wood was not aligned. He extended his right hand. His hand shook fiercely, as it closed in on the edge while the water chilled his body to the bone. He touched the ship, but his hand slipped off the wood. His face slapped the water. He was adrift but still close to the ship. He silently said a prayer of thanks, grateful he was next to the ship and not under it. He tread water for a moment to catch his breath, creeping his way closer to where the wood bent away from the ship. His boots and clothing pulled him downward. His chin bobbed in the water as he forced his head back, so his nose and mouth pointed upward out of the water. His boots filled with more and more water and weighed him down further.

As he heaved himself forward, a wave rose behind him and pushed him closer to the ship. This time his hand connected with the small irregularity, and he grasped it as the life saver he needed. The wave pushed his left shin and knee into the ship, ripping open his skin and hyperextending his knee. He secured his left hand onto the ship and prayed not to slip. He pulled his right hand out of the water and touched the side of the ship, and nearly laughed when his hand went through the wood. He found the bilge, a small round opening easy to hold on to. He turned his nose away from its stench, as he moved his left hand to the opening and held himself secure as he caught his breath. Pain soared from his left shin to his knee, but he was alive.

He surveyed his position to determine his path. He needed to tread around the stern and prayed that the captain, who was likely in the cabin, did not look out and see him. Christoph hoped Van Doorn would be pre-occupied with business matters, planning, loading, and unloading of cargo. But since the captain barely saw him when he was on board and told Christoph "if you float you can go," it shouldn't matter. Before he started to transfer his hands along the ship, Christoph assumed the captain would never think about him again.

Chapter Forty-Two

Weary, queasy, and mourning the loss of her second husband, Anna Barbara struggled to stand. She thought her seasickness would ease, but the ground on the island of Kronstadt swayed, rocked, and bobbed below her as the Ursa Major had for the last eleven days. She held onto Kristina, her rock. She dreaded walking into this country without Christoph by her side, knowing that a new husband would be assigned to her shortly. Three women succumbed to illness on the ship. Women who dreamt of a new life and strived to live long enough to see the shore of a new home. One was lost during childbirth. Another was in her forties and had been ill for a week before departure. No one knew what happened to the last woman. Three men were widowers, one with a newborn.

She noticed Maria was nervous, too. Maria fussed as she pushed loose hairs off her forehead when there were none astray. She moved her hands constantly as if seeking a chore to complete. Yet Anna Barbara believed the odds were in Maria's favor that she was likely to get a better husband than what she had. While she did not want to tempt fate, Anna Barbara struggled to imagine a man as kind as Christoph. She looked straight ahead at the other ships in Kronstadt's naval port. Was she still determined to create a better life without Christoph? Tears quietly coursed down her cheeks, but she refused to sob. Could she see this journey through to a new home and life? She had to. For her children.

The Wächters were a few families ahead of them. When they finished processing, they moved toward a line of boats on the southern end of the island. Walpurga turned, seeing something in the distance and pointed at it. Walpurga pulled her mother close and whispered, "Herr Schmidt."

Johann turned around to face the direction where Walpurga pointed. He could barely believe what he saw.

"Mama." Johann tugged at Anna Barbara's hand. "I think I see Papa."

"It must be someone else, Johann. He is being held on the ship." She knew Christoph's fate. Kristina turned in the same direction as Johann and caught her breath in her throat. "Mama, you need to see this."

Anna Barbara turned around and faced the direction her children looked. In the distance, she saw a filthy, water-soaked man limping along, searching the crowd as water dripped off every inch of him. He stepped in the opposite direction, and Anna Barbara recognized his walk.

"Christoph!" Anna Barbara bolted out of line, yelling to Maria and the children, "Stay there, I'll be right back." The man walked farther away from her.

Her nausea and weariness faded into the background. She found the power to run, run as fast as her legs could carry her. He continued to walk farther away from her. She lost sight of him as the dock was crowded with many people coming and going. She caught up to the first spot she had seen him and looked to the ground at the water trail he left behind. If she did not see him, the water might lead the way. She followed the wet trail.

Anna Barbara stopped to catch her breath, not losing sight of the splashes of water. She breathed deeply and started to walk as fast as her body would let her. He walked faster.

She yelled, "Christoph," again and this time she saw the top of his hat turn toward her. She assumed he could not yet see her in the crowd, as she only saw the top of his head. She called his name again. He stopped. There was so much noise in this port, she hoped he had heard her.

She called his name one more time. He backtracked a few steps but was not looking in her direction, and Anna Barbara gained ground on him.

As she ran, she called "Christoph," again. He turned and looked in her direction.

He saw her.

Despite the weight of the watered-down clothes and boots and his left leg dragging, he hobbled to her with arms open. As they neared each other, she flung herself in his arms and he swooped her close to him. They clung to each other, sobbing, and laughing that they were together again.

He pushed her away from the wet clothes. "I am making you as watered down as I am."

"I don't care. I saw you jump off the plank. I never thought I would see you again. This is a miracle."

They stood in the puddle created by his dripping clothes, overjoyed to be together. They gazed deeply into each other's eyes to make sure they were not dreaming.

"I didn't think I would ever see you again, but I made it back to you. I do not think I have ever been so happy."

"You have made me the happiest woman in the world." Anna Barbara sobbed.

Christoph clutched her hand to his heart. "We better get in line. We need to be together as we enter our new country."

***

After they reached the entry point, and confirmed their names to the Russian guards, they were boarded onto smaller rowboats to transport them from Kronstadt Island south to Oranienbaum. The Titular Counselor, Ivan Kulberg, confirmed their names, tracked their origins, their relationships, and their religion. He recorded the Schmidt's information succinctly, then searched for Maria's information.

Kulberg asked, "Maria Schumacher, where is your husband? He was listed on the ship's manifest when you departed Lübeck."

"He died, sir."

"You have no husband. We need to match you with a new husband to keep you safe during your travels."

"She is with us," said Christoph.

"How is that? She had traveled with Martin Schumacher."

Anna Barbara never spoke without being questioned, but she could not lose Maria. "Yes, sir, you are correct. And he is now gone. But she is my sister, she is part of our family. Can she stay with us until a husband is identified?"

"We are not able to match her with a husband at the moment. A new arrangement will happen when you are assigned to your village before you travel on the Volga."

"Assigned?" asked Christoph.

"Yes. You cannot roam around the country. You will be grouped to form a colony by religious affiliation." He recorded a few notes. "Walk along this canal until you see the palace. Stay in the garden near the stairs to the balcony. You must swear your oath of allegiance to Russia."

Boats delivered them safely to Oranienbaum. They walked from the port entrance following the canal as directed. Feelings of freedom and good fortune surged within Christoph no matter how much his leg hurt or how long he stayed wet.

As they neared the palace, the crowd thickened, and they listened to many conversations, mostly in German.

"This is the Czarina's Summer palace."

"Summer palace, does she have a palace for every season?"

"It was Peter III's palace, but now it belongs to Catherine."

"I've never seen anything so grand. Russia must be a wealthy country. We will be wealthy, too."

Anna Barbara stopped mid step and her jaw dropped open. She had seen palaces and castles before but none of this size nor grandeur. The glorious white columns stood solemnly before synchronized rectangular windows with circular accents, and the broad garden landscape was bordered with life like white sculptures. So realistic, the artwork emanated a power and pride she never considered possible. I could gaze at this building for my entire life, she thought, and find new beauty in it every day.

When Anna Barbara looked at Christoph, Maria, and the children, they looked as dumbstruck as she felt. Maria flushed.

"I've never seen anything that big and yellow," said Johann, "except the sun. That could be why they call it the Summer Palace."

"The brick is solid and bright, it shimmers in the sunlight," said Kristina.

Christoph enveloped Anna Barbara's hand. "Did you think you would see anything as grand as this?" Anna Barbara shook her head.

They stared at the building which represented generations of history, pageantry, and sovereignty.

The hum of the crowd was suddenly split by the sound of trumpets. Everyone looked toward the balcony where guards marched in rigid formation. Ten heralds followed the guards. They assembled around the outer edges of the balcony, each assuming an exact position with clockwork precision. Once in place, they stood motionless, waiting.

Johann stood next to another young man.

"Hello," said the young man. "My name is Konrad. Konrad Reimer."

"Hello Konrad, I am Johann Kal...I mean, Johann Schmidt. Isn't it exciting to be here?"

"Yes, I have never seen anything like it."

"Can I show you something special?" asked Johann.

"Yes."

"I have a knife. Look at the engravings on the handle."

"That's a beauty," said Konrad.

"Yes, and I can store it in its own special leather case."

"You are fortunate." Konrad saw Anna Barbara watch them. "Is that your father?"

"Yes, now he is. Actually, my stepfather," said Johann.

"I am excited to get to our village. Will you settle in a Catholic or Lutheran village?"

"Catholic."

"Oh, no, I hoped I had met someone who would live near me. I will be assigned to a Lutheran village. I am traveling with my mother and stepfather, too."

"I understand. Hopefully, our paths will cross again." They smiled at each other, understanding it was unlikely they would see each other again.

After five minutes, a man strode to the center of the balcony. The crowd was quiet in anticipation, leaning closer to hear his address.

His erect posture and elongated nose added dignity to his blue and red uniform decorated with a multitude of silver stars, crosses, and medallions covering his broad chest. A royal blue sash was offset by the silver leaf edging down his sleeves. He did not just shine, he glowed strength and confidence. He was taller than the guards and musicians, with muscles pushing against his jacket. His blue eyes darted across the crowd, assessing everyone in the audience at a glance. To say he was an attractive, engaging man did not suffice. His smile and persona were magnetic. He could lead an army to their deaths and the soldiers would be happy to die for him.

"I am Guardian Potemkin. I welcome you to the empire of Russia."

The crowd applauded despite how tired they were from their journey. They cheered until Potemkin raised his arms for silence.

"It is not only me who welcomes you to your new land. I would like to introduce the one who is responsible for your journey and re-settlement in this splendid country. Someone who traveled here before you and now leads you to embrace your new homeland. Welcome our fearless leader, the Empress of all Russia, Catherine II."

The crowd shouted as a beautiful woman appeared on the balcony. She wore a silver gown that dazzled in the sunlight. Her royal crown glittered with emeralds and diamonds. Her deliberate yet delicate movements demonstrated elegance and style indicative of a Czarina. She glanced at Potemkin and nodded to him. Their eyes connected and Anna Barbara felt a spark of the power generating from these two Russians. Catherine glided to the front of the balcony where her small frame assumed half the space of Potemkin, but her presence conveyed a power more formidable than his.

"Welcome, compatriots. You have traveled far to come to your new home. Your journey mirrors what I encountered more than twenty-three years ago when I left Anhalst-Zerbst to begin my life anew in the Russian court."

The crowd applauded. The Empress nodded acknowledging all her soon to be Russian citizens. She waited for silence.

"As Empress of All Russia, I share my good fortune with you. In return for your allegiance, you shall create your new home, you shall settle new lands, and enjoy the prosperity of the empire of Russia with our assistance. I, as Empress, and your new country, Russia, offer you this joyous opportunity with many freedoms. First, freedom from military service in perpetuity for you and your descendants. Second, freedom of religion, you can choose to worship as you desire. Third, freedom to speak the language you choose, be it German, Finnish, Danish or Russian. And finally, freedom to live within your cultural values, to educate your children as you see most appropriate. You realize that these freedoms are unavailable to many people on earth." The crowd cheered her, arms waving above their heads, enthusiastic and ready to start their new lives. The uproar continued for five minutes, as the newly arrived travelers realized their hopes from reading Catherine's Manifesto were true.

Christoph smiled. "My priest in Ansbach read these promises to me. I thought if even half of these promises were true, it would be worth coming here." Anna Barbara nodded, still in awe of the energy, the palace, and the Empress of Russia herself welcoming them to their new country.

"I never saw an Empress before," Kristina said.

"Me neither." Anna Barbara hoped it wasn't the last time.

Catherine II said. "Now the regents will lead you in the Oath of Allegiance to Russia, first in German, then Danish, French, and Finnish."

The Empress turned and walked back into the palace. The regents stepped forward and each recited one line of allegiance in each language, and the crowd repeated it.

Within twenty minutes of standing at the palace, the Schmidts and Maria were now Russian citizens.

* * *

After Christoph received their allotment of wood, they were directed to construct their own housing on open land about ten minutes from the palace. Anna Barbara asked the guards if they had alcohol or honey to help Christoph's wound. They gave her honey, and she applied it to the broken skin and then she wrapped an old cloth around his knee.

Christoph worked assembling the boards, asking Johann to hold the wood in place as he built a shelter with the limited tools given.

As they ate their midday meal, Anna Barbara saw that Maria lifted the food to her mouth, but nothing passed her lips. When Maria thought no one saw, she slid her food off her plate to Johann. As Christoph watched Maria give Johann her food, he noticed the leather case tied to Johann's waistband.

"Johann," said Christoph after their meal, "where did you get that knife?"

"Maria gave it to me on the ship when you were away. She said she would ask for you to approve."

Maria turned to them. "Christoph, I apologize. First Mate Hertzinger gave it to me, it was Martin's only belonging besides his bag. I asked Johann if he would like it as he was interested in Martin's carvings. I have no reason to keep it for myself." She looked at her empty plate. "I meant to ask for your approval, but with our arrival in Kronstadt, Oranienbaum and all of the excitement, it slipped my mind."

Johann extended the knife to Christoph for a close-up view. "Martin showed me how to use it carefully, so I do not hurt myself. He carved these beautiful edges on the handle."

Christoph observed the knife, and he hoped it was not cursed. His brief encounter with Captain Van Doorn implied Martin's knife was used. Only the murderer knew for sure. And there was Johann, so happy to have something to call his own. Johann looked expectantly at Christoph for his decision.

"You believe it is a treasure, Johann, and if you use it carefully, yes, it is yours."

Johann sighed with relief.

By midafternoon, their boards aligned into a small structure. Their new home was not as sturdy as Christoph hoped, but it was spring, and he was optimistic they would travel to the Volga region soon. They would not face the harsh, Russian winter in this minimal shack. But they were safe, they were together, and they were a family.

Christoph was grateful to be with his family and grateful Anna had the solid earth beneath her feet. Their stay in the crudely assembled shack would last only a few weeks.

Chapter Forty-Three, October 2014, Arizona

Not knowing the time of day was an eerie feeling for Rosalind. More eerie was the thought that the beautiful knife, which was a hand-me-down for generations, may have taken a human life. Many lives could have been lost to that sharp blade. She calculated the knife must have passed through at least six generations to end up in her possession.

She stood up to stretch, twist, and bend her body forward, backward, downward, and upward. Rosalind breathed deeply in and out until she felt her body relax to normal after about ten minutes.

No sound came from the hallway. Her stomach growled and she couldn't remember the last time she ate. She didn't eat dinner at the Daily Planet although she ate an energy bar yesterday morning. Had she spent an entire night in jail?

She walked to the door and knocked. She called out, "Hey, can I get some food in here?"

Rosalind pounded on the door again. No answer. She doubted anyone heard her.

Someone planted a vision board and oleander in her casita. Perhaps the branch through her window was merely a diversion to cover up someone breaking into her home. She must tell Hamilton about the window.

The hollowness of the empty room struck her as ominous as she sat down on the bench. If she ever got out of here she would search for Captain Van Doorn, First Mate Hertzinger, Ivan Kulberg, Grigory Potemkin and any other names that could have left a trace of their existence. She lay down gently on the bench. "Please help me return to where these visions left off. I need to determine if these are my ancestors. I seek a sense of belonging, a sense of home, and a need to find family again."

Chapter Forty-Four, Russia, 1766

Three weeks later, the settlers had been grouped for their village, by religious affiliation. The Schmidts were assigned to a Catholic village on the wiesenseite or meadow side of the Volga River. While they lived in the shack in Oranienbaum, they met military officers who would protect and lead them to their colony. As they headed to territories unknown, they dreamed of their destination, their new home.

Maria was not assigned a new husband. Of the three men who had lost their wives on the Ursa Major, two were assigned to different villages. The third man died in Oranienbaum.

"Frau Schumacher, there are no eligible men of marrying age heading to your new village. We will continue to look for the best match for you, but it could take weeks," said Kulberg before they left Oranienbaum.

So, the five initiated the next stage of their travels. They were happy that the Wächters and Asselborns traveled with them as did forty-five other families.

They had sailed to St. Petersburg, then climbed onto flotillas heading up the Neva River, through Schüssberg Canal to Lake Ladoyga, then up the Volkov River to Novrogad. Next, they traveled overland to Torshok.

In Torshok, the northern most navigable point on the Volga River, they stayed as guests in the houses of Russian peasants. Kristina noted the crumbs in the beards of the Russian Orthodox men. At first it did not disturb her, but by the second day of seeing the same crumbs, plus a few new ones, she diverted her eyes. She realized at a deeper level that the Russians with whom they stayed did not have the same manners that her family did. She saw them as crude, with backward habits, not as fastidious as her culture. Poor or not, there were certain cleanliness standards. She looked forward to leaving these homes even though she understood the next part of their journey was back to water travel on the Volga River.

The boats floated in the gently flowing water heading south on the longest and widest river in Europe. They boarded the barge and settled in for a long stretch of water. As the vessel sailed, singing filled the air. On the port side, she saw a barge pulled by eleven men who walked on the shore, tugging ropes tied to the vessel. Their rhythmic song complemented their steps, syncing their time, so the barge moved north against the current, opposite the route for the new settlers.

Four of their fellow travelers died after leaving Oranienbaum, but no one had been killed. Christoph was saddened by the deaths, especially the two children who had passed. He still believed they made the right decision to move. Only God knew what would have happened if they had not left. Here they had food and the dream of freedom.

After days on the Volga, the sailors said they were at an unnavigable tributary of the big river, the Karaman. As they disembarked at Saratov, Maria remained in her seat. Her face was tight, her pallor pure white.

"Maria," said Kristina, "We need to go now. We are close to our new home."

Kristina extended her hand. After a few moments, Maria noticed and edged her way off the bench. With every ounce of remaining energy, Maria slid her hand into Kristina's and pushed herself erect. Kristina wrapped her arm around Maria and led her to the shore in Saratov.

* * *

They waited three days for transportation from Saratov to their village, three days which helped Maria recoup. A shade of rose slowly emerged across her cheeks.

Anna Barbara asked, "Maria, how are you feeling? You look more rested than you did when we arrived."

Maria nodded. "Thank you, I am feeling a bit better. I have no idea how you so gracefully managed this journey in your condition. I cannot say I have fared as well as you."

"Maria?"

"I am with child. I didn't feel well on the Volga River, and I cannot imagine how you endured the open sea."

Anna Barbara drew Maria near and hugged her. Maria had new hope and Anna Barbara prayed there would be a husband as kind and generous as Christoph to help her with this child.

***

Christoph watched the two women and noticed how Anna Barbara gazed at Maria's midsection in awe. He understood. Maria needed a husband.

There was only one single man close to age twenty who was not married. Henry Wächter, recently turned sixteen years old, was Kristina's friend, the oldest son of the Wächters. He was tall, dark and demonstrated impeccable manners. He helped his parents with the younger siblings. There was an age gap, as Maria was at least twelve years older. But, in this isolated area of Russia, eligible spouses were limited by availability.

Christoph approached Henry's father as he finished breakfast. "Joseph, when do you think Henry will marry?"

"I do not know. No one is close to his age who would be a good fit." He pushed his plate away. "Henry enjoys time with your stepdaughter Kristina, but she is too young for marriage, correct?"

Christoph nodded his head then glanced down at his feet. He whispered to Wächter who shook his head. The military officer in charge of the transportation walked toward them and asked, "What is the issue, gentleman?"

"Nothing, sir."

The officer's eyes moved back and forth from Joseph to Christoph. He checked them from head to toe. "Herr Schmidt, you are the man who murdered Martin Schumacher, aren't you?"

"No, sir. I was held briefly. I was released. I did not kill him."

"Why did they think you killed him?"

"I cannot answer that, sir. Captain Van Doorn allowed me to leave. He rules the sea on the Ursa Major, so his decision was final."

"You need to stay on the straight and narrow. No odd business here."

"Yes, sir," said Christoph as the officer turned on his heel and headed in the other direction.

Wächter was silent for a moment, confirming the officer was out of earshot.

"Christoph, I know that Schumacher was difficult. What he said about your wife was wrong. If you did not kill him - and I could understand if you did - but, if you did not kill him, who did?"

Dead Reckoning

Christoph thought for a few seconds. "I was so grateful to get away, I did not think about it. Schumacher upset the sailors when he won their wages in card games. I assumed one of the crew killed him because of gambling losses."

"Do you know how he was murdered?"

"No, what did you hear?"

"Not certain. There was a rumor his throat was slit, with his own knife."

"Oh, that is awful." Christoph would never tell Johann. If the knife were used to kill Martin, the secret would have to go with Christoph to the grave. "Was his money missing?"

"Frau Schumacher received Martin's purse from First Mate Hertzinger, with half of the money she expected. Now I am not a killer, but if you wanted revenge, would you leave half of the money?"

"Good question. If the killer risked murder, one would assume theft wouldn't be frowned upon. If it were one of the crew, why only take half?"

"There is no way to prove it. Perhaps it was one of the crew. If not, we could be traveling with a murderer."

Chapter Forty-Five, Mariental, June 16, 1766

Leaving Saratov a few days later, they crossed the Volga River at dawn, landing on the wiesenseite, stepping foot onto a sandy shore filled with grassy overgrowth and bushes. Wagons from the barge were unloaded and reloaded with passengers and their small belongings.

Maria, Anna Barbara, and the children were on board the carts, the men walking close to their families. Christoph insisted on walking despite his sore left knee and steered clear of the military officers. Henry walked next to Christoph while the Wächters sat closer to the front of the wagon.

As the sun set, the wagon stopped. Grateful for the break, the passengers climbed off the wagons. The wagon driver said, "You are home now."

The settlers looked around at the openness of the land, a wild landscape. The grasses of the steppe bent with easterly winds and were wider than the sea.

Everyone except the escorts looked confused. Where were the houses? The roads? Where was the farmland that was promised to them? There were no building supplies, no provisions outside of what they carried. Something must be wrong.

"It is best you sleep in or under the wagons tonight. The wagons leave to return to Saratov at dawn tomorrow. Tomorrow you start to build your homes."

Anna Barbara looked at her children, and then into Christoph's eyes. Despite all the challenges of the journey, she now felt broken as her vision of the plains and farmland evaporated into a grassy, scrub terrain.

"Many in this part of the country build homes in the ground, called mud huts. We call them semlinkas. We will show you how to create your houses tomorrow. You are fortunate it is the sixteenth of June, not the dead of winter. Digging will be easy and you can make yourselves comfortable in your huts tomorrow."

Peter Asselborn looked at the officer and walked up to him. "This is not what we were promised. We were told there would be housing and supplies to assist us."

Dead Reckoning

"You build mud huts. This is the direction we were told to give to you. Supplies are on their way to help you. You can live in the huts until more supplies arrive. See the forest toward the north? There is plenty of wild fruit, apples, black cherries, red whortleberry and strawberries. There are beam trees which sprout fruit more precious than apples."

"Where are the seeds, the tools? We were promised much more than this."

"And you shall have it all in good time. You are here now, and you start your new lives tomorrow. You have had a long journey. Relax tonight, things will look different in the morning."

Christoph pulled the slip of paper from his pocket, the paper that was folded so many times, that he had it memorized, and, despite getting soaked in the Gulf of Finland, the words remained etched in his mind. Freedom, freedom, freedom. He lowered his eyes, held his head in his hands, and cried, "What have I done?"

Part Three

"If you look deeply into the palm of your hand, you will see your parents and all generations of your ancestors. All of them are alive in this moment. Each is present in your body. You are the continuation of each of these people."

Thich Nhat Hanh

Chapter Forty-Six, October 2014, Arizona

Rosalind awoke. The date June 16, 1766 was stuck in her head along with Christoph Schmidt's image. Desperation sank from her head to her stomach. She shook her head. Her imagination during meditation had gone off the skids. With two deaths hanging over her head like an invisible guillotine, she had invented fantasies of murder and disappointment. It was ridiculous.

She sat upright trying to forget Anna Barbara, Christoph, and the settlers. But the desperation did not pass despite the details fading. She continued to be immersed in their emotions. She must have a direct blood line to Christoph. Why else did she think so much about him?

Outside she heard footsteps and rattling. Slowly the door was unlocked and opened. Detective Hamilton stood at the doorway. "Ruth Hoffman posted bail for your release."

Rosalind rolled her eyes jutting out her jaw. "I'm free to go?"

"Yes, you are released on bail. Stay close to home. And Sedona is not close to home."

Behind him Officer Enders approached Rosalind holding her phone and purse, handing it to her.

Rosalind accepted the items and turned back to Hamilton and Enders. "I'm not a flight risk. And someone planted a vision board and oleander in my house. When I returned from Sedona Saturday night, a mesquite branch had fallen through the sidelight. It appeared to be caused by the storm, but someone purposely broke my window to enter and plant those materials. If I did kill Tony, I could think of better ways to dispose of evidence. I need to report a break-in."

Aunt Ruth walked up to them. "Rosalind has a good point. Her window was broken. You can check with the window repair company. She paid extra to have them fix it on Sunday. And who looks under their couch every day?"

After Officer Enders filled out Rosalind's statement about the break-in, she looked at her and calmly said, "You may leave."

* * *

Rosalind was still annoyed when she and Aunt Ruth drove onto the driveway and parked near Rosalind's casita. "I'm so grateful to be out of that building. I was there a full day and night, but it felt like an eternity. Are you ready for a mimosa?"

Ruth nodded and they entered the casita. Hercules jumped for joy when he saw them and landed in play stance, ready to play fetch. Rosalind hugged him. Then she opened the back door, picked up a blue tennis ball, gently tossing it in the yard. The Doberman ran after it and brought it back to Rosalind.

Ruth pulled the cork off the sparkling wine. "I cannot believe they would haul you in and charge you before we got you an attorney." She poured the liquid into two glasses, added orange juice, and filled it to the top.

She handed one of the glasses to Rosalind who swallowed the drink and sighed. "The mimosa helps to ease the pain. I need to put my freedom to good use and find Tony's killer." Rosalind popped bread into the toaster.

"That could be the best way to look at it. No one can change the situation." Then for the fifth time, Ruth said, "I cannot believe they would haul you in there before we got you an attorney. Which is why we need a good attorney now. You cannot talk to Max or any of the officers again without the attorney by your side."

"Max? Now you are on a first name basis with Detective Hamilton?"

"I guess as of this morning."

Rosalind swallowed her drink, remembering how the murder of that man on the ship haunted Christoph's life. She refused to live with Tony's murder linked to her forever.

"Well, I'm no longer waiting for 'Max' or anyone else to solve this case. I will talk to every person who ever knew Tony and figure out who did it and why they killed him. I refuse to have Tony's death hanging over me for the rest of my life."

"Well, whatever you do, stay in the area. I don't want to lose my house over the bail bond. You were lucky the judge allowed bail. Normally first-degree murder suspects are not permitted out, but I guaranteed her that you were not a flight risk. She heard my pleas. Thank goodness Max agreed."

Dead Reckoning

"You know I won't let you lose your money." Rosalind put her elbow on the table and her chin in her hand. "Aunt Ruth, do you know if any of our ancestors were accused of crimes, crimes they didn't commit?"

Ruth looked confused at the question. "No. Why do you ask?'

"Just a feeling I have." She grabbed the toast that popped up, spread avocado on it, set each piece on a plate, and served one to Aunt Ruth. After waffling down breakfast, her phone chimed, and she checked the display. She held it up for Aunt Ruth to see Josh's name. Ruth nodded. "You better answer that one."

"Hello? Rosalind? I called you like forty times. Are you okay?"

"I am now. I haven't had access to my phone since yesterday afternoon. I was in jail and charged with murder. But they released me on bail this morning."

"That's crazy."

"Is your offer to help me find Tony's killer still open?"

"Of course. When do we get started? I can leave the office at any time. I've would love to get away for a few hours."

"Give me a bit of time to recoup. How about 2 p.m.? Can you come here?" She tossed the ball again for Hercules to retrieve.

"That works. I'll see you at two."

Rosalind disconnected the call and before she could set the phone on the table, it rang again. It was Audra. Rosalind cringed. She didn't want to keep explaining what happened, but she needed to answer.

"Hello?"

"Rosalind. Thank goodness I reached you. How are you?"

"Ok as I can be for spending the night in jail."

"Oh dear, I'm so sorry. Did you get any rest?"

"It wasn't comfortable, but I did sleep." Hercules dropped the ball at Rosalind's feet hoping to continue the game.

"I'm so sorry. The rumor is that you were charged in the murder. Is that true?"

"Unfortunately, yes. But now I have to find out who killed Tony to clear my name." Rosalind picked up the ball and tossed it toward the bed. Hercules sped after it. "I'm ready to fight for my freedom."

"Is there anything I can do to help?"

"I guess let me know if you hear any tips. Someone committed this crime. I need to find out who that person is. And thank you for stopping over last night and this morning to care for Hercules."

"You're welcome. If I hear anything, I will let you know."

"Audra, who do you think wanted Tony dead?"

"Let me answer that question with another question. Tell me, how long is a piece of string? I'm sure any number of people were irritated with him. But my best guess is someone connected to the nightclub. There are a lot of sordid characters in that business."

"I will check out the nightclub connections. Thanks, Audra. We still need to set up that lunch date. I will call you back when I know what my schedule will be. Talk to you later."

As she clicked the end call button, she glanced at Aunt Ruth who was scrolling through her attorney contacts.

"Rosalind, I found the perfect attorney for you. A woman, she has overseen sensitive cases before. I will call her." Ruth drained her glass. "And don't forget to make a list of suspects."

"Of course, Aunt Ruth. I have no other way of accomplishing anything without a list."

"Good, I will set up an appointment with the attorney. And send me a copy of your suspects so I can review it, too."

"Will do. First I'm giving the love of my life, Hercules, a treat. Then I need a shower. Until I do those two things, I cannot think another thought."

After asking Hercules to sit and rewarding him with a small biscuit, Ruth and Rosalind downed the last of their mimosas and hugged goodbye.

Before her shower, Rosalind took a detour to her laptop, opened her emails and started to compose. "Dear Margaret, by any chance are you aware of any of my ancestors being accused of a crime they didn't commit? Are there any records for the ship they sailed on from the Germanic states to Russia? Is there a chance the vessel could have been the Ursa Major?" She wrote a few more comments and asked Margaret if Friday worked to meet for lunch.

Next Rosalind wrote down the visions she remembered about Christoph, Anna Barbara, Kristina, Johann, Maria, and Martin. She needed to keep what she could remember as fresh as possible. She didn't understand why these dreams, hallucinations, or past life memories happened, but she believed she must track the details. If it was a real flashback, it had to be documented. And, if she was losing her mind, at least she would have a record of it.

Chapter Forty-Seven

Gravel crunched under the tires of Josh's Jeep. Rosalind peered out the window and felt a new sense of freedom. Life was short. Life was unpredictable. Life was short and unpredictable whether you played it safe or lived a bit dangerously. Playing it safe had gotten her charged with murder. Could it be worse to live a bit dangerously?

Josh knocked and Hercules raced to the door. He scratched near the bottom of the door frame, ready to play with someone new. Rosalind opened the door, clipboard in hand.

"Where are we heading first?" asked Josh.

"I wrote a list of key suspects but would like your input. I'm not certain who I suspect the most, but these people knew Tony and would have an opinion as to who murdered him." Rosalind motioned for him to sit at the table, and she handed the clipboard to him. Hercules laid down at Josh's feet.

"Ok, so you have Jennifer Sorsetti, Pamela Findley, Ralph Findley, Cassandra Starmer, and the Nightclub. It's a good start. Do we just show up at their home?"

"I think so. If they murdered Tony, they wouldn't help me avoid conviction. But I think they will open their doors to us. Hopefully, they'll provide us with perspectives which could lead us to more people we need to meet."

"Ok, let's head out."

"Water?" Rosalind held out a bottle for Josh.

"Yes, good idea."

Hercules walked with her, jumping in circles ready for a car ride.

"Not today, baby. You can come with me soon. I promise." She bent down and held his face in her hands, rubbing her head against his. Hercules understood, walked to his day bed, and laid down nestling the blue ball between his paws.

Thirty minutes later Josh and Rosalind parked outside Pamela Findley's house in Paradise Valley. The smooth stone walls and perfectly trimmed flora and fauna matched Pamela's meticulous attention to her appearance.

"Whoa," said Rosalind. "Imagine how much the landscape alone costs."

They walked through the arched gate, around the curving stone path to the front double oak doors. The security camera recorded their presence. Josh knocked and a tall woman with light gray hair wearing a plain black dress answered the door.

Josh introduced himself and Rosalind. The woman introduced herself as the housekeeper, Lucy, and surprisingly, she let them into the house. Lucy said she would alert Mrs. Findley and check if she would be available to see them.

They walked on the marble flooring illuminated by the round skylight over the atrium foyer. Lucy led them to a room on the left and asked them to wait there. They sat on the white leather sofa surrounded by exquisite furniture. After five minutes, Lucy returned. "Mrs. Findley will be with you in twenty minutes." They thanked her.

Josh turned to Rosalind. "Such precision timing. I'm setting my timer for twenty minutes."

Exactly twenty minutes later, the click, click, click of heels descended the semi-circular staircase, crossed the foyer, and stopped at the entrance of the room. Pamela reached out her right hand to the mahogany door jamb and placed her left hand on her hip. Her nails sparkled, her smile was perfect and as always, not a hair was out of place. She wore a meticulous oceanic blue jacket and skirt that matched the shade of her impeccable and stylish heels. "To what do I owe this honor?"

Josh stood up when he saw her. He stretched out his hand to her, but she hugged him instead encircling him a cloud of jasmine. "Pamela, Rosalind and I want to extend our sympathies to you. How are you holding up during this tragedy?"

"You have no idea how lonely it is to not be a widow." Pamela put her hand over her forehead and perched on a wing chair. "No one sends their condolences to the first wife, the one who made the man. Oh, it's too difficult to discuss. I have sunk into a deep depression. When Tony died, my alimony went with him." Pamela bent down to adjust her shoe, which dangled from her toes, back onto her heel.

Rosalind leaned forward, her hands on her knees. "When was the last time you saw Tony?"

"Two months ago. If Tony and I needed to communicate, we texted. We knew each other's moves so we didn't have to meet face to face."

"Where did you last see him?"

"In court. Tony had a gigantic commission check on its way and I made sure my portion of the payment was secure." Pamela's shoe dropped off her foot landing on the tile.

"Did you talk to Tony that day?"

"No. It was purely a financial court appearance. Nothing personal." She picked up her shoe and put it back on her foot.

"When was the last time you talked directly to him?"

"Oh goodness, who knows? A year or two ago? As I said, we typically texted."

"What were you talking about the last time you texted him?"

"It was a financial discussion."

"What kind of financial discussion?"

"I asked for an alimony increase. We didn't quite see eye to eye on it."

"Did you argue?"

"I wouldn't go that far."

"Who inherits his estate?" Rosalind kept her expression neutral, despite feeling impatient with Pamela's answers.

"Unfortunately, I don't know. The day you saw me at the bank, I looked for his will in our safety deposit box. I was always due to inherit, even after the divorce. He trusted me. But the copy left in the box was never signed or notarized."

"How old is the will?"

"It's a few years old. Anthony hated updating these things."

Rosalind jumped on Pamela's last comment. "That's a long-time to not update a will, especially after a second divorce. I noticed Ralph Findley did not talk to you at the funeral. Why is that?"

"Oh, poor Ralph. He always was a sore loser. I suppose he still misses me desperately."

"Desperately?"

"Ralph introduced me to Tony. And the rest is really none of your business."

Rosalind exhaled slowly. "Who do you think killed Tony?"

"You." Pamela reached into her pocket and handed a photo to Josh. "Haven't you been charged with his murder?"

"The police are grasping at straws, using me to draw out the real killer who thinks he, or she, is off the hook."

Dead Reckoning

"Tony kept that picture of the two of you at the bank. I had others but must have misplaced them. Strange isn't it?"

Rosalind pulled out an envelope. "I picked this up after you dropped it at the bank. Tony's choices of pictures and CDs has nothing to do with me. I don't think you'll want to drop that envelope again. Especially the CD. I read the title but didn't watch it." Pamela's face reddened and she swallowed a little bit of her pride.

"Where were you the morning Tony died?"

"I was fast asleep in my bed. The housekeeper vouched for me when the police questioned her."

"Lucy lives here, too?

"No. But she is more than a housekeeper. She helps me with everything from running the house, to social events, to overseeing unexpected guests." Pamela's smile did not appear forced, but it was clearly an expression she had practiced in front of the mirror.

Josh disregarded the phrase unexpected guests. "So, Lucy was here? She verified she saw you Tuesday morning?"

"Yes, she verified. She doesn't have to see me to know where I am."

Rosalind shook her head trying to interpret Pamela's logic and then realized it existed only in her mind. "Was there information Tony had? Could he have been bribing someone?"

Pamela laughed. "If Tony had blackmail worthy information, he would have found a more sophisticated way to profit from it." She pushed a blond bang off her forehead. "Rosalind, certainly you don't think you can find the killer, do you? And the fashion sense you display fits in well with prison garb."

"Pamela, you loved Tony for his money. You hoped to live off his success for the rest of your life. I heard what you said when they wheeled you out on a stretcher. Perhaps the police need to hear it, too." She stood up and stepped closer to Pamela and looked her straight in the eye. "Your arrogance is a fine cover for the fear you face. But what do you do without Tony's money? Go searching for a new trophy husband?"

Pamela's jaw dropped as she shrunk back from Rosalind but quickly regained her composure. "You don't understand, Rosalind. Fear is not in my nature."

"You smell of fear." Rosalind walked toward the foyer, then turned. "And you don't have an alibi. You are a top candidate for murder."

Pamela gasped. Josh nodded to Pamela, thanked her for seeing them and followed Rosalind. When he caught up with her, he said, "Where did that come from?"

"I'm tired of people thinking I'm a pushover. I'm not, and I will track down Tony's killer."

As the door closed, Pamela picked up her phone, pressed speed dial one, and connected to her attorney.

* * *

Jennifer Sorsetti, Tony's second wife, lived closest to Pamela. Her house was not a mansion, but a beautiful Southwestern ranch surrounded by blooming bougainvillea, purple Texas sage and golden barrel cacti. Neat and sturdy with an understated elegance.

Josh knocked on the door. After a few minutes, an older man opened it. His dark eyes and salt and pepper hair seemed a bit old for Jennifer. He held a hammer in his hand and nails fell out of his back pocket. "Hello, can I help you?"

"We are looking for Jennifer Sorsetti, is she at home by any chance?" asked Rosalind.

"No, she is at work. Can I ask what this is about?"

After introductions, Phillip Sorsetti, Jennifer's father, explained he was finishing some minor repairs for his daughter. He remembered Josh's name from the agency, as he was the creative one and the brains behind Tony's successful customer campaigns. He was sorry Rosalind had found Tony, but he didn't know much about the case.

"Too bad someone didn't do the deed when Jennifer was married to him. With that timing she would have inherited everything. I told her to take the money and run, and she did. Got a good settlement. Who wanted to kill Tony? I know I did when Jennifer was married to him, but why now? Jennifer had her cut, and the man wasn't worth prison time. But I'm sure a lot of people wanted him dead."

"Where were you from Monday evening to Tuesday morning?"

"At my home alone. Who else are you going to see?"

"Cassandra Starmer, his girlfriend, is next on our list."

"Oh, yes. I wonder if I could ask a favor. Jennifer wanted to deliver a box of old items to Tony. The items were packed up with Jennifer's belongings by accident when she moved out. I'm sure Tony didn't miss it. It's nothing important, but Jennifer now feels uncomfortable keeping it and more uncomfortable throwing it away. Could you take it with you and deliver it to Cassandra?"

Josh looked at Rosalind and she tilted her head to the left. "We can try. We don't know for certain if she will see us."

Mr. Sorsetti returned with a cardboard box. He handed it to Rosalind.

"Thank you so much. Do you have a card? I could ask Jennifer to call you."

Rosalind handed him her card believing Jennifer would never call her.

* * *

When the elevator stopped at Cassandra Starmer's penthouse, the doors opened slowly, creating a bright spotlight blinding Rosalind and Josh. Unable to leave the lift until their eyes adjusted, both blinked until the floor appeared in front of them. As Rosalind looked up, she could not decide what shimmered more, the sun, or the huge diamond on Cassandra's left ring finger.

"Hello Cassandra, I'm Rosalind Schmidt, and this is my co-worker, Josh Bartholomew. We are so sorry for your loss. How are you doing?"

Cassandra raised her shoulders, then breathed out slowly. "Just trying to survive one day at a time. I'm missing Tony desperately and stuck in limbo. This is the best place I ever lived but I have no idea if it will last."

Despite the bright Arizona sun blazing through the floor-to-ceiling windows, the room was a comfortable seventy-two degrees. The light reflected off the white furniture, white walls, and white floors. Even Cassandra's outfit was a shimmering shade of ivory. Everything in the apartment was white except Cassandra's dark auburn hair.

"I understand it is difficult. Is there anything we can do to help?"

"Nothing I can think of." Cassandra's eyes moved up and down assessing Rosalind. "Wait, I recognize you from the memorial service. Didn't Theresa accuse you of killing Tony?"

"Ah, yes, your memory is correct. But I did not kill Tony."

"And then you both bolted out of the memorial. Like you were guilty. How dare you come here to visit me? I should contact security immediately."

Josh stepped between the two extending the cardboard box toward Cassandra. "We were asked to bring some items over by Mr. Sorsetti, Jennifer's father." He held out the box. "This box was inadvertently moved with Jennifer after she left Tony. She didn't realize it until after the divorce. She meant to get it to Tony earlier, but she always thought there would be time and now she felt awkward about it. The items may not be important, but Jennifer believed you were the best person to receive them. Can I set it down here?" Josh motioned toward the glass coffee table.

Cassandra nodded her approval. She walked to the box, glanced through it. She casually moved items which banged against the side of the box as she dug through it to the bottom.

"Did you look through these items?"

"No," Rosalind said. "The box was for you, not us."

Cassandra held up a small black case. "I guess he won't be needing this anymore. If Jennifer had it, it's no longer useable."

"What is it?" asked Rosalind.

"It's Tony's insulin kit. He always traveled with one as he was diabetic. He tried to treat his condition with diet, but that didn't always work. When he knew he had to use it, he normally asked me to do the injection. He had friends help him, too. These kits were his lifeline, but Tony hated needles."

She rustled around papers, scanned a few photos, then turned back to them. "This isn't a treasure trove. And I can't say I'm pleased to spend the day looking at photos of Tony with his ex, and one also with you. You are Rosalind, correct?"

"Yes." She held out her hand to take the photo from Cassandra who placed it in Rosalind's palm. "It's odd. This is the third time I have seen this photo since Tony died." She stared at the photograph then flipped it over. Her name was written on the back. "This makes no sense. Someone photographed us the one time we met outside of the office for coffee. I wonder who took it?"

Cassandra and Josh shook their heads.

"Well, it could have something to do with this all. Would it be ok if I keep the photo?"

Dead Reckoning

Cassandra nodded, then pulled an ink pad and stamp out of the box. She laughed bitterly. "Well, I wasn't the first to use one of these things with Anthony, but I didn't expect to ever see another one." She held out the stamp which was a full-blown image of lips in the shape of a kiss. Rosalind cringed as she remembered the kiss imprint on the copies of Tony's buttocks that spewed from the copier.

"This one is a little smaller than mine. Let me show you." Cassandra walked to the bedroom and rustled through a drawer. She returned to the living room.

"Maybe I'm crazy, my kiss stamp is missing," said Cassandra. "We must have left it somewhere other than the nightstand."

Rosalind wondered how many kiss stamps existed and who had copies. "How big was it?"

"Oh, about an inch bigger than this one."

"Do you know where he bought them?"

"No, and I didn't realize there were multiple stamps."

"Cassandra, I know the timing is difficult, but could we ask you a few more questions?"

"I'm not keen on it." She sighed. "Well, you did Jennifer a favor by bringing me this box so go ahead. What do you want to ask?"

"Can you think of someone who wanted Tony dead?" asked Rosalind.

"I loved Tony dearly, but not everyone did. I imagine many people didn't understand him. Who would want him dead? Who would think it, much less actually do it? I'm not certain."

"When did you last see him?"

"He left the apartment around 8 p.m. to go to the nightclub."

"You didn't go with him?"

"Usually I would, but I had a headache and stayed here. He wasn't feeling well either, but he insisted on going to the club. He said he had been queasy since lunch. I stayed in bed and slept until security called and told me police officers were here."

"What time did the police arrive?"

"It was around 8:30. I still had a headache, but I was stunned. My whole future vanished before my eyes. I keep waiting for someone to tell me this is only a dream." Cassandra played with the diamond bracelet on her left wrist. "He should have been back here after the club closed. I have no idea why he went to the office."

"You were here all Monday night and Tuesday morning?"

"Yes, the police checked security videos to prove I did not leave the building." Cassandra strode to the couch, sat down propping her elbows on her knees, putting her face on her open hands. Then she slowly raised her head to look at Josh and Rosalind. "You chose a good day to come here since any other day I might still be sitting here in my pajamas wallowing in my sorrow. I can't imagine why anyone would kill Tony. He was generous by providing for his ex-wives. Tony sent money every month to a single parent with three sons struggling to make ends meet. He helped them, he mentored them. He compensated his employees at the nightclub fairly. The only person I can think of who may be able to help you is the manager at the nightclub, Don Jansen. Something must have happened at the nightclub that led to his death."

"What is the person's name he sent money to?"

"Paulette Mason."

"Did you mention this to the police?"

"No, I don't think so. Didn't think of it."

"Would it be possible to get Paulette and Don's contact information?

Cassandra nodded and walked to the kitchen area to pick up her phone. Rosalind wondered if Paulette's children were the result of an affair with Tony.

"I can text you the contact. What is your phone number?"

Rosalind shared the digits and Cassandra sent the contacts via text. Without any further questions, Rosalind and Josh thanked Cassandra for her time.

"If you do uncover anything, please stay in touch," said Cassandra as the elevator doors closed between them.

Rosalind looked at Josh and shook her head. "I can't think of any reason Cassandra wanted Tony gone unless she was the beneficiary in his will."

Josh nodded. "Her tears seem genuine. I never knew Tony was diabetic, did you?"

"No, I didn't. Not certain that plays into this investigation but it's good to gather all the facts. I will add Paulette Mason and Don Jansen to our list. Let's keep to our plan and talk to Ralph Findley next."

Dead Reckoning

As they drove to Tempe from downtown Phoenix, the sun was at their backs and the traffic was light.

"Josh, do you remember your dreams? Do you ever write them down?" asked Rosalind.

"Sometimes the dreams are memorable, sometimes I wake up with feelings leftover from the dream, and other times I remember nothing. Why do you ask?"

"I never remembered my dreams. I did as a kid, but not as an adult. I had dreams in jail, but I didn't have a pencil or paper to record it. I wrote what I could remember this morning." Rosalind held back the details unsure how Josh would react.

"I doubt most people think about it. I'm sure dreams mean something. I just don't know what." He hit the brakes and parked the car outside Ralph's condominium.

Ralph answered the doorbell after the second ring and after quick introductions, he led Rosalind and Josh to the living room. Ralph wore a suit without a wrinkle and sat in his recliner with his legs crossed. He exuded wisdom, knowledge, and humility as they sat opposite him. Rosalind winced as his resemblance to Tony was uncanny, but his energy was on the opposite end of the spectrum. Ralph was calm and collected, whereas Tony was always high strung and raring to go.

"Please sit." Ralph motioned them to the couch while he eyed Rosalind closely. "Aren't you the woman accused of killing Anthony? The one who bailed out of the funeral without a single retort?"

Rosalind nodded. "Yes, that was me. I was shocked at Theresa's outburst. I didn't want to create a melee, so I left. I found Tony dead, but I swear to you I didn't kill him, and I need to prove my innocence. Which is why we are here to ask you a few questions. Were you and Tony close?"

"Ha," Ralph burst out. "We were close many years ago. As I told Detective Hamilton, I hated Anthony. I didn't kill him, but it grieves me not in the least that someone else did."

Rosalind was surprised but then she remembered how quickly he walked out of the funeral home after viewing Tony.

"Who wanted him dead?" asked Josh.

"I have no idea. How many people did he meet since 1999?"

Josh laughed. "Tell me more."

"Anthony loved pranks. He loved embarrassing people. I grant you, I haven't seen him since 1999, or early 2000. I doubt he changed much since that time."

"What kind of pranks did he do?" Rosalind was familiar with Tony's office pranks but wanted Ralph's perspective.

Ralph looked down at his well-manicured fingernails as he tapped his fingers in rotation on the arm of the couch. "I don't think there was a woman Tony met that he didn't try to seduce." Ralph's voice cracked. "And he was quite successful."

"How did you feel about that?" asked Rosalind.

Ralph gazed at the floor to regain his composure. He swallowed and met Rosalind's eyes. "Did you ever experience pranks identical twins play? As I told Detective Hamilton, Anthony used to pretend he was me. He would act like me with my girlfriends taking it well beyond the prank stage into more intimate territory. The third time he did it, I was engaged. He swept my fiancé away with deception and then with money."

"I'm so sorry to hear that." The high jinks Rosalind experienced were nothing in comparison.

"Yes, we were together about six months, I was convinced Pamela and I were in it for the long run. Their affair was the ultimate betrayal. The next time I saw Anthony and Pamela was at his funeral."

"You were engaged to Pamela Findley?"

"Yes, she was the one."

"Where were you last week Monday night and Tuesday morning?"

"I was here reading, reviewing lecture notes for my next class."

"Can anyone vouch for your whereabouts?"

"Nope, I'm pretty much a loner."

"You have quite a motive for revenge."

"True, but if I wanted revenge why would I wait so long? Wouldn't I have done it years ago? And while I do not mourn him, it is payback for Anthony to have his lucrative life cut short."

Ralph's phone rang. "Excuse me." He stood up and sauntered to the dining room to answer the phone.

"What? Oh, my God. This is insane. Are you sure?" After a few beats, he accepted whatever the news was. "I'm on my way."

Ralph looked back to Rosalind and Josh. "I'm sorry I must leave right now. I have an emergency." Ralph waved Rosalind and Josh to the door.

"Thank you for your time," said Rosalind. "Is there anything we can do to help?"

"I doubt it. That was my mother's housekeeper. She just found my mother dead."

Chapter Forty-Eight

It was nearly 6 p.m. when they left Ralph Findley's house. Despite shock at the latest turn of events, Ralph Findley had one of the best motives for murder they had heard today.

Rosalind looked to Josh barely comprehending what Ralph told them. "Now Tony, Theresa, and Tony's mother are all dead. What the hell is happening?"

"If there is a link, I'm not seeing it. And his mother? We only know she is dead, not necessarily murdered."

"I need a break from the investigation. Some time to recap what we learned today. Why don't we grab dinner at the Daily Planet?"

"Great idea. I need to stop at the office first, to pick up something I forgot. I doubt anyone will be there this late. If anyone is working, they're wining and dining clients off site."

"True, I would love to get in my office to grab a few items of my own."

There were no cars parked in the lot. As they approached the door, Josh used his ID on the card reader to gain access.

Rosalind followed him. "Looks like everyone left and forgot to set the security system to away."

"Yeah, that happens way too often. I'll meet you back in the lobby in five minutes. Ten at the most."

"Ok." Rosalind pulled her keys out of her bag. She walked to her office and turned the key in the lock. She listened for the click, but footfalls sounded in the hallway behind her. She softly opened the door, moved inside, closed it ever so gently, and stood behind it frozen in place. She didn't hear anything. Not even the rattling air conditioning unit.

As she moved to the center of her office, Rosalind sensed an anxious energy around her desk. She was certain someone had rifled through her entire office. Perhaps the police? Perhaps someone else.

On her desk she saw file folders she didn't recognize. She glanced through the side door window frame again, concerned that someone would see her and report her to management. The hallway was clear. Rosalind scooped up the new files, pulled open a drawer, and grabbed a small box. As she put the box and the files in her bag, a door closed softly. She turned, expecting to see Josh, but then she heard voices, followed by footsteps. She ducked under the desk, grateful for two things: the vanity plate blocking her from view and the dark room that cloaked her presence. Thank god she hadn't turned on a light.

"I told you this would take time," said Bob.

"I don't have more time. What is your best guess on resolution? Next week?" asked Audra.

"I can't confirm that it will be next week. This is a tricky situation since Tony was the sales lead. It takes time to undo it. Tony played hard ball. Who knew what he was capable of?"

Audra sighed. "I kept your secret. My work kept this branch alive."

"I know, you deserve it. But it's not as easy as it seems. The payment requires board authorization."

"I need assurance that I will be compensated for my efforts."

Bob sighed then exhaled slowly. "I will call home office tomorrow. Then I will negotiate the transition to you. I already feel better that it will be paid to you as it should have been. I will confirm when I hear back from corporate."

A pen scratched on paper and a rip detached a sheet from the notebook. A door swung open and hit the wall.

"Please don't be upset with me. These are stressful times. We'll get through it. Now let's get out of here." Rosalind heard a phone ping. Bob continued, "Perfect timing, the driver is waiting outside for us."

Rosalind listened as someone clicked off the lobby lights. The keypad chimed as the security system was set to away. She remained crouched in her hiding spot. Any motion would set off the alarm, resulting in sirens and flashing lights, with police arriving in less than ten minutes. Of course, one of those police officers would no doubt be Detective Hamilton since this was a recent crime scene. She was stranded and was left hoping Josh exited the building before the alarm was set. Did he even know Bob and Audra had been in the office?

* * *

Rosalind heard the security chime but wasn't sure who entered the building, so she stayed hidden. Within a few minutes, she heard Josh call, "Rosalind?" from the hallway. She crawled out from under the desk, stood up and breathed a sigh of relief as Josh looked through the side door window. She rushed out and hugged him.

"I thought I might be stuck for hours. I'm so happy to see you. Did you talk to Bob and Audra?"

"No, I heard voices, I knew it wasn't you, and I dashed out the back door. I moved the car before they left so they wouldn't see it. What did you see?"

"I didn't see much but I'll tell you what I overheard on our way to the restaurant. Right now, I'm too hungry to think. Ralph Findley has a strong motive and is a top suspect. But somehow Bob McMahon has messed up things at the office."

* * *

Inside the Daily Planet, they scanned the room for an open table, and saw Graham waving to them.

"We haven't ordered yet, please join us," said Issy who was seated next to Graham.

"This is a surprise running into both of you," said Rosalind.

"My team ditched me for a concert, so when I saw Graham we decided to join forces for dinner."

Over dinner, Rosalind and Josh recapped their day. Graham and Issy concurred. There were plenty of suspects and not a lot of clear answers.

Rosalind laid her fork across her plate. "I'll make phone calls tomorrow instead of driving around the Valley. I need to follow up with Paulette Mason and Don Jansen. After that, I'll check in with Detective Hamilton for updates and ask him about Tony's mom."

"Another busy day," said Josh. "Keep me posted. If needed, we can head to the Lantern Escapade nightclub tomorrow night to scope out Tony's other life."

"It's a plan. Thank you for your help today, Josh." They waved to Ernie when the group of four exited the Daily Planet.

After Josh opened her car door, he walked her to her doorway and said good night. She retreated into her casita as he drove away. She was surprised how much she enjoyed Josh's company and assistance today.

After letting Hercules outside and feeding him, Rosalind looked at the files from her desk, not ready to dive into her new assignment that

Dead Reckoning

no one discussed with her. So, she climbed into bed and despite all she learned today, she just had one thought. *Can I trust him?*

Chapter Forty-Nine

The next morning Rosalind jerked straight up in her bed. Dreams? What crazy dreams. She grabbed her notebook and pen ready to write. When she looked down at the sheet, she expected it to be blank, then she saw "BOB" and "JOSH" written clearly in all capital letters.

The word secrets circled in her head. Secrets, commissions, payouts, what did it all mean? She sat still and wrote what dreams she remembered, chasing clouds, running from Bob, cowering next to a rock. Words and scenes that did not connect with meaning...yet.

Hercules stirred next to her, nudging her to move out of bed, ready for his morning meal. She swung her legs to the floor, slipped into her sandals, and let Hercules into the yard for his business. When she opened the back door Hercules bounded straight to his bowl to devour his breakfast.

Despite yesterday's interviews, she wasn't closer to identifying the murderer. No wonder the police needed time to ask questions, record notes, eliminate suspects, and provide tangible proof.

Hercules curled around her feet when she sat at the kitchen table. Notebook in hand, she saw her scribbled BOB. She slowed her thoughts and her breath. She turned on classical music and let the notes of Beethoven's *Für Elise* soar around her. She breathed in, breathed out, crossed her arms over her heart and tilted her head to her chest. Bob, promises, secrets. She asked for assistance, ideas, suspects. As instructed, she sat quietly and waited. And waited and waited. Nothing came.

After a few minutes Rosalind noticed the folders from her office that she left on the table. She flipped through their titles and opened the one labeled, "Theresa Mars Settlement." It read:

Theresa Mars hereby agrees to pay Kelco Marketing thirty-three thousand dollars for funds misused during business. Without admitting guilt, Theresa agrees to the arrangement of paying $550 each month, garnished off her wages, until the full sum is repaid with no interest incurred. In consideration of these payments, no charges in civil or criminal court will be filed in connection with this event. Payments will commence upon Theresa's return from an authorized paid six-month maternity leave.

The file papers slipped through her fingers fanning out over the kitchen table. Theresa had a child. She had never been married or in a relationship to Rosalind's knowledge. Theresa stole money from the company. And it happened more than twenty years ago. If Theresa followed the agreement, she was never criminally charged and paid back every dime, within five years. Theresa had signed the resolution along with Bob McMahon and was witnessed by Anthony Findley. Why did the folder end up on her desk now? Secrets were coming out of the woodwork.

Rosalind signed into her laptop and typed Arizona birth records into her search field. Would entries from twenty-five years ago be available? She had no idea what she would find as she pressed enter.

She searched the links for more than twenty minutes then realized looking for birth announcements with only the last name Mars, if that was the correct last name, was futile. She worked through a few months' worth of newspaper births, without connecting anything to Theresa. She considered the argument she overheard between Audra and Bob.

She glanced through the second file but had no idea what to make of it. Agreements about payments and reverses made no sense and she had no idea how the dollars were moved without corporate's approval.

Josh asked her to meet him for lunch today. Certainly, it was not a crime to meet Josh at the office. It had been more than a week since Tony's death. And Theresa could not scream at her since she was also dead. This was her chance to talk to Bob. She hoped he was in the office.

Bob was her boss. He hired her years ago when he saw her business and organizational acumen as the missing component needed to elevate Kelco Marketing to the next level. She balanced out a strong, creative team by adding process and integrity to the customer experience. Bob recognized her contributions. Now her challenge was to find out why the folders were left on her desk. She also needed to know if Bob and Audra drove together the morning Tony died. If not, had he planned for her to find Tony? Was that his way of trying to leave himself in the clear?

The office was her north star. It had guided and directed her life since she moved to Arizona. Without it she was sailing into unchartered waters. Suddenly the term dead reckoning came to her, but it was only a fuzzy memory. She didn't know the meaning of the words.

Rosalind picked up her phone and searched for Josh's contact. Her call went to his voice mail.

"Hey Josh, about lunch today, I'll meet up with you at the office. I need to stop there..." she paused, "well, I just need to stop there. I will text you when I arrive."

She hung up the phone and her stomach fluttered. Bob had no idea how the rest of his day would go. Neither did Rosalind.

* * *

Before Rosalind left the casita for a delayed morning run, her plans changed again. A knock on the door interrupted her thoughts. It was Audra carrying two coffee cups.

"I finished a customer breakfast meeting early and had a few minutes between appointments. What better way to relax before my next call than to bring you a caramel latte?" Audra handed a latte to Rosalind and leaned over to greet Hercules with a scratch to his head.

"Thank you. What a great surprise, a couple lattes. I'm sure we have a lot to catch up on." Rosalind would love to ask her about her conversation with Bob yesterday, but how could Rosalind bring it up without giving away that she was in the office?

"Unfortunately, I can't stay, the line took a lot longer than I planned. Just wanted to say I'm glad you are out of jail. Oh, and I almost forgot. I brought a treat for Hercules. Can he have it now?"

"Sure," said Rosalind.

Audra opened her purse and pulled out a small bone shaped dog treat. She bent down to Hercules with the snack on her open palm. Rosalind heard him crunch the biscuit.

"Sorry to have such a short visit, but I have an appointment in ten. See you later."

Rosalind drank her latte and reviewed her options, but thoughts spun round her head without clear focus. Without her run, none of these ideas would align into order. She had to run, and she had to go now. She slipped on her left knee brace and wondered if she still needed it. It had become her security blanket after years of pain, but no serious issue existed per her doctor.

She grabbed Hercules leash, but he was busy snoring. "Ok, baby. I will run enough for the two of us. You rest today."

Dead Reckoning

After her run, she moved to the patio with her phone and laptop and sat at the outdoor table. She dialed Paulette Mason's number. There was a click and then she heard, "You have reached a number that is disconnected."

She typed Paulette's address into Google earth. The map showed an empty lot. She checked the number and address twice and the info matched. How odd since she received the information from Cassandra yesterday.

Next she called Don Jansen's number at the nightclub.

"Hello. Don Jansen here."

"Hi Don, this is Rosalind Schmidt. I worked at Kelco with your former partner, Anthony Findley. I know this sounds weird, but I'm following up on Tony's last night at the club. Do you have a couple minutes for me to ask you a few questions?"

"Unfortunately, I can't right now. Why don't you come to the club around 4 p.m.? I should have a few minutes to meet with you then."

"Ok, I'll see you later."

Chapter Fifty

Rosalind was grateful no one was in the lobby when she arrived at the office shortly before noon. She used her ID to sign in and noticed two cameras near the entrance. She was sad to see Theresa's reception area empty during working hours, knowing she would never return again.

Rosalind turned to the right, keys in hand, hoping to unlock her office and escape into the room undetected. As she approached her workspace, she saw the lights on and the door wide open.

"Check by the cabinets, there could be something there," said Hamilton.

Her heart sank to the bottom of her stomach. She would need some gastroenterology work if she ever climbed her way out of this mess. Well, there was no turning back now.

She walked into her office. "Hello, Detective Hamilton. Can I help you find something?"

Hamilton spun around, and, despite his usual composure, he was surprised to see her. "Good morning, Rosalind."

"These are important papers you have tossed about here. Could I help you to find what you are looking for? To be clear, my offer doesn't include cleaning up your mess."

Before Hamilton could answer, Rosalind heard footsteps behind her and turned to see Bob. She raised her head, pushed her shoulders down and back, then summoned every ounce of courage she could muster. She inhaled deeply and remembered Issy's words. *I request a most benevolent outcome.*

"Rosalind, what are you doing here?" asked Bob.

She smiled graciously. "I wanted to talk to you, Bob. Can we go to your office?"

"Certainly." Bob led them to the corner office. He sat behind his desk and motioned for Rosalind to sit in one of the two adjacent chairs. "What's up?"

"I have a couple questions. It's about the last day I was here."

"You mean yesterday when you sneaked into your office and hid under your desk? That is until Josh came to your rescue."

Rosalind tried to hide her discomfort. Her hands trembled. *How could he have re-directed the conversation so quickly?*

"We now have security cameras for the building. I clearly saw video of you and Josh entering and exiting the office."

"Security cameras?"

"Yes, after Tony's death I had the cameras installed. We need to know what happens in the office at all times. I only wish I had the foresight to have the cameras installed years ago, then we would know why Tony is dead, or maybe, he wouldn't have been killed here."

Rosalind tried to absorb this new information before she moved forward with her questions. Her stomach churned as she felt betrayed by Josh who must have been aware of the cameras. She would follow up on that later.

"Everyone wants to believe I killed Tony. They feel safe to have a storyline that solves this murder. The only problem is I didn't kill him. He was dead when I found him. And I won't let the story continue until I find his killer."

"Who did it?" asked Bob, with a look of genuine surprise and intrigue on his face.

"First, I have a few questions." Rosalind leaned forward in her chair. Bob pushed himself a bit farther back in his seat.

"Did you drive alone to work that morning? Or did you and Audra drive together?"

"I drove alone, Audra pulled into the parking lot just after me."

That meant Bob did not have an alibi from the time he left his house.

"What did Tony know about you? What did he use against you to always get his way?"

"Nothing. He was always more drama than reality, you know how he loved to rant and rave."

"Bob, Tony knew something. It always kept you on edge around him. What was Tony going to reveal?"

Bob jumped up and pounded his fists onto his desk exploding the stress that he always contained. "You have no cause to suspect me of killing Anthony."

Detective Hamilton ran to Bob's office. Rosalind stood, trying not to tremble or lose eye contact with Bob.

"I asked one question. I did not say you killed Tony, but your reaction implies differently."

Hamilton interrupted. "Let's relax here for a moment. We aren't going to solve this case by yelling at each other. Rosalind, you come with me."

She wanted to ask Bob more questions. But she reluctantly followed Hamilton's request.

"Let's go to my car. This isn't a good place for you."

They left the building, both signing out of the security system. In the parking lot he opened the car's passenger door and Rosalind sat down. He walked around, then climbed into the driver's seat.

"What were you doing?" asked Hamilton.

"Trying to save my skin since no one else can."

"Of course, we are trying to save your skin. Why do you think we were searching in your office?"

"I have no clue."

"You're interfering with a murder investigation. You need to stop interrogating people."

"You charged me with murder, and I'm out on bail. I can't go to work so what else can I do but try to clear my name?"

"Not when you get Bob out of sorts. I have to follow a procedure here and you are throwing wrenches in the plan. He says you have some important the files we need which were on your desk, and you were in your office yesterday. Did you see these files?"

Rosalind shook her head and lied. "No, I don't know about any files. Even if I did I wouldn't do anything to help Bob right now. He didn't need to make a scene."

"I need to find the files now before Tony Findley's will is read at 3 o'clock. Those files could build the final piece of our case."

"Good luck, Detective Hamilton." Rosalind immediately regretted her lie. She opened the car door and headed to the back parking lot. She texted Josh to meet her at his car. She walked to the back of the parking lot and found Josh standing outside his vehicle.

"You avoided any scenes today, right?" He laughed.

"I guess you heard Bob and me?"

"Everyone heard Bob and you. Lucky the police were there to intervene."

Rosalind laughed. "Yeah, this stuff gets stranger and stranger. And, why didn't you tell me Bob had security cameras installed at the office?"

"What? When was this done?"

"Sometime after Tony's murder and before we stopped there yesterday."

"I had no idea. I should have paid closer attention."

Rosalind was comforted by his response but remained on edge. "I also don't understand why Bob told the police those files were on my desk. The information is extremely confidential. And why leave the files out now?"

"What was in the files?"

"The first was an agreement between Kelco and Theresa Mars to pay back Kelco money used 'inappropriately' and giving her a paid six-month parental leave. Did you ever hear of Theresa having a child?"

"No, she devoted her life to Kelco and, of course, Tony. But Tony had so many relationships. It was a revolving door for him. I never heard about Theresa in a relationship or with a child. She could have given the child up for adoption."

"It's possible, but unlikely since she was granted six months of parental leave."

"What was the date on the contract?"

"'It was signed in November 1988."

"Depending on how far along she was, the child was born in 1988 or in 1989. That would make the child twenty-five years old. Know anyone who fits that description?" asked Josh.

"There are plenty of twenty-five-year-old people around. I checked for birth announcements but couldn't make a match."

"By any chance, has Tony's will been read?"

"Hamilton said the reading is scheduled for this afternoon."

"And what about the second file?"

"It was an employee-initiated lawsuit that challenged why Tony was paid commission on the Smithson sale two years ago. They settled out of court and there was a non-disclosure agreement, just like in Theresa's settlement."

"Wow, that's something I always wondered. I know the entire team supported that campaign with great ideas."

After lunch at the Daily Planet, Rosalind was the happiest she had been since she discovered Tony's body. Josh brightened her day despite the storm clouds on the horizon. He agreed to visit Don Jansen with her later today, yet Rosalind kept thinking about the cameras. Josh seemed surprised to hear about the cameras, but it still nagged at Rosalind. He regained some of her trust, but not all of it.

***

Rosalind's mind spun with more questions. Hopefully, Tony's last will and testament will focus the attention on another suspect who is his beneficiary. But why had her dreams so focused on Bob? What was the connection that pulled him in to be responsible for Tony's death?

"Hercules, it's time to clear our heads. Let's walk to the mailbox and accomplish something today." As she and Hercules walked to the end of the drive, she noticed Hamilton's car was parked near Aunt Ruth's back door.

She turned to Hercules. "Guess he has more questions about me for Aunt Ruth," and then her phone rang. She didn't recognize the number, but it could be a lead. So she answered.

"Hello?"

"Hi, Rosalind this is James Simon. I completed the full evaluation on the knife. Whenever you want to stop by, we can discuss what I discovered."

"Ok, sounds good. I will come in during the next couple days." She thanked him, and then unlocked the mailbox.

She glanced through the envelopes and noticed another package of census lists from the historical society. Also, inside was a set of keys to the larger parcel delivery boxes. She unlocked the compartment, grabbed the box, and checked the return address. She smiled. The frames for her family pictures and passenger lists had arrived. At least three things went right today. One more stop to meet Don Jansen at the nightclub. Will she be able to pinpoint Tony's killer tonight? She hoped so.

Chapter Fifty-One

As Josh parked his car outside the nightclub, the music reverberated through the walls. Rosalind felt the vibrations pommel against her as they walked. A purple Lamborghini was parked near the entrance.

They were surprised to see the host who looked up to greet them. It was the strawberry blond woman from the Daily Planet who usually sat at the end of the bar.

"Welcome to Lantern Escapade. Two of you tonight?"

"Actually, we are here to meet with Don Jansen. But don't I recognize you from the Daily Planet?"

"Yes, you're right. I hang out there often. I'm Tiffany. And you are?"

"I'm Rosalind, and this is Josh."

"It's nice to meet you. I'll let Don know you are here."

After calling Don to confirm the appointment, she escorted them back to his office. Josh asked, "Whose Lamborghini is out front?"

"Oh, that's Don's. It's his favorite car."

As they entered the office, Don motioned for them to sit on the two chairs in front of the polished mahogany desk. Rosalind was impressed with Jansen's desktop which had only three items: a purple Monte Blanc pen, a closed purple day timer, and a clay pot filled with purple Baja Ruellia. The room's calm quiet contradicted the high energy of the club.

"How can I be of service?" Don asked.

"As I mentioned this morning, I worked at Kelco with Tony Findley and hoped you could tell us about his last evening here at the nightclub."

"It was a typical night, nothing to distinguish it from any other, really. Anthony was here, visited with our guests, our friends and enjoyed a couple of drinks, like usual. He left about an hour before closing. He mentioned that Cassandra wasn't feeling well. He didn't look like himself, he was a little under the weather, too."

"You close at 2:30, so he stayed till about 1:30?"

"That's what I remember, yes."

"Do you know anyone who wanted Tony dead?"

"Tony could drive some people crazy, but was it enough to want to kill him? I have no idea, which is exactly what I told the police."

"Who did he spend the most time with that last evening?"

"Tony moved from table to table, connecting with all customers. There were a few people from Kelco."

"How many? Men? Women?"

"Theresa was there, which was routine. Then there were two others, one might have been named Bob."

"What did they look like?" asked Rosalind.

"Suits. Non-distinctive. Brown or dark haired, tall, not memorable."

"What time did Theresa leave?"

"She left about a half hour after closing."

"Why did she stay after hours?"

"Theresa? She typically stayed late. She was one of our partners."

"One of your partners?"

"Yes, she, Tony and I created this place. We have a few other small investors, but we run, or ran, the show."

"So, who runs the show with those two gone?"

"That will depend on to whom they left their shares. I certainly hope it is me."

"Did you care enough to kill him for that share?" asked Josh.

"Murder sounds like too much work to me. I like to make money the old-fashioned way with food and drinks. Tony was my pal. And, hey not for nothing, if I killed anyone, I wouldn't leave the body at Kelco. If I killed Tony, his body would not have been found." Don leaned back in his chair without a care in the world.

*　*　*

As Rosalind and Josh drove to her casita, her cell phone rang. The caller ID was unknown. "Hello," she answered.

"Rosalind, this is Jennifer Sorsetti."

Rosalind recuperated from her shock. "Hi Jennifer, thank you for calling me."

"I doubt I can help you, but my dad mentioned you were trying to help solve Tony's murder and you wanted to talk. Also, I wanted to thank you for delivering the box to Cassandra."

"You're welcome. Yes, I'm trying to touch base with as many people who knew Tony as I can. I know you may not have seen Tony recently, but do you have any idea who would have wanted him dead?"

"I know I wished him dead when we were working through the divorce settlement. I should have listened to my dad and never married Tony in the first place. He was simply too much. Too much of everything." The phone line went quiet.

"Are you still there?" asked Rosalind. Looking in the side mirror she noticed a purple Lamborghini two cars behind them.

"Yes, just dwelling on the past. Unfortunately, the man I married was not at all the man I thought he was. I chose to see what I wanted."

"You aren't the only person in the world who can say that about their past."

"I don't have an alibi as I told the police, but I was done with him once the divorce papers were signed. I have no idea who was in his life now or who would have risked prison time just to see him dead."

"I understand. If you think of anything that might help, please let me know."

"Thanks for understanding. Knowing he is gone breaks my heart all over again. I fell in love with the man I thought he could be. Not the man Anthony Findley really was."

Chapter Fifty-Two

Bright and early the next morning Rosalind lay in bed mulling over yesterday's conversations. She squinted open her eyes and noticed a few scribbles in her dream journal. Rubbing the sleep from her eyes, the writing was unreadable. She didn't recall any dreams. Her phone rang interrupting her thoughts and she saw the screen lit up with Bob's name. Three more rings and Rosalind answered.

"I'm coming over to see you. Be there in five minutes." Before she could stall him, he hung up.

Stunned, Rosalind jumped out of bed, throwing on the first pair of leggings and oversize sweater she saw in her closet. She pulled open the back door to let Hercules outside. No need for him to greet visitors by peeing on their legs even if Bob might deserve it for being so rude giving her only five minutes notice before he arrived at her door.

Surveying her casita, she tolerated some clutter since she barely had any advance notice. She scrambled to jam her interview notes together, slid them into her accordion folder, and tucked it under her mattress.

She grabbed the Kelco files and threw them into her purse. When a strong fist banged on her door, the sound echoed through the room. She let Hercules back into the casita and he settled onto his bed.

Rosalind swung the front door open, and Bob rushed inside. She sensed his abrupt demeanor. Her hands shook and she clasped them behind her back so he wouldn't notice her concern. He was on a mission. Rosalind believed more than ever that she was in the presence of a killer.

Bob noticed Hercules on his bed, turned to greet him, scratching the top of his head. Rosalind quickly spun around to check her casita one more time to make sure nothing more was left out.

Rosalind turned back and cleared her throat. He was still focused on Hercules. "Well, to what do I owe the honor of a visit from you?"

Bob slowly faced Rosalind. "Give me the missing files."

"What files?" Rosalind clenched her left hand with her right to hide her shaking.

"I know the files were there when you entered the office. We have cameras throughout the building. What did you do with the files?" His gray eyes bore into her as she tried to resurrect her bravado.

"Many people go in and out of my office. Including the police. I wasn't the only one."

"You are the only one charged with Tony's murder." He edged closer and closer to her until their noses were only inches apart.

"Are you threatening me?" A surge of fear ran through her from head to toe. If only she was holding her phone. Why hadn't she thought to set it to record before he arrived? Rosalind slapped her thigh and Hercules ran to her barking aggressively, positioning himself between them, forcing Bob to back up.

"Whoa, Whoa, dog. Nothing going on here."

"Really? It doesn't feel that way to me. There's a lot going on here." She turned to Hercules and was grateful she had the best Doberman guard dog. "Good boy."

"The files are confidential. You know confidential files cannot be released without a warrant."

"Well, leaving the files on my desk was not wise, nor indicative that it was confidential."

"Anyone could have left the files. Why do you think I did it?"

"Not everyone has access to the office keys. You do. Theresa held the passkey to the vault. She didn't leave the files since she is dead. The person who left the files had to unlock my office since the files weren't slid under the door."

His eyes showed his only desire was to control everything. If only she had concrete proof that he killed Tony.

"Rosalind, your cooperation would have been appreciated. I was going to recommend that you come back to the office if you had provided me with what I needed, but given these current circumstances, you are still suspended from the office. And no visits after hours. The cameras would record you immediately."

Without giving it thought, Rosalind blurted out, "Are you here to suspend me for not having files you left on my desk?"

"You are jumping to irrelevant conclusions. However, losing those documents is grounds for dismissal."

Rosalind shook her head slowly. Of all of the issues with her employer these files had to be the least consequential item to impact the murder investigation. Unless she was looking at it from the wrong perspective. She glanced at Hercules back on his bed, eyes closed. "Okay, now I understand. You wanted this to happen. You wanted to have cause to dismiss me."

"Until the police investigation is complete, Kelco officially suspends you without pay."

Rosalind gasped. She was a great employee, loyal to all. Even Tony. The files were full of corporate secrets she never knew. How could she continue with an organization that had so many hidden surprises? She loved her work, but there was a limit. She breathed in deeply and exhaled.

"Let me make this easy for you, Bob, just like everything I have done for you since the day I started at Kelco. You don't want me in the office, you don't trust or believe me. In the meantime, I have a full-time job trying to clear my name in a murder investigation. I'm done with Kelco. I quit, Bob."

"That's quite a rash decision."

"Rash? This is the first logical thing I have done. The company does not support me through a murder investigation. You accuse me of stealing something you put on my desk. You are still supporting your dead star, Tony. And you were trying to find a convenient way to get rid of me. Well, you succeeded. And you can ask Audra to organize all the lunches, dinners, client meetings, and entertainment just like last Monday for Tony's customer meeting."

Bob's expression softened, but no apology came from his lips. He walked out the door. "I will pack up your belongings and have them delivered to you."

Her hand shook as she closed the door behind him. The balance of their relationship always leaned toward Bob's wants and needs. Yet, for the first time in years, she felt relief and exhaled her tension. Bob was entrenched in dubious management maneuvers that had gone awry. The Theresa Mars settlement, and whatever other money matters, was a web of intrigue Rosalind no longer wanted to think about.

Chapter Fifty-Three

Rosalind locked the door and walked to Hercules ready to give him a hug, more to comfort herself. He rested on his bed, and she noticed he breathed quite heavily and looked lethargic. She grabbed his bowl and filled it with his regular breakfast.

Despite the food she set next to him, Hercules stayed asleep, completely oblivious to her. She checked his ears, his nose, yet he was unresponsive. Then she noticed vomit laced in the crease of his bed. She stroked his back to comfort him.

"Hercules, this day just gets worse and worse. We're going to the vet immediately."

Frazzled, she picked up her phone trying to hold back tears.

"Aunt Ruth, something is wrong with Hercules. Can you help me get him to the vet? Can you drive us?"

"I'll be right there."

Ruth pulled her car as close to the wide-open door without treading on any plants.. As she entered the casita, Hamilton's vehicle stopped next to her car. Rosalind picked up two edges of Hercules' blanket and held tight to her purse as Ruth picked up the other two corners. They hoisted the blanket up and Rosalind crawled into the car guiding Hercules headfirst. Ruth held the tail end as Rosalind positioned Hercules gently onto the back seat. He groaned deeply. Rosalind bent to cradle his head, tears running down her cheeks.

Detective Hamilton stood next to Ruth glancing at Hercules. "This is not the playful Hercules I've seen before. Where are you heading?" He exchanged glances with Ruth.

"To his vet."

"I'll follow you." Hamilton pulled on his hat brim to shield his eyes from the sun.

* * *

He helped Rosalind and Ruth carry Hercules into the veterinary office. Once in the examination room, Rosalind wiped the tears away trying to compose herself. The technician took Hercules vitals and listened to Rosalind's account of his morning. "The doctor will be in as soon as possible."

Rosalind wrapped her arm around Hercules' back, willing him to awaken. They took turns scratching his head, and whispering to him as he laid still.

Hamilton looked toward the door which remained closed. "I realize this is not important now, but I was coming to your house to tell you who inherits Tony's estate."

Rosalind nuzzled Hercules' head. "Could his heir be the murderer?"

"It's unlikely, since she had no idea she was the main recipient of his estate."

Ruth and Rosalind exchanged glances. "Please don't keep us in suspense," said Ruth.

"Cassandra Starmer receives the apartment and some cash. The bulk of Tony's estate...his boat, his cabin, his portfolio, and his share of the nightclub goes to Antonia Tiffany Findley."

Rosalind gasped. "Tiffany? The blond woman at the Daily Planet?"

"She does live above the Daily Planet. Ernie, who owns the Daily Planet, is her uncle."

"She lived with Theresa?" asked Rosalind.

"Yes, she did. Tiffany is the daughter of Theresa Mars and Anthony Findley."

"What?" Rosalind shook her head in disbelief. Now Theresa's six-month parental leave made sense. Before she could ask for more details, Hamilton said, "I need to get back to the station. Please keep me posted on Hercules."

"Wait." Rosalind pulled the Kelco files out of her purse. "I have to confess I wasn't quite honest with you yesterday. These are the files Bob wants. I don't see how the files impact Tony's murder, but you can have them since I resigned from Kelco."

"Thank you, Rosalind." Hamilton opened the files paging through it slowly. "Is there anything else you haven't told me? By any chance, do you know Paulette Mason?"

"Funny you should ask. I got her phone number and address from Cassandra. She said Tony supported Paulette and her children. When I called the line was disconnected and her address is an empty lot. Is she involved?" Rosalind held Hercules paw in one hand and nuzzled his ear with the other.

Dead Reckoning

"She could be involved. I only have her description. Tall, sunglasses, a green jacket, black jeans with a floral scarf covering her hair. She visited Cassandra late Monday night."

"That description doesn't remind me of anyone. I can text you the contact info I have, maybe you will have better luck."

"Thank you, please send it. I have also been assigned to investigate the death of Leona Findley due to the timing and Ralph's history with Pamela Findley."

"Ralph had a quiet rage within. He didn't kill both Tony and his mother, did he?"

"I'm working through that case, not certain where it will lead. But there is bad news about Theresa Mars's death. We have reason to believe it was not suicide."

"What happened?"

"I'm not at liberty to say, but evidence points to murder."

"You know I didn't kill her, right?"

Hamilton smiled. "We are headed in another direction. It doesn't hurt for the murderer to think we are not chasing them directly. They might get sloppy." He tipped his hat to Ruth and Rosalind, then said, "Keep me posted on Hercules."

"Will do." Rosalind noticed quick eye contact between Aunt Ruth and Detective Hamilton. He walked out the door and nearly ran into the doctor.

After each apologized to the other, Dr. Barrett greeted them and checked Hercules' vitals. "What did he eat today?"

"He refused food today."

The doctor examined Hercules from head to toe. "He is so lethargic, If I hazarded a guess without further testing, I would say he ingested some type of poison."

"Poison?" said Rosalind and Ruth simultaneously. They looked at each other wide-eyed. Rosalind stretched her hand to Hercules side and steadied herself with her other hand on the examination table.

"His heart rate is abnormal, he is drooling, and you mentioned he vomited. He experienced some tremors while he was lying here, too, from what the technician told me."

Then Rosalind remembered that Bob had blocked her view of Hercules when they greeted him.

"It could be, perhaps, that a co-worker gave him a poisoned treat?" Rosalind realized she no longer should refer to Kelco employees as co-workers. "But I don't understand. If he did have a treat, could the treat have caused him to become this tired, this ill?"

"Depends on what it was."

She looked at Hercules half closed eyes. "What if it was oleander?"

"Oleander? There are blood tests we can run but the results take time. We need take immediate action. What makes you think oleander?"

"Just my instincts kicking in. But I would feel better if you treated him as if it were. I can't prove it, but it could be oleander."

"Based on his condition, we need to keep Hercules overnight. We will try to get him to pass what he ate and monitor his status for any changes. We will induce emesis, give charcoal to him to attempt to bind the poison for elimination, then administer IV fluids with an electrolyte solution for rehydration and cardiovascular support. We'll monitor his heartbeat and give him medication to improve the condition of his heart. We'll observe him for at least twenty-four hours."

"Overnight? Can I stay with him?" Rosalind ran her hand through her hair.

"I'm sorry, insurance coverage prohibits overnight stays except for employees and patients." Dr. Barrett looked into Hercules' eyes. "I understand your concern. We'll call you immediately with any updates. We'll move him to a bed, so he is more comfortable. I'll call you before I leave today. Our night staff will check in on him, at least once every hour."

"Can I visit him later this afternoon before you close?"

"He should rest. After twenty-four hours, we will see how he responds to the therapy. The next few hours are critical, so it is good you brought him in now. We want to do everything we can to help him beat this situation."

Dr. Barrett nodded to his assistant who returned with IV bags. "We will draw blood to determine if it is oleander poisoning, but we won't have the results for at least a week.

Rosalind shrugged as the tears fell. She looked toward Ruth who reached out to hug her tightly. After Ruth released the hug, Rosalind leaned over Hercules, touched his paw, kissed him good-bye, and

Dead Reckoning

headed toward the exit. At the threshold she turned and blew him a kiss, but he was unaware she was leaving. She looked toward the doctor and nodded. "Save him."

As she rode in the car with Aunt Ruth, she noticed a purple Lamborghini stopped behind them at the intersection. Rosalind texted Detective Hamilton: *Hercules terribly ill, Dr. thinks he was poisoned. Bob was at my place earlier; I fear he may have slipped him a treat with oleander. And I see a lot of purple Lamborghinis in traffic since I talked to Don Jansen.*

Chapter Fifty-Four

Once home, Rosalind needed her daily run more than ever. She locked the door behind her, jogged down the driveway, and took a right at the corner.

She looked up at the towering mesquite trees surrounding her. Issy always described the mesquite as the epitome of survival. The tree was composed of rough bark with shallow fissures, thick scales, and deep roots. Mesquites were desert survivors not easily damaged by disease or insects. She watched as the limbs of the drought resistant mesquite swayed in a soft breeze. The warm days shortened as the autumn equinox passed weeks ago. She prayed Hercules was a desert survivor, just like the mesquite.

On the lookout for purple Lamborghinis, she ran past the silver Jetta parked near her neighbor's driveway. She sprinted toward the parkway then headed south toward the Desert Botanical Gardens. Ahead on her right, the Papago Buttes jutted out of the earth reminding her of gigantic potatoes submerged halfway into the desert. Hercules loved this part of the run and Rosalind missed her companion. She said another affirmation for his good health making it the eleventh time today. Detective Hamilton hadn't responded to her text, but she hoped it gave him the backup to arrest Bob, or at least to make him spend twenty-four hours in jail.

She turned into the Garden's entrance. A visit with Issy would settle her mind. She owed Josh a phone call, too, since she needed to tell him she resigned. But she had to run off this nervous energy first.

As she hurried toward the greenhouse, a silver car drove into the parking lot. Guest services waved her through when she showed her volunteer badge. She ran to the greenhouse and threw the door open. "Issy, are you here?"

Rosalind heard some rustling of clay pots near the back of the greenhouse. Issy stood up holding two large planters, one in each hand. "Good morning Rosalind. No Hercules with you today?"

"Hercules is at the vet."

"What is wrong with him?"

After recapping her resignation and the vet visit, Rosalind held back tears again. Issy set the two planters on the rough wooden table. "I don't understand, how could anyone want to hurt that beautiful dog?"

"I know, I'm so upset. I ran to clear my head."

Dead Reckoning

Issy sat down on the stool closest to her. "Rosalind, you may have solved the case. If both Hercules and Tony Findley were poisoned, you had the prime suspect in your home this morning. But why hurt Hercules?"

"I have no idea. Another way to torture me?"

"Could someone be coming after you? Without Hercules by your side, you aren't defenseless, but you are an easier target without him."

"And Bob could have murdered Tony, and then pretended to arrive after I entered the building." Rosalind sat on one of the stools and ran her fingertips through a pile of soil on the table.

"By the way, your resignation has my full support."

"Thanks. I may need a job here." Rosalind laughed then sat back in her chair. "Remember those files I found on my desk? The first one detailed how Theresa embezzled money from Kelco and how it was settled with repayment, a six-month maternity leave, and a non-disclosure agreement. Detective Hamilton told me Tiffany Findley, the daughter of Tony and Theresa, inherits his estate. What I can't figure out is how Theresa kept her daughter hidden from so many people. Of course, maybe everyone was quiet for fear of losing their jobs. Maybe no one else knew."

"Geez, what was the second file?"

"The other file was another lawsuit where employees sued Kelco for contesting the Smithson sale to Tony."

"Two lawsuits? Both settled by contracts outside of the court of law. What else are they hiding?"

Rosalind traced designs with her fingertips through soil on the table. "Who knows? I'm not sure. After I resigned, a huge burden lifted. Simply knowing I wouldn't have to return to the office gave me an incredible sense of relief." Rosalind laughed softly.

"What happened to your hyena laugh?"

"Ha, I guess the hyena escaped, probably while being chased by a bear."

"Thank goodness." Issy wiped dirt off her apron. "The situation with the files reeks of a setup. I foresee their day of reckoning will be coming soon."

Rosalind nodded. "My thoughts exactly."

"Ok, before we go any further, I have two important thoughts."

"Shoot."

"What is Detective Hamilton doing with the files?"

"His staff is digging into the details. The information did involve Theresa, Tony, and Bob. But not in any way I anticipated."

"You need to sleep on it and ask for some answers. You got good direction before, it's worth trying."

"Ok, but first, I have to get the latest update on Hercules. What's your other thought?"

"I think you need to go through all of your interviews again and focus on only the people who do not have alibis."

"You're right, like Bob, Ralph, Pamela…"

"And me." Issy laughed.

Chapter Fifty-Five

The wind in her hair and the beauty of the open sky were the best therapies for which Rosalind could ask. Before she reached the Zen garden, a silver car edged out of the parking lot.

Rosalind was on foot. It looked like the same car that arrived when she did. Issy's comments echoed in her mind. She didn't want to be followed by anyone and maybe the silver car was just a coincidence. Aunt Ruth left for work after getting back from the veterinary office and was out of town until the next day. She could run back to Issy, but if it were a threat, she didn't want to jeopardize Issy, too.

Rosalind reversed her direction and headed back into the gardens. She ran on unpaved stretches that would not allow vehicles. If she headed south, she could lose the silver car, then she could wrap around Papago Park and run through the neighborhoods to get back home.

The terrain was an open desert with cacti, teddy chollas and notwithstanding the metropolitan area, coyotes. Not that the coyotes would bother with her. She hoped.

She pulled out her phone. She had one bar of coverage. The connection was slow, but it finally started to ring.

"Hello?" said Josh.

"I'm so sorry to bother you at work. I might be losing my mind, but I think I'm being followed. It feels strange, like I could be in danger."

"Where are you?"

"Walking to Ramada 8 in Papago Park. Can you pick me up in like fifteen minutes?"

"Sure. I will get there as soon as I can. Just try to stay out of sight until you see me."

"Thank you." As she hung up the phone, she jogged further south. She looked ahead and saw the Hole in the Rock. Today is a good day for a climb.

Chapter Fifty-Six

Rosalind stopped at the opening of the Hole in the Rock, and she savored the view of the valley from over two hundred feet above the earth. The palm trees, the beautiful, clear lakes, and the Foothills mountains in the distance gave Rosalind a sense of peace and serenity. She clung to that feeling. She eyed traffic passing on the parkway, travelers who were oblivious to her dilemma. She didn't see the silver car from the garden parking lot. But there were lots of silver cars. She wished she had looked closer for the make and model, but it was too late now.

Josh's car would approach from the south. As she peered through the oblong opening, she was happy to be hidden from view. She noticed a police vehicle heading north and wondered if it was Enders or Makowski. She glanced at her phone. The battery showed less than half a bar. She dialed his number as she heard a jet overhead and when she looked back at her phone, there was no service.

Did she just see the same silver car head south on the parkway? It might have been her imagination, but Rosalind hoped that it was not the same car. All cars approaching this butte would enter from the south. Rosalind watched every vehicle and hiker. Come on, Josh, she thought. Now would be a perfect time to get here. She imagined Josh being delayed with questions before he could gracefully leave the office. After the jet descended near the airport, she dialed Detective Hamilton's number again.

When she heard steps behind her, she assumed it would be more hikers heading up for a view from the Hole. She was wrong.

"Hello, Rosalind," said a familiar voice. "Didn't you think I had the strength to run along with you?"

Rosalind turned slowly around to face her stalker. The sunlight shone directly into her eyes. For the first time in a long time, pieces started to fall into place. The tall woman wore sunglasses, a green jacket, black gloves, and black jeans with a floral scarf covering her hair.

"What brings you to the Hole in the Rock today?" Rosalind slid her phone into her pocket hoping it might connect.

"Ha, funny. Don't you think I know you have poked around in too many places to not have figured it out?"

"Figured out what?"

Dead Reckoning

"Figured out that it is time for you to jump from this rock due to your sorrow at the two murders you committed."

"What?"

"You heard me. It would be an appropriate conclusion to wrap up Theresa and Tony's murders by having the nice girl Rosalind take her own life by jumping out the hole and onto the desert floor. Of course, after having written a sweet, all confessing suicide note for the police to find in her pocket."

Rosalind stalled. She was furious she hadn't considered Audra a suspect. "I am not writing a note."

"You won't have to. It is already written. That's why it took me a few minutes to get here. Once I saw you back track into the gardens instead of heading home, it was just as easy for me to run behind you. So, you die here. Instead of at home with a gunshot wound to the head. Makes no difference to me. This is a bit more public, so it's good I brought the silencer. Traffic on the trail is quiet today. Good timing for me."

"This story may sound like the way out for you. I don't think you understand the karma and horrendous future you will have trying to live with yourself after killing three people."

Audra's head tilted back, and she laughed so hard, Rosalind thought she could run past her and escape. Of course, Audra had longer, stronger legs combined with great stamina and, unfortunately, Audra would catch her quickly. So, Rosalind stayed in the same spot to consider her options.

"Living with Tony making commissions off my creative campaigns would be a horrendous future. He stole every ounce of life from my career, leaving me the table scraps to fend for myself. He deserved to die."

"How did you get him to ingest the oleander?"

"Ah, that was the easiest part. Tony leaves his insulin kit unattended. It was just a matter of watching and waiting until he left his desk for lunch. He's always gone for at least an hour giving me plenty of time for a few days of poison to be injected straight in his veins. Since I arranged his customer lunch in the office on Monday, slipping fresh oleander leaves into his salad went completely unnoticed. The bitter taste was drowned out with his request for massive amounts of dressing. That's what he gets for having us order the food."

"You killed him for the commission money?" The wind whined as it rushed past Rosalind's ears.

"Primarily, but like you, I had endured years of tirades and abuse. The money and the frustration of collaborating with him was inexcusable. And Kelco didn't care. It finally overwhelmed me. I never stood up to him as you did, which made it that much easier to pin the murder on you."

Rosalind sighed. How did she miss this side of Audra? Desperation clawed inside her and realized that Josh was delayed or wasn't coming. She was alone, scared, and needed to stall for time to figure a way out.

"But how did you lure Tony to the office? And how did you get the kiss imprint from Cassandra?"

"Ha, you know Tony. It was like another conquest for him. While he partied at the nightclub I visited Cassandra and borrowed their kiss imprint. When I texted him to meet me at the office to create a surprise for Cassandra, he was game. He was already feeling queasy, and he was like play doh in my hands. He would do anything to keep Cassandra by his side and I convinced him this was exactly the type of prank his fiancé would adore. She is quite a few years younger than Tony and he wanted to keep up with her at all costs."

"Are you Paulette Mason, the single woman Tony sent money to?"

"You mean my alter ego, Paulette. It was a way Tony could direct small funds to me without raising anyone's suspicion." Audra smiled.

"But why Theresa?"

"Frankly I wanted to put her out of her misery, she was so lost without him. I didn't want her to uncover my scheme, so it was easier to eliminate her. I told her you had a vision board about Tony, and it was easy enough to plant it in your casita when you were in Sedona. She happily informed the police about it, and it turns out she had one of her own. There were too many contradictions from her stories to the police. It was easier to get rid of the noise." Audra pushed her hand into her pocket as if she hid a gun.

"And you broke my window to gain access to my home? You planted the vision board and oleander and you purposely damaged that beautiful tree."

"Of course, easy enough to do with the storm blazing through the Valley. Anyway, enough chitter chatter." Audra pulled a gun out of her pocket and pointed it at Rosalind. "And put this suicide note in your pocket." She held out a piece of white paper. "Don't think I won't shoot you dead. Take this note. I need your fingerprints on it." Audra held the gun steady, and her long arm reached out with the note to Rosalind who took it and slid it in her pocket.

"Ok, move to the edge now. Then you need to take your final swan dive right into the Sonoran Desert."

Rosalind searched the cliff in front of her seeking any way out. If she charged, they'd both end up going over the side. Could she survive the fall? Unlikely. Maybe death was the answer to get her out of this situation. Rosalind's knees wobbled. She prayed and requested a most benevolent outcome for this jump.

Before terror won out, Rosalind turned and rather than jumping out face forward, she turned toward Audra and dropped to the ground. She would try to grab onto any edge, limb, or rock on her way down. She stretched out her right leg, bent her left leg and slid right foot first down the butte.

The rocks scraped her hands and face as she grasped along the stone without finding anything to hang on to. She felt her hands bleed. She squeezed her eyes shut into the darkness wondering about Josh. She heard Audra yell, "No!"

Rosalind slid down against the earth, her hands clenched trying to catch an edge. She slipped a few more yards, then her foot hit a small extension. Her weight dragged her past it.

Still she saw the edge and she stretched out her hand to the potential lifeline. She caught it with her right hand and then clasped both hands around the miniature spire. She clung to it for a moment before she realized her feet dangled away from the rock. Rosalind glanced down to see a good portion of her legs had passed beyond a wide crevice opening in the rock.

Rosalind tried not to look down. She breathed in and exhaled slowly. She wondered if she could swing into and hide in the crevice. She focused her energy to swing her legs toward the gap and then slightly back out to gain momentum like a pendulum. Back and forth she moved until her hands started to slip.

This is it she thought. She took in one big breath, rocked back and forth toward the opening, and flung herself toward the fissure. As her feet lifted, she curled as tight as possible then she half back somersaulted into the gap.

She hit the floor of the opening with a loud thud and hoped Audra would think Rosalind plummeted to the earth. Pain coursed through every bone and muscle in her body. It hurt now, but she knew the real pain would be felt tomorrow, if she lived that long.

"I saw that move, Rosalind!" she heard Audra shout from above. "This isn't done yet."

Rosalind ached but crawled deep into the opening. She looked at her torn skin, the blood on her hands, and her ripped clothes. She huddled back as far as she could in the crevice.

The view from the opening was not as wide as the vantage point from atop the Hole in the Rock. Rosalind watched the cars rolling past on the parkway, still hoping Josh's car would come into view. She silently prayed for help from anyone.

As she remained still, she discovered the walls were covered in petroglyphs likely from hundreds to more than seven thousand years ago. As Rosalind caught her breath, she saw deer, turtles, and a kokopelli. In the center of the artwork, she saw a huge bear and bear paw print with a magnificent star overhead. She traced the outline with her fingertip, blinking a few times to confirm what she saw.

She pulled back when she heard a rustling from a rock near her foot where the crack was only a foot high. She turned to see a triangular head with dark diagonal lines from the eyes to the jaw poking out behind the rock. A soft rattle confirmed her fear. It was a diamondback rattlesnake. Her breath caught in her throat. She had never seen one this close. She swallowed the panic ready to overtake her.

The creature glided between the rocks showing off its black and gray diamond pattern which Rosalind estimated at five feet long. She breathed in and out trying to control her reaction as she backstepped gently hoping the snake would find the path to her left more attractive. Adrenaline electrified her, but she had nowhere to run so she tried to control her breath and hoped that would control her body. When she had a few feet of clearance, she grabbed her phone to check if Detective Hamilton answered.

"I doubt you have cell service here."

Dead Reckoning

Rosalind jumped at Audra's voice and dropped her phone.

"I knew one day my rock-climbing experience would come in handy. Why slide down when you can simply climb right up." Audra aimed the handgun directly at Rosalind.

"You don't want to be here, Audra. It's not safe."

"Don't you mean you don't want to be here because you are not safe? Once I shoot you, you won't be found for weeks, months, even years. Who would look for you here? But when you are found, a hundred years from now, the suicide note will be with you."

Rosalind backed up, tilting her head to avoid hitting the top of the opening. She checked the whereabouts of the snake before each step. She figured a snake bite could give her a chance to survive where a gunshot wound to the head would not. She sidestepped closer and closer to the rock until she was next to it.

"Stop moving. And don't bother to try to wrestle the gun from me. I will shoot you and no one will hear the shot with this silencer."

Audra walked closer and closer and when she was within a foot, Rosalind ducked behind the rock, grabbed the middle of the snake, and threw it at Audra's face. Rosalind fell on her side behind the rock. Audra, caught off guard, fell back screaming as the snake hit her. At the same time her finger pressed on the gun's trigger releasing the bullet. The bullet ricocheted off the ceiling and straight down into Rosalind's left leg.

Rosalind screamed in pain, edging away from Audra who fell flat on her back as she wrestled with the snake that continued to bite her. Rosalind saw the gun land on the ground, and she lunged toward it dragging her wounded left leg which felt like it was on fire. As she reached the gun, Rosalind heard sirens and for the first time she hoped that Detective Hamilton was on his way. She grabbed the gun then slid it under her body. Her pain was excruciating, the worst she had ever felt. As she looked toward Audra still juggling the snake, she saw the hazy image of a man walking toward her. She didn't recognize him, but he looked familiar. As her head landed on her outstretched arm, she heard a man scream her name. Was it Hamilton? Josh? Christoph Schmidt? The voice echoed in her ears until the fire surging in her leg caused her to slip into unconsciousness.

Chapter Fifty-Seven, Mariental

Christoph returned home after walking Kristina and Johann to the Wächter's house to spend the evening. He stood near the entrance not knowing if he should go in or stay out. There wasn't much room for the three women who hovered around Anna Barbara while they tried to keep her comfortable. As Christoph waited, he overheard Anna Barbara say between breaths, "Maria, if anything happens to me, you must take care of my children." Anna Barbara stopped to catch her breath between contractions, then she whispered, "And Christoph."

"Shush now, you have a baby to deliver, save your energy for this babe."

Anna Barbara clung tight to Maria's sleeve. "Maria, you must promise me."

Maria was startled by the fierceness in Anna Barbara's grip as her hand pulled Maria back. Maria looked at the desperation in Anna Barbara's eyes. "Of course. I will do whatever is necessary to care for your family. But you are going to be fine, I feel it in my bones."

Maria held Anna Barbara's hand and sat on the ground next to her where she lay on blankets provided from all the ladies' households. "And you must promise me when my time comes, you will do the same. My child will be alone in the world if I am not here. Promise me, sister?"

Anna Barbara immediately nodded. "Yes, of course. You are part of our family as your child will be."

Christoph walked to distance himself from the commotion. Joseph Wächter came up behind him. "Come with me. Let the women tend to your wife. You will only get in their way."

Christoph was grateful for the distraction. Joseph handed him paper and loose tobacco and both men started to roll cigars. They walked through the high grasses surrounding the mud houses, which were hastily dug within weeks of their arrival. They carefully rolled the paper around the tobacco. Joseph reached into his pocket for his tinderbox, pulled out the flint, struck it against the metal, and lit the tinder. Next, he lit a small candle, then held the flame to Christoph's cigar as he inhaled deeply. The cigar lit. Joseph followed the same procedure until he breathed in the smoke of the cigar. He doused the flame in the tinderbox. They walked slowly, circling around the twenty mud houses that made up their community. The early evening was calm outside, in contrast to the frenzy of activity surrounding his wife indoors.

Joseph motioned back to the house, cigar in his hand. "It is good Maria Schumacher is with child, too. It provides distraction from the loss of her husband."

"Yes. She is grateful it proves she is a viable wife for another husband. It will help her survive here."

"And do you still think my son is that man?"

"He is the only single man of marrying age. Is there any other?"

"Not one I know. He would rather wait a few years for your daughter Kristina's hand. Has Kristina mentioned Henry at all?"

"Kristina is quiet around me, but I will ask her mother once the affairs of the day are settled. I realize the age gap between Henry and Maria could be difficult."

"It is not always easy for a man to accept another man's child as his own. Even with the best intentions it can be difficult," said Joseph.

"Are you familiar with such a situation?"

"Not personally, however I have seen other families, some work out well, others do not."

"What makes the difference between working well or not?" They passed the planted fields which they prayed would provide a harvest this year.

"It is not easy to say, but from what I have seen it is the heart of the man, his wishes for all his children whether they are of his seed or not. That makes the difference."

They circled the community a few more times then sat down in the center of the village around the fire pit where colonists gathered to discuss town matters. A hawk glided through the air looking for dinner but not finding anything worthwhile it headed south. The grasses bent their seeded tops as the wind caressed each blade. The sounds of each stalk brushing against its neighbor was the only noises they heard. Except for the occasional scurry and muffles from the Schmidt's mud house.

They sat in silence for a few hours. Christoph tried to keep his nerves calm, but he was worried for Anna Barbara. He considered the long journey, the rolling sea, the bumpy travels overland and now this grassy meadow where they were trying to build a home and a family together. He could hardly imagine his luck at drawing her for his wife, the two ending up in line across from each other at exactly the right time. Was it fate? Was it pre-destined? Christoph did not care. He wanted his wife's childbirth to be over and for her to be back in his arms where he would protect her always.

A few hours later, when both men were nearly dozing, a shout erupted from the Schmidt house. Was it a happy shout or a sad shout? As Christoph sprang to his feet and ran toward the house, Maria met him at the front door. "Give us a couple minutes to clean up in here. I will call you when your wife and child are ready to see you."

"My wife and child." Christoph couldn't contain the joy inside of him. He wanted to jump, he wanted to run, he wanted to embrace his entire family now. His family. In his home. Less than a year ago, he was alone and bitter toward starting over, but now he was in a new land, with a beautiful wife and a new child. This child was the best thing that had happened since they arrived in Mariental.

Maria, Katharina, and Magdalena left the mud house, their arms filled with blankets for cleaning. Christoph laid next to Anna Barbara on a new set of clean blankets. Anna Barbara dozed on and off with the child, only minutes old, in her arms, a boy they named Georg Johannes. Christoph knew he was home now.

* * *

Four months later the cold forced the families inside their huts for all but a few hours each day. Christoph was grateful for the potatoes and dried fruit they had stored. Anna Barbara wrapped Georg in blankets. If Anna Barbara had food, Georg had food. Johann and Kristina played on the floor.

Maria sat in her chair, afraid to move. The child inside her who had been so active had felt quiet the past few hours and she felt an ache from her stomach to her knees, unlike anything she had experienced before. As Anna Barbara boiled the potatoes, Christoph noticed Maria looking pale. He walked to her and sat down.

"Maria, how are you?"

"Weary. I am close to my time."

"Should I send the children to the Wächter's house? You look like you need to take to bed."

"That might be wise."

Christoph walked to Anna Barbara. "We need to go to the Wächter's house now for dinner. I will bring the meal. We will eat there."

Everyone bundled up in layers of garments, leaving Christoph and Maria behind them. Christoph assisted Maria to the blankets and helped her lay down gently. Maria groaned in pain.

"You should have said something sooner."

"As always, you are right. There is much I should have said sooner but I was afraid of my husband and of being alone. Now I am afraid for my child."

"Maria, you will be fine. We will support you."

"I am afraid for my child's future, but I must tell you what I should have told you many months ago. Martin was an evil man; he was not kind like you, and he humiliated me whenever he could. It broke me, Christoph, and I let you take the blame. You see, I am the one who killed Martin. I could not bear another minute around him, pretending to be the humble wife. He was rude and arrogant, and you know he wanted Anna Barbara. I could not let that happen."

"You killed Martin?"

"Yes, and I have to confess it now in case I do not make it through this ordeal. I cannot go to my grave without confessing. Can you please listen to my story before Anna Barbara returns?"

Christoph nodded and reached out to hold Maria's hand. She continued. "Thank you. I went on deck unnoticed after you and Martin. I left my blankets wrapped so it looked like I was asleep. I hid until you went below deck. I was so appalled, but I couldn't let him know I overheard him talk about Anna Barbara. I pretended to come up the stairs after you left. He was upset and he yelled at me that I was not worthy to be his wife. I tried to placate him by asking if I could admire his knife. As you know it was his pride and joy. It soothed his ego a bit and he handed it to me. I flattered him, admired it, and did everything I could to calm him. He suddenly turned against me and asked me if I could swim. He walked closer and closer to me as he backed me up to the deck railing. He definitely wanted me gone and he picked me up to toss me overboard."

Maria paused to breathe through the pain until it subsided. "I knew I was with child at that point, and I wanted the child and me to live. I hadn't planned to kill him, but I knew I had to act. I was enraged at him, and the will to survive gave me strength I never knew I had. I used his knife to strike out wildly at him, again and again and again until he lay still on the deck. I dropped the knife and ran." Maria sobbed. "Christoph, I am so sorry they accused you. I told Hertzinger they could not issue a sentence without letting me know. When we disembarked from the ship, I thought they were letting you disembark, too, because Hertzinger did not tell me otherwise. I would have confessed to save you, but I missed my chance."

"Oh, Maria, I would have stayed in that cell to save you from that fate. I am sorry you had to be that man's wife."

"Christoph, from the moment we stood in line until the last breath Martin took, I understood that man." She paused as a contraction took all her concentration. "I have never said these words before, but he was petty, self-centered, and he cheated at cards. He had two decks. I don't know how he did it, but he always had the cards in his favor."

The door opened and Anna Barbara and the women who were to help Maria came in carrying more blankets. The same women who helped Anna Barbara were prepared to help again. Maria and Christoph nodded to each other. They would never speak of this again.

"Ladies, I will go to the Wächter's house. Please let us know as soon as you have news." Christoph turned to wave at Maria and nodded to her for the last time.

* * *

Tears streamed down Anna Barbara's face as she caressed a baby girl in her arms. She had promised Maria. Now she needed to convince Christoph to have two babies, neither of which were sired by him, in his house. The women departed a few minutes ago to alert Christoph he could return home. They did everything they could. Maria gave her all to ensure her child survived. She never held her daughter in her arms.

Christoph opened the door seeing his wife in the rocking chair he had built. The women had cleaned the room as best they could. They wrapped the blankets for washing. They laid out Maria with her hands over her heart, finally at peace.

Dead Reckoning

He walked to Anna Barbara wrapping his arms around her and the baby. "Anna Barbara, you have been through so much tonight. The children are staying at the Wächters."

Anna Barbara looked into his eyes. "She's a little girl, Christoph. I …I promised…" But she sobbed and could not continue.

"We will raise Maria's daughter. She was a good friend and like a sister to you. What is one more child in our home? I am sure Maria would have wanted us to raise her child and tell this little girl how wonderful her mother was."

Anna Barbara loved Christoph before but in this moment, love overflowed in her heart. "Thank you, Christoph, thank you. And I would like to name her Maria."

"Welcome, Maria." Christoph pulled aside the blanket to see his newly adopted daughter's face for the first time.

Part Four

"When we heal ourselves, we heal the past, the present, and the future."
Dr. Steven D. Farmer

Chapter Fifty-Eight, Arizona, October 2014

Rosalind awoke with her body aching from the crown of her head to the tip of her toes. She tried to remember what happened at the Hole in the Rock but the dream vision of Anna Barbara holding a baby girl tugged at her heart. And she kept seeing snakes around her. Even her eyelids hurt as she opened them, trying to gain her bearings and determine her surroundings. The aroma was antiseptic. Her left leg was elevated as was her right arm. An IV was streaming fluids into her left arm. She glanced around a room she did not recognize then turned when she heard a familiar voice.

"I was so worried about you," said Josh as he reached out and took her hand in his.

"Not worried enough to reach me before I was nearly killed." Rosalind pulled her hand away and turned to the other side of the bed.

"By the time I got to Papago Park, I heard a gunshot and couldn't see you at all. I was so frantic on the drive there, I ran a red light and hit another vehicle. I couldn't leave the scene of the accident. I'm so sorry." He walked to the other side of the bed. "I called your phone three times then remembered your battery was dying. I called Detective Hamilton for help. He arrived before me. I stood next to you as the EMTs were carrying you into the ambulance. I followed behind and have been next to you ever since."

Rosalind wanted to believe him. But she was still upset that he had not arrived sooner. Treading carefully, she said, "How long have you been here?"

"Since you arrived." He pushed closer to the edge of the chair. "How are you feeling? How is your leg?"

"My whole body is in pain, but my left leg is on fire." Rosalind looked at bandages wrapped around the bullet wound. "What did they do to my leg?"

"They removed the bullet and stitched up the wound. No vital nerves were damaged, but the bullet did hit the femur right below your knee, hence the cast on your leg. The bone isn't completely split, but you will need to take it slow. I bet they will get you walking today."

"Yay, more pain to look forward to." Rosalind laid her head back on the pillow. After a few minutes she remembered the snake. "What happened to the snake I threw at Audra?"

Before Josh could answer, Detective Hamilton walked into the hospital room.

"How are you feeling, Rosalind?"

"I've had better days. Can't say being in a hospital bed is my idea of a fun time."

"Well, to answer the question you asked before I walked in, the snake also has seen better days as it didn't survive. Audra, on the other hand, did survive with bites. She has chosen to remain silent for now, and she is recovering in the hospital, too. She will visit jail as soon as she is medically released."

"She did it all, Detective. She told me how she used Tony's diabetic kit to feed him the oleander poison and she added oleander to his salad on Monday. No wonder Tony wasn't feeling well. She also killed Theresa because she was getting close to the truth."

"Yes, we suspected her. And thank goodness you called me when you did. We heard her confess to you and we recorded most of it. We were on our way just moments before Josh called us. He told us your exact location. It helped us find you faster."

Rosalind finally relaxed as she realized Josh had helped her.

Hamilton continued. "We had suspected her when found Tony's diabetic kit with Audra's fingerprints in the trash at Kelco. At Audra's apartment we found some photos of you that Audra took from Theresa's apartment. Not certain how she was going to use it, but it was there."

Hamilton handed the photograph of Rosalind and Tony to her. She flipped it over. Again, there was no documentation on it. "Oh my, did everyone have a copy of this picture except me? Theresa must have followed us and taken the photo."

"From what we gather, Theresa and Tony had an on again off again relationship despite his two marriages. They were business partners, and she was one of the original investors in the nightclub. She carried a torch for him all these years and raised his daughter alone. Now that she and Tony are gone, their assets belong to Tiffany." Hamilton sat in the other open chair.

"Tiffany?" asked Josh.

Hamilton nodded. "Antonia Tiffany Mars is the daughter of Tony and Theresa, the one who required Theresa's parental leave twenty-five years ago. Theresa and Tony accepted the contract with Bob and

Dead Reckoning

the payment terms to cover up Bob's misuse of funds in exchange for the extended leave. Theresa never admitted guilt, but she was loyal to Bob and Tony. She didn't want the Kelco management team to discover Bob's indiscretion, so she agreed to these terms. Bob repaid the funds, and the contract gave him the leverage he needed to keep his job. He finally admitted all to us when we questioned him again with the files you gave us."

"Whoa, is Tiffany the blond woman at the Daily Planet?" asked Josh.

Rosalind smiled through the pain. "Yes. Since Ernie was Theresa's brother, that also makes him Tiffany's uncle. Tiffany lived with her mother, and Ernie helped Theresa raise her child. It was only natural for her to be at the Daily Planet. It was home for her."

"It's a small world of invisible relationships in this case," said Hamilton. "Also, Leona Findley's death was of natural causes, so it is no longer a murder investigation. Just wanted to make sure you were on the road to recovery. Of course, all charges against you have been dropped. Thank you for your help in leading us to Audra."

Hamilton turned to head out the door but circled back. "I hope you get out of here soon. When will your aunt be back in town? Will she be able to help you?"

Rosalind checked the time on her phone on the nightstand, where Josh had plugged it in to charge. "I can't believe I have been here a whole day. She should arrive home in the next few hours."

"Good, she can help you when you are discharged. I'll check back with you after you are released."

"Thank you," Josh and Rosalind said at the same time as Detective Hamilton left the room, his heels clicking against the floor and echoing until he reached the elevator.

As she started to lay her head back on the pillow, she jerked upright. "Hercules. I need to call the vet about Hercules." When she saw two missed calls from Dr. Barrett, a shiver of fear shot down her spine.

***

Two days later Rosalind sat at her kitchen table. Her left leg propped up on a chair, her crutches leaned against the wall behind her.

Tchaikovsky's *The Queen of Spades* filled the room with its familiar crescendos and rhythms.

Next to her in the softest dog bed she owned, Hercules snored softly as he rested. Dr. Barrett confirmed he suffered from oleander poisoning and now both Rosalind and Hercules were sidelined from their daily run for at least a few more weeks as they mended.

The once vacant walls were now filled with framed family photographs, key census records, and a 1941 map of Mariental. On the opposite wall Native American art petroglyphs of a large bear, a bear paw print and the Polaris star took center stage. Photos also covered the table as she tried to perfect the chronological timeline of scenes from the 1950s.

Next to the photographs were three different census records for Mariental. From these lists she hoped to connect her grandfather all the way back to Christoph Schmidt. Depending on the timing of the census, she did not know what she would uncover, but she was optimistic about getting her family tree linked through more generations. She appreciated the freedom she now had to organize her historical pictures and make sense of how her family moved from the Germanic states to Russia and over a hundred years later to the Americas.

She opened her laptop and saw a new email from Margaret.

Dear Rosalind,
No need to apologize for missing lunch. Solving a murder comes first as does your recuperation. Will next week Wednesday work for you?

As far as one of your ancestors being accused of a crime, I'm not aware of any society lists that would help. There could be records on the ship Ursa Major, or on the Hanseatic League, and captain logs might give you the background you seek. I recommend using Google to search for these. I will keep my eyes open for any new discoveries and try to locate Kristina and Johann Kälberin Schmidt.

I encourage you to consider attending the society's convention next summer. The convention gathers descendants of many German Russian families, and the sessions are great opportunities to learn about every

Dead Reckoning

generation of German Russian history. It is great to link up with relatives you may not know you have and discover more of your ancestors' history.
Good luck on your search.

Sincerely, Margaret

Rosalind sighed. So much information and so many angles to consider for future research. Hopefully, Josh or Ruth would be able to drive her to the luncheon with Margaret since her leg injury prohibited her from driving. She emailed Margaret that their lunch meeting was on and made a note to call her later.

She decided to try out the search her friend recommended, typing out Ursa Major + Captain Van Doorn + Baltic Sea. As she glanced at the hits, she saw the name Captain Van Doorn, the commander of the Ursa Major. Rosalind clicked on the Wikipedia link and read:

Captain Galin Van Doorn, (1724-1767) commander of the Ursa Major for all its journeys, was a respected sailor of his day. Despite numerous successful travels, Van Doorn went down with his ship during a nasty storm in 1767 in the Baltic Sea.

Captain Van Doorn was a real captain. Despite his sad demise, she was ecstatic to confirm that at least a part of her visions were true. A warm energy filled her chest as awe and happiness overwhelmed her spirit. She believed now that all her insights were true, and she simply needed more time to find confirming documentation. She would follow up if any of his logs survived. Perhaps she could discover if First Mate Hertzinger was with Van Doorn at the end. Her heart craved confirmation of the past but before she could read further, a knock at the door interrupted her search.

"Come in," Rosalind called as Aunt Ruth opened the door carrying a tray filled with covered plates and glasses of orange juice.

"Ready for breakfast?" asked Aunt Ruth.

"Yes, thank you, but you have to stop pampering me. I need to start to do things for myself."

"You can go to the bathroom by yourself, feed Hercules, and keep your leg elevated just as you are. I only pamper you when I'm here, and I'm only off work a couple more days. Rest is what you need. I'm so happy that you are not going back to work at Kelco that I made your favorite breakfast, eggs benedict."

"It smells divine." Rosalind stored the photos into the archive safe boxes and moved the census records to an empty chair. As Ruth slid the tray on the table, removed the plate lids, set the juice and plates on the table, Hercules woke, sniffing the aroma of fresh food.

"I didn't forget you, Hercules. Here's a special treat for you." Ruth placed a bowl with turkey bacon treats next to Hercules. He devoured them as Rosalind picked up her fork.

They dined as the music soared around them savoring every morsel of food that Ruth prepared. The hollandaise sauce created from scratch, the eggs poached to perfection, Canadian bacon sauteed in light oil with a side of broccoli.

"I'm enjoying the hollandaise sauce on the broccoli, too." Rosalind scooped the final bite dipping it in the sauce.

"Thank you, it did turn out rather well. Oh, I nearly forgot, here is the package I picked up from James Simon with his full analysis of the knife. He said he cleaned it without damaging it. His team estimates the knife is two hundred and fifty years old. His certificate of authentication is attached."

"Wow, that's remarkable. The knife matches the timeline and could have been given to Johann Kälberin Schmidt. I can't prove what I saw, but it gives me hope that I will find more documentation to authenticate my stories."

"All in good time," said Ruth. "What are you doing the rest of the day?"

"This morning I'm taking it slow. I invited Josh over this afternoon to talk. There isn't much more Hercules and I are up for." Rosalind laughed.

"I'm delighted to hear it."

"What are your plans for this gorgeous fall day?"

"Nothing much, going to the Botanical Gardens for a walk with James."

"With James? The antique dealer? Your social life is certainly busy between James and Max."

"And why not? Some good has to come out of you being charged with murder. I met two interesting men."

"Would you consider marriage again?"

"Posh. Marriage, me? Why would I consider marriage? And, seriously, Rosalind, me with a police officer? I couldn't deal with the stress of being his significant other."

"I have seen you with him and I know you like him, detective or not."

"James and I are going for a walk today. Max and I have dinner later this week. I can spend a nice afternoon and evening with two attractive men, especially now that you are no longer a murder suspect, correct?"

"Correct. I wish you the best on your walk in the park."

Ruth loaded the empty dishes onto the tray and walked toward the door. As she grabbed the doorknob, someone knocked. Ruth swung the entry open, and Tiffany jumped back. "Did you see me coming? I never had anyone answer the door that fast."

"I was on my way out."

"I'm looking for Rosalind. Is she here?"

Ruth moved back allowing Tiffany to see into the casita.

"Rosalind, I hope you don't mind the intrusion. We met at the Lantern Escapade."

"I remember. Aunt Ruth, stay for a few more minutes?" Rosalind motioned Tiffany to sit at the kitchen table and introduced Ruth to Tiffany. "What brings you here?"

"I came to apologize for my mother's accusations. I wished she hadn't put you through that tirade at my Dad's funeral. She desperately missed him, and she lashed out at you. I know it doesn't make sense, but she was lost without him. His marriages did not destroy her like his death did. She dealt with the infidelity as long as she was part of his life. She believed he would always return to her." Tiffany stopped to catch her breath. "I'm sorry to run on like this, I just had to get it all out before I changed my mind and ran away. It's difficult to talk about."

"Of course, it's difficult. You lost two parents and your grandmother in a few weeks. You are brave to visit me, and I appreciate it. How are you holding up?"

Tiffany shook her head from side to side. "It's been difficult for me. I had two unusual parents with vast commercial interests. I have a lot to figure out. Between my mother's estate and my father's interests, I need to determine if I sell it, keep it, turn it over to management, or something completely different. Lots of pending decisions. Uncle

Ernie thinks one way and Don Jansen thinks another. And my Uncle Ralph, who I met for the first time at the funeral, sees other opportunities. The money is good to have, but how do I manage it? I have no idea whose recommendations I should follow."

Aunt Ruth coughed. "Sounds like you need an objective financial advisor who does not have a vested interest in the outcome. I could suggest a few good ones."

"That's a great idea, I know everyone means well but I really don't know what I'm doing."

Ruth pulled out her phone, checked for two contacts and air dropped the info to Tiffany, who smiled as she accepted it.

Rosalind saved Tiffany's phone number in her contacts. "I'm texting you my number, too. I also lost my parents at an early age. If you ever need to talk to someone, you can call me."

"Thank you, both, for listening. I need to head out and continue my soul searching. To help me do that, I have planned a vacation."

"Where are you going?" asked Rosalind.

"I always dreamed of going on an Alaskan cruise. I leave in a few days, so I need to start packing. I invited Cassandra to join me, so I won't be alone."

"Have a wonderful time. Enjoy your travels."

"Thank you, Rosalind."

As Tiffany left the casita. Rosalind and Ruth looked at each other. Rosalind said, "I know how she feels, thank goodness you gave her good options."

"Yes, I hope she investigates in depth before she lets love capture her heart and get herself into a whirlwind of trouble."

Rosalind looked at her aunt sheepishly. "I know, I didn't listen, it wasn't my strong suit at that time. But she is a bit older than I was. I bet she will do better."

"True. And in the end, I succeeded. You are here with me. That's all that matters."

"You have been my sanity through all of this. How can I ever thank you?"

"You need to be happy, and I think this friend of yours, Josh, is part of the key to it, don't you?"

Rosalind grinned. "Time will tell." Ruth hugged Rosalind goodbye.

Dead Reckoning

***

After finishing her genealogy work for the morning, Rosalind got an email that made her breath catch in her throat. She called Aunt Ruth. "Come here now, it's urgent!"

Ruth burst through the door with enough energy that Hercules barked and ran toward her.

"What is it? Are you hurt?"

"No, I am shocked. We've received our DNA results."

"Wow, I nearly forgot we did that with everything going on. What do you see?"

Rosalind pointed her trembling index finger at her screen. "The DNA results show we are related, by blood, not just by adoption. You and I are at least third cousins, maybe more closely related."

Chapter Fifty-Nine

Two weeks later, Graham and Issy sat at a corner booth at the Daily Planet with Ruth and Max Hamilton. Tiffany, now on her Alaskan cruise, was absent from her usual barstool, but Ernie was behind the bar. Josh swung and propped open the door as he assisted Rosalind on crutches to their table.

Rosalind landed abruptly on the chair. "Whew, please remind me not to get shot in the leg ever again. Thanks, Josh, for helping me get here."

"You're welcome. So, what's on the menu today?" asked Josh.

"A delectable combination of superb food, extraordinary drinks and unparalleled camaraderie." Max poured margaritas for Josh and Rosalind from the pitcher and passed their drinks. "Let's toast to the closing of the Findley and Mars cases, and to the speedy recuperation of Rosalind's leg."

Glasses raised and clinked in all directions. Sips of satisfaction circled the table as Ernie delivered two heaping platters of super nachos smothered in onions, peppers, and cheese with guacamole on the side. Plates were passed and nachos disappeared.

Rosalind said, "Before I drink my second margarita, I want to thank all of you for your support during this crazy time. I appreciate your listening, your suggestions, and your patience with me."

Before she could continue, the entrance door burst open. Pamela Findley entered followed by a tall, dark, and attractive man in a custom suit. Pamela turned to her right and recognized Josh, Rosalind, and Max so she strode over to the table.

"Goodness, Josh, have you lost your touch? I see you haven't gathered quite as many Kelco employees as you used to draw in the past."

"Hello, Pamela. This isn't a Kelco meeting, just a group of friends."

"Oh, seriously, Josh, based on my late husband's career, there wasn't a single meeting without Kelco taking the forefront."

"Not this time." Josh smiled. "Will you introduce us to your friend?"

"Friend? This is my fiancée, attorney Harold Gladstone. Harold, this is the Kelco gang." Harold shook hands accepting congratulations around the table, then said, "Let me scout out the best table for us. I'll be right back, dear." Pamela nodded.

"Thank you for your kind wishes. I have a new life to pursue. I have my beautiful house, my priceless jewelry, and a new man on my arm to provide for my future. All in all, it's a win-win for me."

Harold approached Pamela and held out his arm as she swooped her hand in to link elbows with him. "See you later, Kelco gang." Pamela walked away with the new man in her life.

"You know, I thought she might end up back with Ralph Findley. She seemed taken with him at the funeral," said Rosalind.

Hamilton smiled. "You are perceptive about Ralph and Pamela except he would not make the same mistake twice. When I saw him last, he was having coffee with Cassandra Starmer. Maybe this is his turn to get one of Tony's girls."

"How is Audra faring?" asked Rosalind.

"She has a good attorney, but the D.A. believes he has a slam dunk with her recorded confession and your deposition yesterday. Audra's admissions at Papago Park filled in gaps for both murders." Hamilton tasted more of his margarita.

"Good to hear. I wish I had seen through the situation from the beginning."

"No one saw it from the start. It takes time to pull together enough facts and evidence to identify a killer."

"Yeah, who would have guessed that this would result in Bob McMahon resigning. The whole team at Kelco will change. The corporate executives will bring in someone new to replace him. Everything will be different, but I won't miss it." Rosalind refilled her plate with nachos.

"Bob admitted giving Hercules a treat when he visited you. He received it from Audra, so it all tracks back to her. She also gave Hercules a poisonous snack earlier in the week."

"That makes sense because the day before he was too lethargic for his run. Anyway, my doctor confirmed Hercules had a small amount of oleander in his system. I would have lost him without the vet's help. So glad he was strong enough to recoup from it."

Issy looked at her phone. "I have been checking your horoscope as you heal, Rosalind. Here's today's forecast for you. '*As you heal from past trauma, you are surrounded by friends and your future is brighter than ever.*'"

"Wow, I'll take that one, better than a few I had earlier this month."

"After you are fully healed, and since your future will be brighter than ever, what's next?" asked Issy.

"I want to take time to reflect and review my options." She sipped more of her second margarita. "I'll seek answers as Madam Damara recommended. I plan to study genealogy. Perhaps I will help others and become a professional genealogist once I learn more. Or maybe I will finally put my minor in English to work and write about family history. My ancestors faced so many challenges, I'm amazed they survived. Their stories need to be told. Plus, there is a ton of research I need to do based on our DNA results. It turns out Aunt Ruth is not just my aunt, but also my third cousin. I have to figure out how we are blood relatives."

Issy laughed. "You have come a long way, my friend. I propose another toast. To Rosalind's next adventure. May it reach beyond her wildest dreams."

Everyone clinked their glasses and said, "Wildest dreams," and drank their margaritas.

Josh leaned over to Rosalind. "Whatever you choose, I will be by your side, just as long as you let me."

She turned to face him. "From what I have learned, and from what you have seen so far, it's not always a comfortable ride."

"Comfortable? I was the one who ran from the funeral with you. I know life with you will not be easy. But I don't want to miss it."

Rosalind kissed his cheek and smiled. She was finally home.

Dead Reckoning

Anna Dalhaimer Bartkowski

Schmidt Family Tree

Descendants of Christoph Schmidt

```
1-Christoph Schmidt b. 1741, Ansbach, Bayern
  + Anna Barbara Kalberin b. 1741, Germanic States
   2-Georg Schmidt b. 1766, Mariental, Russia
   2-Maria Schmidt b. 1766
  + Walpurga Wachter b. 1764, Germanic States
   2-Margaretha Schmidt b. 1793, Mariental, Russia
   2-Matthias Schmidt b. 1797, Mariental, Russia
   2-Magdalena Schmidt b. 1800, Mariental, Russia
   2-Peter Schmidt b. 1804, Mariental, Russia
     + Unknown
       3-TBD Schmidt Sr
         + TBD
           4-Tbd Schmidt
             + TBD Mother
               5-Christopher Schmidt b. 1888, Mariental, Russia, d. 1955, Wisconsin
                 + Maria Schoenberger b. 1894, Mariental, Russia, d. 1972, Wisconsin
                   6-Christopher Schmidt b. 1925, Wiscosin, d. 1978, Wisconsin
                     + Rose Spies b. 1927, Wisconsin, d. 2004, Wisconsin
                       7-Christopher Schmidt b. 1950, Wisconsin, d. 1999, Wisconsin
                         + Elizabeth Herzog b. 1952, Wisconsin, d. 1999, Wisconsin
                           8-Rosalind Maria Schmidt b. 15 Apr 1982, Wisconsin
```

Rosalind's Follow up to do list:
- Were Christoph and Anna Barbara the parents of George and Maria, born a few months apart?
- Which descendant of Christoph ties to Christopher Schmidt born 1888?
- Who was Kristina and Johannes' father?
- Wedding date for Christoph and Anna Barbara?
- Wedding date for Christoph and Walpurga?
- Find her mother's yearbooks.

Dead Reckoning

Anna Dalhaimer Bartkowski

Acknowledgements

Dead Reckoning is a modern-day and historical fiction multi-generational genealogical mystery. History is portrayed as accurately as possible and most of the major events in the Germanic States and Russia hold true to actual events. Hindsight leaves gaps and any interpretation of historical events generates risk, but the essence of my interpretation holds closely to the truth.

Many recognizable historical characters, Catherine II, who became known as Catherine the Great, Gregory Potemkin, Ivan Kulberg, LeRoy and Pietet are part of this story and play their part according to their historical roles. Their appearances in small segments cannot be considered a full essay on their lives. Village names are accurate and correspond to the dates of settlement. If there are any historical flaws, they are entirely mine.

The books cited are real books detailed in the bibliography and are excellent sources for further learning about the ancestry of the Germans from Russia and the historical figures who played dominant roles in their lives.

As for Rosalind's ancestors, their personalities are fictional. I created their lives as I interpreted and imagined the actions of my ancestors, the Dalhaimers. My fourth great grandfather was Johann Christoph Dahlheimer who settled in Mariental in 1766. Rosalind's family tree does not match mine, but my family tree was the inspiration for the Schmidt's timeline. Rosalind, the modern-day characters, and the Germanic travelers are works of fiction.

Special thanks to my editor, Becky Bartkowski, and my sounding board, Ashley Bartkowski.

Many thanks to my beta readers: Ashley Bartkowski, Becky Bartkowski, Laurie Fagan, Timothy Geiger, Rex Gygax, Margaret Morse, Karen Odden, Karen Randau, Hayley Sherman, Frank Sortelli, and Sandy Wright.

Dead Reckoning

I owe a debt of gratitude to the following friends and mentors who have helped me on my journey to learn German from Russia history and track my family tree. Thank you to: Judy Gareis, Timothy Geiger, Carmen Gill, Wladimir Herrman, Lewis Marquardt, Dona Reeves-Marquardt, Dr. Timothy Kloberdanz, Alex Herzog, Nancy Herzog, Jerome and Jan Siebert, Dodie Rotherham, Karen Soeken, Leona Mann, Irma Eichhorn, Kevin Rupp, Denise Gassman Grau, Thelma Mills, Ed and Doris Bischoff, Herb Babitzke, Ed Babitzke, Leo Sitter, R. Dale Copsey, Frieda Purvis, Larry and Eleanor Haas, Mary Dotz, Brent Mai, Michael Miller, Fabian Zubia Schultheis, German Sack, Ray Weinberger, Don and Lorna Kraemer, Ed Hoak, and Isabel Kessler.

Bibliography

Websites

American Historical Society of Germans from Russia, retrieved from https://www.ahsgr.org, too many dates to list.

Germans from Russia, Mariental (Tonkoschurovka), Russia. Retrieved August 29, 2021 from https://www.volgagerman.net/mariental-russia

Pioneers on Two Continents: Germans to Russia and America retrieved on August 8, 2020. from https://library.ndsu.edu/grhc/research/scholarly/meetings_conventions/pioneers.html.

Religions of Germany and the German-Russian Volga Colonies. Retrieved August 9, 2020 from https://books.google.com/books?id=_ZHXuaP0yEcC&pg=PA47&lpg=PA47&dq=budingen+marriage+1766&source=bl&ots=dfpLW3RAlK&sig=ACfU3U3MP7lWWQbBOlO38R9gtvxbP610Pg&hl=en&sa=X&ved=2ahUKEwiKhN7jpYzrAhXFHDQIHeO8DhwQ6AEwAXoECAoQAQ#v=onepage&q=budingen%20marriage%201766&f=false

10 Facts about the man who made Crimea part of Russia. Retrieved May 9, 2021, https://www.rbth.com/history/331267-10-facts-man-who-annexed-crimea-potemkin.

Voyage to Russia 1766, retrieved from https://www.norkarussia.info/voyage-to-russia-1766.html, on August 8, 2020.

Dead Reckoning

Publications

Catherine the Great, Robert K. Massie, Random House, an imprint of The Random House Publishing Group, New York, 2011.

From Catherine to Khrushchev: The Story of Russia's Germans by Adam Giesinger.

German Migration to the Russian Volga (1764-1767): Origins and Destinations by Brent Alan Mai and Dona Reeves-Marquardt.

Heal Your Ancestors to Heal Your Life: The Transformative Power of Genealogy Regression, Shelley A Kaehr, PhD, Llewellyn Publications, Woodbury, Minnesota. 2021.

Healing Ancestral Karma, Free Yourself from Unhealthy Family Patterns, Dr. Steven D. Farmer, Hierophant Publishing, San Antonio, Texas. 2014.

Lists of Colonists to Russia in 1766 "Reports by Ivan Kulberg" Igor Pleve, Saratov State Technical University. Saratov. 2010.

The History of Mariental, as told by Nicholas Thalheimer to his son Johannes, 1908. Saratov Archives. Translated by Elli Wise. Published in the *American Historical Society of Germans from Russia,* Spring 2023.

Most Benevolent Outcome used with permission from Tom T. Moore per email of November 21, 2022.

Transport of the Volga Germans from Oranienbaum to the Colonies on the Volga 1766-1767, translated and edited by Brent Alan Mai, 1998, American Historical Society of German from Russia, Lincoln, Nebraska.

St. Petersburg: Architecture of the Tsars by Dmitri Shvidkovsky

Anna Dalhaimer Bartkowski

The Merchant Seaman of Bristol 1747-1789. Branch of the Historical Association of the University, Bristol., Hon. General Editor: Peter Harris, Assistant General Editor: Norma Knight, Editorial Advisor: Joseph Bettey. Retrieved on September 7, 2020 from https://bristolha.files.wordpress.com/2019/09/bha038.pdf.

Traditions from the Past, Traditions for the Future: Folklore of the Germans from Russia, by Dr. Timothy Kloberdanz. AHSGR Winter Journal 2022.

Wir Wollen Deutsche Bleiben The Story of the Volga Germans by George J. Walters, edited by Christoph D. Walters, updated by Charles Walters. American Historical Society of Germans from Russia. 2021. Lincoln, Nebraska.

About the Author

Anna Dalhaimer Bartkowski is a descendant of the brave souls who answered Catherine II's call to relocate from the Germanic states to the Russian Empire. She traces her paternal line to Mariental and Louis and her maternal line to Reinwald, Rosenfeld am Nachoi, and Balzer with most lines back to their Germanic Origins as early as 1699. She is an enthusiastic family historian and grebel lover. For more information, visit annabartkowski.com.

Other books by the author include:
Maggie Visits Grandpa
Maggie Visits Argentina
Value Meals on the Volga
Grebel & Gemütlichkeit
Forty Years in the Desert, Editor

Made in United States
North Haven, CT
30 September 2024